THE BLOOD'S CHILDREN

ELI RAINWATER

THE BLOOD'S CHILDREN

The Blood's Children
Eli Rainwater
Copyright @ 2024 by Eli Rainwater

Cover photography by Eli Rainwater
Taken at Hutchin's Garage
402 W. Geer St.
Durham, NC
27701
First edition August 2024
ISBN 979-8-9874168-2-2 (hardback)
979-8-9874168-3-9 (paperback)
979-8-9874168-4-6 (ebook)
Library of Congress Control Number: 2024906994
Eli Rainwater
www.elirainwaterbooks.com

Trigger Warning

This book contains material that may be disturbing for some readers. While I do not include highly detailed descriptions of or about the acts, they are central to the plot. The material includes:

- Kidnapping of a teenager and children
- Dismemberment in which the kidnapping victim loses a finger
- Brainwashing/cultists
- Coercion

*To
Sherrie,
Carlos,
& Brandy*

Nothing will ever fill the holes you left in my heart

Acknowledgments

For Brenda who, as always, keeps me sane, grounded, and focused. You're the best inspiration I could ever ask for, and I don't know how I would still be doing this without you.

For Sarah for keeping me going during long events, making sure I have time to talk to my fans, and being just overall amazing.

For Richard and Kim, the best brother and sister-in-law in the world. I can't wait to drag you to more author appearances!

For Sandra, Beth, Meghan, JD, and Aron for always being the first to read the books and cheer me on.

For Casey and Malachy for lighting the fire under my ass that got these books going. And to Tracy and Jim for always making sure I have the time I need to pursue my passions.

And, most importantly, for Dave and Erin for making sure these books are worthy of being seen by the public. Your tireless efforts to proofread and edit and help me stay true to my vision are invaluable, and I don't know what I would do without you.

Fae & Cryptid Index

This list consists of fae and cryptids either mentioned or who appear in the stories:

Banshee: Celtic fae, although there is speculation on whether they are actually cryptids, banshees are harbingers of death. They are always women who scream or wail to foretell the death of a member of an Irish family and are solitary creatures. Reports of their physical appearance vary.

Brownie: Brownies are Scottish and Irish fae and are classified as household spirits. They are known for cleaning and cooking in exchange for compensation (usually a bowl of cream, milk, or bread; no other gifts are considered acceptable).

Centaur: Greek cryptids with the body of a horse and torso and head of a human, these creatures are renowned for their wisdom, medical advancements, and fighting prowess, particularly with a bow and arrow

Dragon: Dragons fall under Western or Eastern. Eastern dragons are more sinuous and tend to be benign by nature. They are revered, unlike Western dragons who have been hunted almost to the point of extinction. Western dragons are covered in armor like scales and use their fire breath to defend themselves in battle, destroy, or purify.

Dryad: Spirits of nature who originated in Greece. They are mostly commonly equated with trees and are tied to their trees and groves for life. They can manipulate wood and are typically wary of humans.

Fir Darrig: The Fir Darrig (pronounced "fear dare-ig") are Celtic fae. Also called Rat Boys, they are characterized by a ratlike appearance, red coats and hats, and living like rats. They are generally looked down upon and considered to be malevolent, but they can provide aid and protection when treated with respect.

Gargoyle: Gargoyles are stone during the day but appear human at night. Their skin and hair are dark gray like stone. They are some of the oldest cryptids in existence and are the keepers of the balance of good and evil in the universe. No one knows where they originated or how old they are.

Ghosts: Not a lot is known about ghosts, although thanks to Charlie, we now know that they can express emotion through color, they can't leave the site of their death, and they can recreate scenes that are highly emotionally charged, such as a death, murder, or other traumatic event.

Hobgoblin: Celtic household fae, they can be helpful when rewarded, but mischievous, spiteful, and destructive when they do not feel appreciated. They love playing pranks and are related to pucks and brownies as well as goblins.

Kitsune: Japanese fox spirits that originated in China as the huli jing, the Kitsune could be classified as fae. They can appear as beautiful women or men or as a fox, and they grow a new tail every hundred years until they have nine tails total. Their coats change from red to gold to white as they age. They possess magical abilities and great wisdom.

Lamia: The original Lamia is a Greek cryptid who was one of Zeus' many victims. She was a beautiful Libyan queen, but after Zeus became enamored of her, Hera, in jealousy, forced Lamia to kill her own children. As Lamia went mad, she began to steal and eat other women's children until she became a monster, snakelike and bestial and living in shadows.

Leprechaun: Leprechauns are Irish fae, believed to be descended from the god Lugh, who was the god of the sun, arts, and crafting. Known to be skilled craftsmen, they tend to be solitary. They can be kind and helpful, but they are tricksters and can be malevolent. If captured, they can be forced or persuaded to grant three wishes.

Matagot: Matagot are spirit cryptids from France who typically prefer the forms of a cat, crow, or dog. They can sometimes appear human as well. They can bestow fortune and aid to those who treat them with respect or kindness, but they can also attack or ruin those who treat them unfairly or with disrespect.

Naga: The Naga are Hindi and Buddhist cryptids that are part human, part cobra. They can work on the side of good or evil, depending on how they are treated. They live in an underworld realm and are very wise and usually considered to be benefactors.

Nain Rouge: The Nain Rouge are North American fae from Detroit and are hybrids of French dwarves or goblins and Native American spirits. They are said to be omens, appearing before disasters and with the power to strip fortune or luck from humans when attacked or antagonized. They are the same shape and size as dwarves but with red eyes and a disheveled appearance.

Nisse: A Norse fae similar to a brownie, the Nisse is a household spirit who takes the form of a small, old man and has one eye in the center of his forehead. They offer aid and assistance in return for payment.

Ogre: Ogres were once Oberon's Honor Guard until they disappeared right before the first cabal uprising; it was believed that they were extinct. They are over six feet tall and close to 300-pounds with grayish-green skin, humanoid faces, and horns similar to a bull's. They rampage in battle, at which point they grow to over nine feet tall, their eyes turn red, and their skin becomes diamond hard.

Puck: Old English fae, the most famous Puck is Robin Goodfellow, who serves King Oberon. The puck is a household spirit, known for being both helpful when properly rewarded for their work and destructive and mischievous when they feel they are not properly compensated with bread or milk. Unlike brownies, pucks prefer solitude.

Satyr: Satyrs are half-man, half-goat dependents of the god Pan. They are forest fae with a nose for magic, excellent camouflage skills, and love playing their pan pipes for the local nymphs (and anyone else who wants to drink wine and listen).

Succubus: No one is sure whether the succubi are cryptids or fae. They are part demon and creatures of chaos but not necessarily evil. They are extremely attractive and are drawn to physical beauty as well as intelligence. They possess great powers of seduction which they use to attract lovers or stun and subdue prey and enemies.

Tennessee Red Cheetah: An Appalachian cryptid native to Tennessee whose coat is reddish gold with a spiked, ochre stripe down the back. The Cheetah is said to be very intelligent. Reports vary on its size, ranging from slightly larger and bulkier than an African cheetah to being over six feet tall at its tallest point.

Tuatha de Danann: Pronounced (tooth du dahnahn). The original rulers of Ireland, they are the predecessors of the Aos Sí. They are tall with red or blonde hair and blue or green eyes and worship the Goddess Danu. They were driven underground by humans where they lived in the fairy mounds known as the sídhe.

Vampire: Cryptids that were once human, they now survive off of blood for nourishment. Vampires are supernaturally strong, fast, can fly, and can shapeshift into different species of bats at night. By day they are weak and lose their powers of flight and shapeshifting. They are obsessed with wealth and prestige. They maintain a human facade, but their true form is almost batlike with gray, leathery skin, red eyes, large pointed ears, fangs, and talons.

Wampus Cat: Appalachian cryptid that contains the spirit of Running Deer. This is a very large half cat, half dog creature who frequently walks on its hind legs and is devoted to protecting the Smoky Mountains from demons.

Witch: Humanoid species that can perform magic. Witches are attuned to earth, air, fire, or water, which influences the kinds of spells they can cast. The witch gene breeds true, although male witches are sterile.

Werepanther: Cryptids who can be created through birth or a bite from a fully shifted panther. Werepanthers travel in claws and have a leader, although they are not pack-like. They are great fighters, playful, and tend to keep to themselves.

Werewolf: Werewolves can be born or created through a bite by a shifted wolf. They are human/wolf hybrids with the ability to change at will. Their wolf forms retain their human intelligence and comprehension, and they are larger than wild wolves. They answer to a pack leader but don't necessarily travel or live as a pack in their every day lives.

White Lady: White ladies are spirit cryptids. They are essentially ghosts of women who died through some form of violence, usually at the hand of a jealous lover or husband. They are considered harbingers of death or doom, known to lead people to their deaths.

Character Index

Main

Jessie MacCaverty: Fire witch who was born somewhere around 960 AD in Scotland. She was named Jennet at birth, but due to her unnaturally long lifespan, she remade her identity many times, finally settling on Jessie.

Greta Schmidt: Earth witch who is Jessie's best friend. She was also born around 960 AD in what is now Germany. They met when Greta fled Germany during a French invasion, rescuing Jessie and Isabel in the process, and have been inseparable since.

Nicodemus: Also known as Nicky, he and his brother Mikael were originally from Greece and were turned into vampires almost 3000 years ago at the end of the Helladic period. Nicky is very close to Jessie

Mikael: Nicky's older brother, he is frequently the more levelheaded of the two and close to Greta. He takes great care to dress in the most flattering and expensive suits and amassed great wealth over the millennia.

John Rossford: Local sheriff, leader of the werewolf pack, and Jessie's partner (once she got over her reservations about dating)

LaSalle: a Nain Rouge who showed up to warn them about an attempt to disrupt the Fae, Cryptid, Human, and Witch Alliance peace talks. Then he just never left.

Rupert: A Matagot who prefers the shape of a large black cat. He is also Madame Blanche's companion

Supporting

Annie: A brownie in Mara's court who runs a cleaning service that caters to the fae, cryptids, and witches

Caroline Gregor: Jessie's apprentice and a water witch. She is a twin, which makes her one of the most powerful witches in a century

Cassie Rodriguez: Caroline's human girlfriend and Jessie's tech support. Cassie worked to find ways to bring technology and advancements to the witch, fae, and cryptid communities.

Charlie: The ghost who died in the bathroom at Jessie's bar and now haunts it. He frequently helps out around the bar and can sense emotions and events.

Christopher Gregor: Caroline's twin brother and a fire witch. He is one of the most powerful witches in a century and is afraid of his power after setting a building on fire.

Isabel: an air witch who was born in the same village at the same time as Jessie. She now heads up the Witch Council and is Jared's teacher in the arts of air magic.

Jared Daniels: Jessie's apprentice and an air witch. He is also a table top and role playing game developer

Mara Mac Gabhann: Duchess of Green Orchards and Oberon's great niece, she holds the lands in the Southeast on behalf of Faerie. She is a Tuatha de Danann and one of Jessie's greatest supporters and allies.

Matthias: a fir darrig Jessie and Greta met when they rescued Charlie and Madame Blanche. He became close friends with LaSalle and is glad to help out where he can.

Renard: a vampire who originally went by the name of Hathus when he was a Visigoth; rescued by Mikael and Nicky and believes he owes them a life debt

Riza: A fire witch and the head of security for the Witch Council. She is also a trusted confidant for Isabel

Robin the Puck: Oberon's emissary to the Alliance who was the target of an attack by the cabal. He frequently acts as a liaison for Jessie and the Faerie courts.

Tug: An ogre Jared brought to the bar one day and who stuck around to become Jessie's tenant and security; his true name is Elisian

Vito: The Vampire Sire who also teaches design classes in a local night school outside of Atlanta

Won't Show Up Very Often, So It's Okay If You Forget Who They Are (aka the red shirts)

Astrid: Gertrud's daughter, very young and recruited by the cabal who preyed on her vanity and naivety to convince her to betray her mother. She is now a prisoner of the Witch Council.

Belladonna: Vampire groupie and Marshall's friend who was seduced by Renard

Brigitte: a banshee who was turned into a necromancer and killed after she tried to kill John, Jessie, and Greta

Dain: A Tuatha de Danann page in Mara's service who became good friends with Jared and joined his gaming group

Draig: The oldest Celtic dragon who created the vampire race when he tried to give a human who saved his life immortality

Emma: a hedge witch who runs the Night Market in south Atlanta. She also acts as the liaison for the solitary practitioners and the outside world.

Frank: Emma's husband and a hearth witch. Feels that he owes Jessie a huge debt of gratitude for acting on his behalf when he was framed for a crime against the Council.

Gertrud: A Norse witch called a *völva*, or a type of shaman who lost her powers when her daughter tricked her into making a necromancer. She now assists the Council where she can until her powers are restored.

Ivan: a water witch friend of Greta's who helps out from time to time and teaches Caroline the skills of water magic

Kathryn: Head of the Pisgah National Forest wolf pack; her kids go to the same camp as John's where they get to learn how to embrace their werewolf natures

The Kumars: Fatima (the matriarch) and Rahul (her consort), the heads of the local Naga clan who run the best neighborhood cafe around

Madame Blanche: a White Lady and the European cryptid emissary to the Alliance. She was originally Charlotte de Valois, the original White Lady in France.

Marshall (aka Morticent): a vampire groupie who was bewitched by the cabal to become obsessed with Nicky and kill Nicky's boyfriend

Mary Jo Sutton: A local succubus who accidentally caused Charlie to have a heart attack and is now his girlfriend

Melodium: Tug's oldest brother and Oberon's general and head of his elite guard

The Norns: Ancient Scandinavian witches with the power of foresight and who controlled fate and destiny; each is individually more powerful than any other witch alive

Oberon: The Fae High King who can appear as a beautiful dwarf or a blindingly regal elf

Olav: A Nisse who serves Gertrud and came with her to the Witch Council to keep an eye on Astrid

Robert: A former monk who was turned into a vampire against his will and now believes that he is sent on a mission from God to cleanse the world of blasphemers

Running Deer: Spirit who inhabits the Wampus Cat; she defeated the demon Ew'ah and saved the children of her village

Seanan: John's lieutenant and right hand, makes great cookies and transports the pack in her minivan

Sharon: Jared's mother and a water witch who was persecuted because of her brother's involvement with the original cabal

Stefan: Greta's brother and an air witch; he is a former politician and a businessman

Stephanie: Greta and Stefan's niece who was kidnapped by Robert to try to force Greta to submit to him

Tam: a leprechaun who helped Jessie and Greta rescue Charlie and Madame Blanche

Theodore: Jared's uncle and an earth witch who was trapped with the ogres after he kidnapped their entire race

Zach: a human who began to follow Christopher after witnessing Chris's use of magic. Very rich and spoiled, he believes that magic can be siphoned and used by humans.

Warsaw: The gargoyle who stole Nicky's heart and was murdered to start the war between the cabal and the Alliance

Zelda: the crone who relentlessly torments Jessie and her friends; apprenticed with Jessie centuries ago under the same fire witch teacher

Prologue

The scrawny man glared up at the heavy sky that spat rain in his gaunt face and thin, dirty hair. It fell into his eyes and dripped off the end of a nose that was flushed with burst capillaries from years of alcohol abuse. Why he ever let that vampire convince him to go wander around some godforsaken marsh in Ireland looking for a damned witch was a mystery.

He had no idea how the vampire even knew the witch would be out here tonight. One of those fairy elves showed up at the vamp's hotel room in New Orleans a few nights ago and thrust some kind of package at her before disappearing again, and she had him on a plane five hours later with nothing but the clothes on his back, a letter in his pocket, and a fake passport that somehow got him through customs at Heathrow.

All he knew was that the vamp had better hold true to her promise to turn him when he finished up here. It was about time he gained his rightful place in this merciless world– a narcissistic belief spawned from years of drug abuse and black out nights that ended in a jail cell or worse along with self-inflicted poverty and a string of dead-end jobs.

He pulled the threadbare army coat he had stolen from a homeless man tighter around his shoulders and hunched against the bitterly chill December wind. Wait, was that a howl? Supposedly the banshee who lived in these parts was dead, but you could never be too sure these days. Those damned fae were slippery devils and as likely to skin and eat a person alive as do anything kind for a poor human like him.

No, it wasn't a howl. It was just the wind, but there, just on the edges of his senses, was something else. As he moved further into the marsh, it became clearer. He smelled smoke, like something cooking mingled with a wood fire. Had to be the witch– who else could get a fire to burn in this miserable rain?

He stumbled over the treacherous ground and peered through the gloom until he saw the shadow of a hut in the distance that seemed sturdy enough and sat low to the ground. As he drew closer, he saw that smoke curled from the chimney. The building was made of clay and topped with a neat thatched roof, and the windows glowed with a welcoming yellow light through thick glass. And for a brief moment, this nameless, forgettable man regretted all of the choices in his life that had led him here instead of the alternate reality of happily ever after with his own comfortable home, maybe a pretty wife, some kids. He shoved those thoughts out of his mind as he approached the door.

The letter in its cheap, drugstore envelope burned in his pocket, heat rising as he grew closer to the hut. Yeah, the witch was definitely inside. The vamp told him he would know he was on the right track when the letter warmed to the touch. He'd looked at her like she was crazy; after all, fae aside, magic couldn't really be real, right? But it turned out she wasn't lying. He crept to the hut and knocked sharply on the wooden door, only the howling wind breaking up the heavy silence that fell over him.

When the door opened, he recoiled backward, slipping in the mud and landing heavily on his ass. Like most humans, he had not bothered learning or understanding how much folklore was real when the fae and cryptids came out into the open. He expected some ugly hag of a witch to open the door, not a fur covered, rat faced creature the size of a man wearing a red coat.

The fir darrig bared its yellow teeth as it scowled down at him.

"Strangers are not welcome here," it hissed.

The man scrambled to his feet and sneered in a failed attempt at saving face while trying to shake the mud off of his ill-gotten coat. He looked over the creature's shoulder into the neat, cozy room beyond that struck him as anachronistic considering the... thing that stood in his way at the door.

"I'm not here for you, freak. I'm here for the witch. I have something for her. Something she's going to be very interested in. I suggest you get out of my way before I make you."

The mud and snot running down his face did not sell his bravado.

The fir darrig smiled, a nasty, terrifying snarl of a smile, and called over his shoulder, "Greta, it's for you. But I call dibs when you're done with him, lass."

The man stopped listening. He focused on the woman coming up behind the rat man. She looked so... ordinary. Were all witches like her? Had they really walked among normal people this whole time? This one wore a pair of jeans and a tank top with some fantasy movie quip on the front.

A faded cardigan with frayed cuffs that had seen better days sloped off of her shoulders, adding to her unassuming appearance.

But he felt the power roll from her like a tide. Power that made him inexplicably afraid of the ground on which he stood. Power that made him suddenly regret leaving New Orleans. Power that made him wish he'd said no and walked away when that crazy vamp took him to the cheap hotel room and held out the little baggie of white powder he crammed up his nose to briefly try to feel invincible.

"Thanks, Matthias. What do you want?" Greta asked, tilting her head to one side to pierce the man with a hazel-eyed gaze under the silver fringe of her shaggy, short, bob haircut.

"What's going on then?" said another voice behind her.

This one looked human– but no, he was one of those fairy bastards again. He was almost as tall as the witch, but he had the pointed ears and weird cat eyes and planed cheekbones to prove his damned fae lineage. His hair was all golden curls around his shoulders, and the nameless man could see tools at the fae's belt under his bright red vest.

"I was told to give this to you," the man snapped, thrusting the letter at no one in particular. It was so hot now that it nearly seared his skin when he took it out of his pocket, but the witch didn't seem to notice as she opened the envelope and pulled out a sheet of paper. Silence fell as she read the one carefully written line and the signature scrawled beneath.

"I see," she said, her voice as cold as the endlessly howling wind. She folded the letter and tugged her cardigan back on her shoulders.

Then she looked at him, and some animal instinct deep inside of him knew that he was dead. The brown in her hazel eyes faded away until her eyes were an ugly green, no, now they turned black, the black seeping in from the edges and crowding out the white and now the iris, and oh god, those eyes, he had to get away, why couldn't he run?

Because the Earth had him. He was a prisoner where he stood, and now he will never get away. His screams filled the marsh and were carried through the uncaring air as the witch slowly buried him alive, screaming as he sank into the Earth inch by inch, screaming until his mouth and lungs and stomach filled with the Earth and there was nothing left but the remnants of his screams echoing across the empty marshes.

"Well," Tam said. The leprechaun blinked at the mound of dirt where a man once stood and adjusted his red vest over his tinker's tools. "Killing the messenger seems a bit excessive."

"Aw, I wanted him! I never get the good ones," Matthias complained. His shoulders slumped in dejection and his whiskers drooped as the fir darrig turned away from the door.

"There, there," Tam said, patting Matthias on the back. "You can dig him up when she's done with him."

"I can, can't I?" Matthias brightened at the thought.

Tam shuddered and looked at Greta. Greta hadn't moved, the letter clutched in her white-knuckled fist.

"Greta? Lass?" Tam asked. He exchanged a worried glance with Matthias before they both began to back away.

"I need Jessie," she said in a cold, dreamy, detached voice that was not her own. It was strange to their ears as if she had never spoken before.

"Okay then, let's go to her. Can you use your portal? Do you want me to take you?"

Greta was a statue of ivory, sinew, and bone. Tam and Matthias exchanged another glance.

They hadn't known Jessie and Greta long. It had only been a few months since the witches showed up at the marsh looking for a trail that would lead them to Charlie, their friend and the ghost who haunted Jessie's bar.

When the new cabal rose up and targeted Jessie and Greta, Astrid, the cabal's young, misguided lieutenant and daughter of one of the oldest witches in the world, had captured Charlie in a spirit trap. A spirit trap was a terrible prison designed to destroy a ghost's soul piece by piece until nothing was left to be saved or reincarnated. Charlie would have been lost forever if Madame Blanche, the European cryptid emissary for the Fae, Cryptid, Witch, and Human Alliance and France's most well-known White Lady, hadn't fed him her essence while they were captives together.

Matthias' closest friend, the banshee Brigitte, was a casualty of that fight when the cabal tricked her into becoming a necromancer, an act so repulsive to Nature that it would be centuries before she was free from the karmic punishment. Brigitte had gladly accepted death as an alternative, and Jessie and Greta had vowed to save as many fae and cryptids as they could from the banshee's fate.

"Okay, you hang tight, I'll fetch Jessica," Tam backed away and fumbled for his key to the portal leprechauns used to reach their storehouses and workshops and travel around the world.

"Don't you leave me alone with her," Matthias hissed as he hugged his tail to his chest, holding onto it like it was a long, hairless lifeline. His eyes darted between Greta and Tam. He had very little experience with witches, particularly when their eyes went strange and they buried messengers on his doorstep.

"You'll be fine! We'll be right back."

"Bring Mikael too," Greta said in that flat voice that didn't seem to be hers at all.

"Aye, I'll bring them. Just wait right here," Tam opened a door in the air and stumbled through, leaving Matthias to nervously eye their friend and pray that Tam made it back in time before Greta started to look at him the way she had looked at the nameless man.

Chapter 1

"**I**'m telling you, it should go here!" Jessie argued as she tried to use her shoulder to nudge an errant silver curl out of her bright blue eyes. While the brightly colored knit cap her dear friend Isabel made for her kept most of her hair out of her face, this one lock just would not stay put.

Isabel, air witch extraordinaire and Jessie's oldest friend, had decided to take advantage of her position as head of the Witch Council to knit hats and scarves for her friends during the more tedious meetings. It was a source of endless satisfaction to pull out her craft bag and latest project in the middle of a session; nothing quite deflated some of the pompous asses the Council dealt with like the click of her needles, much to Jessie and Greta's gleeful delight.

Jessie struggled under the weight of a beautifully carved foosball table, her small frame barely big enough to handle her end, and swore profusely when the corner of the table caught her favorite Toadies shirt and almost tore the fabric. She wanted the table in the middle of the room where players would have plenty of elbow room and everyone could appreciate Jared's craftsmanship. Her apprentice had really outdone himself this time.

Jared had a knack for succeeding at anything he tried and making it look easy. He was a handsome, tall, brilliant Black air witch with a promising future as a game developer, and the foosball table was his latest achievement. It wasn't just any table though– it was imbued with magic to bring it to life. He had built the entire base out of oak with cherry wood inlays and, with Greta's earth magic help, made the field out of living turf. The teams weren't just stick figures on rods either. Christopher, a fire witch who excelled at clockwork creations, helped craft the rods that kept the figures suspended while enabling them to move independently. Jared had also enlisted Tam's aid to carve the figurines out of stone in perfect detail and then used air magic to breathe life into each one.

The little figures mostly went where the players told them to go, but then that's where things could get nasty. After he and Greta tested the table to make sure it worked, Jared had to rebuild two of the figurines when one used its skull to shatter an opponent's head, making the ultimate sacrifice for its team. Tam prudently showed up on Jared's doorstep with a large box of spare pieces and set of fae carving tools after that. The table was Jessie's Yule gift. John– and many of the bar's patrons– couldn't wait to play it.

"No, if you want the optimal light and room to play, it needs to go here, by this window and further away from the bar. Jared, you made this thing. Tell her I'm right."

John, Jessie's werewolf boyfriend and the local sheriff, tried to be reasonable, but at this point, he just wanted to put the damn thing down. He also wanted to try it out very badly. His wolf rose at the thought of all of that competition just waiting for him, and his normally green-blue hazel eyes that were set under a shock of unruly blonde curls glinted with a touch of gold.

"Oh, no. I'm not getting in the middle of this," Jared backed away shaking his head and ducked behind the bar where he used the taps and Caroline, one of Jessie's other apprentices and Christopher's twin sister, to shield himself from the impending fight.

John almost dropped the entire table on his foot when Tam popped out of thin air, startling them so much that Jessie lost her grip on her end.

"Jessie, I need you. Greta needs you. You have to come quick, something is wrong. Where's Mikael? She needs him too."

The words tumbled out of the leprechaun's mouth as he grabbed Jessie by the arm and pulled her toward his portal. The bar patrons openly stared, the few humans who braved the unknown or sought thrills in a witch's place of business exchanging uneasy glances. Shania, the widowed wolfpack member Jessie had hired to wait tables part time, paused with the glass she was handing to an impatient werepanther in midair.

"Wait, what's going on?" John demanded, putting down his end of the table and moving quickly around it to Jessie's side.

It wasn't that he had any illusions that his lady love was a wilting flower in need of his protection. After all, as one of the oldest and strongest witches in the world, she had withstood her fair share of attacks, both magical and physical, over the years. But the cabal had targeted her twice in the last three months. He wasn't quite ready to let her out of his sight, despite the fact she was more than capable of taking care of herself, thank you very much.

"We were having dinner, and then this man came out of nowhere and handed her a letter. I don't know what it said.

Her eyes went this strange green and then all black, and then she buried him alive and told me to get you and Mikael," the words fell over themselves as Tam tried to get them to understand this was important and Jessie needed to come with him now.

"Damn," Jared said with a low whistle.

Jessie yelped and hopped on one leg, grabbing John's arm for balance as she pulled up the cuff of her faded, well-worn jeans. The tiny flower tattoo on her ankle, the symbol of her bond with Greta, glowed an ugly, burning red.

"Shit, something's really wrong. I have to get to her now! Jared and John, you guys figure out the table. Caroline, call Mikael. Tell him to get here as soon as he can. Better yet, find out where he is so Tam can go for him. Where's LaSalle?"

"I'm right here," LaSalle spoke up.

The Nain Rouge had popped in seconds before with the trusty, never empty goblet he had "borrowed" from the local fae court grasped in his fist. The court was ruled by Mara Mac Gabhann, Duchess of Green Orchards and Oberon's great-niece. The Tuatha de Danann duchess was also one of Jessie's dearest friends.

LaSalle resembled a disgruntled garden gnome with a matted beard, red eyes, and a cawing laugh. Like all Nain Rouge, he treated others the way he was treated, proving to be a loyal friend and ally to those who earned his trust. While the Nain Rouge usually never involved themselves in others' conflicts, LaSalle's chieftain sent him to unofficially assist Jessie and her friends after the cabal attempted to infiltrate his clan.

He was ready to take his post that he usually shared with Rupert, the erstwhile Matagot who preferred to take the shape of a giant black cat, by the door. They frequently joined Tug, who was Jessie's deeply loyal ogre doorman.

Until the cabal managed to exile the ogres to another world centuries before, they had served as Oberon's elite Honor Guard and were some of the most skilled fighters and craftsmen among the fae. After discovering that his uncle Theodore was one of the witches behind the ogrekin's disappearance, Jared took personal responsibility for their plight. He, along with Jessie, LaSalle, Rupert, the wolfpack, and the Witch Council, was instrumental in rescuing the ogrekin and reinstating them to their rightful place in Oberon's court. Tug still worked for Jessie as the bar's security and doorman. Yes, it made sense that he would be at the bar as a fae liaison in case anything happened, but they all knew he really loved it there.

Rupert was absent that evening– again. During the fight to rescue the ogrekin, he had scouted the battlefield in his crow form while Jessie and her allies fought Theodore and his reinforcements. But the cabal had been waiting for Rupert with the only known substance that could get through a Matagot's almost impenetrable coat and brought him down with a poisoned arrow.

Before they first came to power a few centuries before, the cabal had once hunted the Matagot race to the verge of extinction for their pelts. The compound on the arrow that wounded Rupert in battle was a remnant of those dark times. Madame Blanche was able to get word to the remaining Matagot who went into hiding, but Rupert never quite recovered from the knowledge that his death had been imminent and his kin were, once again, in danger. He had taken to roaming the spirit world in solitary moodiness, something which worried both Jessie and Madame Blanche, his dearest friend and companion. She admitted to Jessie that she was worried he might veer toward the darker side of his chaotic neutral nature (as Jessie put it).

"Go warn Mara that something bad just happened and then find a way to warn Madame Blanche," Jessie ordered LaSalle. "Tell them I'll fill them in as soon as I know more but to be on the alert."

"You got it," LaSalle popped through a dark portal and was out of sight in an instant.

"Tam, where is Greta?" Jessie turned back to the leprechaun.

"Matthias' hut," he told her. "I'll be right behind you with Mikael."

"Thank you. Caroline, you're in charge until I get back." She paused long enough to stand on tiptoe so she could give John a kiss before she ran down the oak paneled hall to her office, gray curls streaming behind her. The others stared at her retreating back.

"You heard her," Caroline flipped her long, curly blonde ponytail over her shoulder and narrowed her big blue eyes at her crew as she dialed Mikael's number while Tam waited, impatiently shifting from foot to foot and fidgeting with his tinker's tools.

Caroline's honey-gold tan and all-American cheerleader good looks masked a no-nonsense attitude and driving ambition, and she and Jared worked hard to prove that Jessie's trust in them was not misplaced after Jessie had agreed to make them her apprentices.

Jared heaved a sigh of resignation and bent to pick up Jessie's end of the table as John resumed his post at the other side. Caroline handed the phone to Tam who spoke a few words to Mikael on the other end and then blinked out of sight.

"This is a masterpiece," John admired the craftsmanship as they struggled to lift the ornate and very heavy table. "Next time do you think you could make it lighter?"

Jared grunted in response.

"Was that a yes?" John grinned, and Jared scowled at him before they managed to get the table in position by the window.

Cassie Rodriguez, Caroline's human girlfriend and Jessie's IT guru, watched as she sipped a neon pink classic Caroline concoction. She was as tiny as she was fierce, her long black hair framing a pretty face with large, dark eyes. Charlie, the resident ghost, hovered next to her along with his succubus girlfriend Mary Jo Sutton. Mary Jo still felt guilty at the part she played in Charlie's death, no matter how many times he reminded her that he hadn't told her about his heart condition when she invited him into the bar's bathroom for a more... personal conversation.

Cassie hadn't always gotten along with the couple. However, Charlie's near destruction combined with Cassie's unprecedented courage and leadership when she recruited Mary Jo's help to save both Jessie and Charlie had caused the trio to form an unlikely, easy friendship.

"You know what I don't understand?" Cassie asked them, stirring her drink and fishing the cherry out with her fingers.

"What's that?" Charlie asked.

"Why no one thought to ask Tug for help," she popped the cherry in her mouth and turned back to the bar. She blew a grinning Caroline a kiss while Jared and John stared at each other in chagrin before looking at the ogre, who just shrugged.

Chapter 2

Jessie burst through the door to her office, colliding with a chestnut-curled vampire and sending them both crashing to the ground.

"Nicky, what are you doing here?" she demanded, exasperated as she struggled to untangle herself from him and get to her feet.

"I came to visit you! Did you have to hit me so hard? That actually hurt!" he complained in a grievous tone as he stood up and dusted off his black velvet, skin-tight pants and the emerald green silk shirt he wore more often than not. The shirt had been a favorite of Warsaw's, he admitted to her one night. He wasn't ready to bury the memory of his dead lover.

The third oldest vampire in the world, Nichodemus hailed from ancient nobility where he had made a name for himself as a flippant, rakish playboy. But despite his flamboyant, mercurial reputation, he was capable of very deep love, and he fell for Warsaw hard. When the cabal made the sweet, serious gargoyle their first casualty in the new war, Jessie and her friends swore revenge on everyone responsible for shattering Nicky's heart into a thousand pieces.

As a result, the cabal's attack on her bar ended in a massacre. None of Jessie's allies had any interest in showing mercy to the group that had so deeply wounded two of their own, for Charlie also suffered when Astrid took him prisoner in the spirit trap.

"Greta's in trouble, I need to go to her now," Jessie snapped, choosing not to question why Nicky decided to crawl through her office window instead of using the front door like a normal person. When he didn't get out of her way fast enough, she snarled in frustration and scrambled over the beat-up, ancient desk.

"Wait, do you want me to go with you?" He reached for her arm.

She paused, considering. Greta had asked for Mikael, but as his younger brother, Nicky was the next best thing.

"Yes, Tam is trying to find Mikael. She said she needs him too, but I don't know why. I just know we need to get to her now!"

"Okay, let's go," Nicky jumped over the desk too, ignoring the fact that it wasn't necessary since, unlike in Jessie's case, there hadn't been a slightly narcissistic and sometimes oblivious vampire blocking his path. Jessie pushed the knot hole in the oak panel behind her desk and opened the portal that led to the Library she shared with Greta.

The Library served many purposes– storage, a workspace, comfort, a home for Jessie's and Greta's cats, and also the ability to operate as a portal to anywhere in the world. Nicky barely had time to glance at the cheerfully roaring fire flanked by comfortable, mismatched, and patched armchairs and six feline heads that poked up over the back of the old sofa before Jessie pushed a panel open on the other wall that looked into Matthias' hut.

Greta was immobile, still framed in the open doorway that looked out on the dark, rain-lashed moors beyond. Matthias hovered nearby, wringing his ratlike hands.

"Oh, thank the Goddess, you've come!" His shoulders sagged in relief.

"Greta, honey, what's going on?" Jessie moved to her friend's side.

The only time she had ever seen Greta like this was after the original cabal attacked Greta's home centuries ago, slaughtering her mother and sister in the process. It had taken five witches to bring Greta down after she succumbed to her rage and decimated a forest and small village.

Her older brother had survived the cabal's attack, fleeing with their infant niece in his arms and using his witching powers and his connection to air to hide the child until Greta and Jessie could get her to safety. He then proceeded to make Greta's attempts at revenge look like a tea party. Jessie was pretty sure there were still old members of the cabal who wet themselves at the mention of Stefan's name. He wasn't called the bogeyman of the witching world for nothing.

Greta did not speak. She simply handed the crumpled letter to Jessie, and Jessie smoothed it out. The black ink of the sharply sloping letters stood out against the stark white of the paper.

"Come to me or the child dies."

A name was scrawled underneath in pencil, written in an adolescent's hand. Stephanie. The daughter of the niece Greta and Stefan fought so hard to save.

"Oh, Greta," Jessie breathed, feeling her heart tighten in her chest as it filled with dread.

"Let me see," Nicky demanded, reaching for the letter. Jessie handed it to him. He read and started to swear, his amber gold eyes turning red and his mouth suddenly filling with teeth.

Matthias backed away from the turning vampire, still clutching his tail. Jessie turned to him and calmly, so calmly, said, "Matthias, I appreciate your hospitality. You are a most gracious host. If I could impose on you for one last thing, I need you to get the Puck for me."

"On my way," he bobbed his head. Either he shrank or the wall grew, but he was through a hole Jessie had never seen before as fast as lightning.

She stood still for a moment, trying to decide what to do next. Jessie and Greta had enemies. They had lived for over a thousand years, taken part in wars and skirmishes, and time and time again fought against conspiracies, ambushes, and betrayals. She knew exactly where this threat came from. But were the perpetrators acting alone, or had they joined the new cabal?

Tam skidded to a halt as he burst through his portal, Mikael right behind him. Nicky's older brother wore dark blue tailored jeans and a deep wine colored silk button up shirt that complemented his long, raven black hair and gray eyes. His outfit probably cost more than a year's worth of profit from Jessie's bar. Even for vampires, Mikael and Nicky's fashion sense and style were legendary.

Mikael looked at the letter in Jessie's hand like it was a snake.

"I heard Nicodemus' rage echo in my head from a thousand miles and another dimension away. Is it true?" he demanded.

Jessie nodded.

"They took her niece. They said they'll kill her if Greta doesn't come."

"They won't," Mikael's voice was flat. "They're desperate. We should have wiped them out when we had the chance before they went to ground."

"Not to intrude, but would someone like to enlighten me as to what's going on?" a new voice spoke up from behind them.

Jessie turned to see the pleasant-faced Robin the Puck with an ever-present mischievous twinkle in his holly-leaf green eyes that, along with his silver and brown-gray hair, like snow-dusted branches, changed color with the seasons. Robin, Oberon's emissary and trusted advisor, had become a close friend after Jessie and Greta saved him from a spell that bound his will and almost ended the peace talks between the factions of the world.

"Yes, and I need you to listen carefully and then go back to Oberon with everything I'm about to tell you. Tell him to warn the rest of the Courts and get word to the Alliance," Jessie said, the serious look on her face driving the smile from his lips.

"A long time ago, just before the war between the Witch Council and the old cabal, witches had to use other skills to try to make ends meet because we were still unknown to humans. Every witch has a skill that can double as a conduit for our magic and provide a means to support ourselves in the human world. For instance, Greta and I busked to make our living. I danced with fire, and Greta accompanied me on the flute. We were able to move around Europe while performing our duties for the Witch Council and stay off the local constabulary and churches' radars. We performed at street fairs and carnivals, and she also played at local inns for our room and board. Fire is energy and passion, and earth is healing and comfort, and we fed those things into our art.

"But then something happened when we were in Paris. We had to stay in a tavern close to a slum where sickness broke out. There were fights; people were scared and angry. When Greta played, she channeled healing and calm so that fights ended as soon as they began, and the sickness fled. The humans never put two and two together– but the vampires did."

Jessie paused in her tale. Nicky hovered somewhere between humanity and monster. Greta still didn't move. Mikael, his beautiful face a mask of rage and hate, took up the thread.

"At the time, witches and vampires were just becoming aware of each other's existence. You have to understand, those of us in the know did not share the information lightly. By this point, Nicodemus and I had made Jessica's and Greta's acquaintance through our work for our respective councils, and we became close friends. However, our affiliation was a heavily guarded secret.

"Unfortunately, as I'm sure you are well aware, all magic leaves a trace, and any creature who performs magic can sense the magic use of another. A vampire's magic is not much, but we still have glamour, compulsion, and transformation."

"To say Greta went overboard at the tavern is an understatement," Jessie glanced at her friend. "She's an earth witch, and an earth witch is a natural healer. She couldn't help herself. It started off as light, gentle magic, but as she sank deeper into the music, the magic became stronger and brighter. At first, we thought we were safe, that no one had realized what she had done. But then *they* showed up."

"A theory had begun to circulate among one of the more unhinged vampiric sects that the ultimate being could be created by turning a witch into a vampire and that whatever vampire could sire and control such a being would have all of the power in the world," Mikael continued. "It has never succeeded. Conflicting magics cannot exist in the same creature without ripping the creature apart from the inside. The Vampiric Council placed a sentence of death on any who tried after a coven of witches was found slaughtered."

"We didn't recognize any of them," Jessie's voice was soft, her blue eyes sadly looking at a scene far away in the past. "It was as if the magic had exploded, destroying them from the inside out."

Robin shuddered. Jessie brought her gaze back to the present and shot a brief glance at the Puck before she continued.

"Anyway," she was spurred by a sense of urgency to finish their tale so she could fix Greta, make Greta move again, make Greta's eyes go back to their normal brown-green. "A new vampire in the throes of turning was in the tavern, and Greta inadvertently healed her through the transition. It's rare that a witch can do that, but it's possible if the vampire is still human enough.

"This vampiric cult's leader, a pathetic idiot named Robert, got it in his head that Greta was the answer to his prayers; the witch he was looking for. He decided that she had to be strong enough to be turned, and then he would rule the world, even though she didn't do anything differently than any other witch. He tried to convince her to join his followers. When that didn't work, the cult kidnapped her, which is when I got him involved," Jessie nodded toward Mikael.

"By the time we got there, Jessica was ready to burn Paris to the ground," Mikael's voice held a low, growling note that made shivers go down Robin's spine. "She told us that maybe a dozen vampires came for Greta. We hunted them to the filthy hole in the sewers they called a coven. They were disgusting. I'm fairly certain that none of them had bathed since they had been turned. You see, Robert believes that he and his followers are the ultimate, supreme beings, and they are above the vampire's instinctive love for material possessions. At any rate, we got Greta back, but we lost Robert. He escaped."

Robin looked confused.

"I was under the impression that the need to surround oneself with material wealth was innate to the vampiric nature."

"It is," Mikael told him. "Our ultimate sire, the vampire who fathered our race, was spawned from the first of the great Celtic dragons. Our need to hoard material possessions and wealth is literally in our blood."

And Greta still did not move.

"We took out the rest of the cult members though. Lots of burning," Jessie said in a matter-of-fact voice. "Robert had plastered the walls with his 'teachings' as he laughably called them. It was the same writing that's on this letter now.

I will remember it as long as I live. That was when Greta and I started to learn how to fight in battle and not just in self-defense. But now he's back, and he took her niece, and he is threatening to kill Stephanie if Greta doesn't do what he says."

"And so he will die," Greta finally spoke, her voice soft and dreamy. Her eyes were like onyx.

"So you need to warn Oberon now," Jessie continued, her urgency creeping into her voice. "You need to tell him what happened and what we just told you. If they still believe that such an act is possible with a witch, it's not a stretch that they'll start to wonder what a vampire fae can do. And we need to launch a rescue mission as soon as possible because please, please believe me when I say that Greta will take the earth itself apart stone by stone to find Stephanie, and she is powerful enough to do it. She will leave nothing behind."

"How did Robert find her niece?" Nicky asked, his face returning to normal.

"We probably have our lovely new friends to thank for that," Jessie said, her voice a shade away from a snarl. "My guess is whoever's behind the new cabal knows the story and pulled some strings to find Robert and his followers. After all, the Witch and Vampiric Councils had to work together to get this threat under control, and it's still talked about as a warning to anyone who wants to indulge in a little cross-species experimentation. It's not hard to find the records in the Council archives."

"Sadly, that would not surprise me," Robin shook his head. "Well, on that note, I had best be off now. I hope to see you again when the timing is more conducive to a lovely afternoon at your pub as opposed to convincing Greta that single-handedly annihilating a coven of vampires may not be the best idea."

Jessie's element may be fire, but her smile was ice cold.

"It's cute that you think we plan to stop her."

Robin stopped in his tracks, looking uncertainly from face to face.

"I'm going to bring popcorn and sell tickets to all of the witches and vampires these assholes have targeted throughout the centuries so they can watch," Nicky piped up, almost cheerful with the anticipation of wholesale slaughter, even if it was of his own kind. Mikael shot his younger brother an exasperated glance.

"I must inform the Vampiric Council. Jessica, I suggest you reach out to Isabel and do the same. I will not be long, and then we will hunt together."

Jessie bared her teeth in a terrible, feral grin.

"As it should be," she said and wrapped her arms around Greta, who stood as still as stone, looking out across the dark, wind-swept marsh with an unseeing gaze.

"Greta, honey, you need to move. You're bigger than me. I can't drag you through the portal. We have to go so we can kill him. Well, so you can kill him. I get to watch though."

"Okay," Greta said in that same dreamy voice. She let Jessie lead her through the portal into the welcoming cheer of their Library. Nicky and Mikael followed close behind.

Matthias, Tam, and Robin looked at each other after the witches and vampires were gone.

"I miss peace and quiet," Matthias said with a wistful sigh. Tam snorted.

"Do you, now? Well, Sir Puck, you'd best be off to the High Courts. I wouldn't want those two witches on my heels for not doing what they asked on a day like this."

"No, you're right," Robin hastily agreed, opening his portal to Oberon's court before he paused.

"How did Greta get the letter?" he asked with a slight frown.

Tam pointed at the mound of dirt outside Matthias' front door.

"A messenger brought it. And then Greta took care of him too," he told Robin, which spurred the Puck to haul ass through the portal so fast that he almost tripped coming out the other side. Tam chuckled and then sobered.

"Well, I suppose it's about time we get involved in this mess. What Jessie said about vampire fae... maybe we should check on some of our old friends. Make sure no one's trying to do any more damage," he said.

"I couldn't agree more." Matthias squared his shoulders and led Tam out the door, taking care to lock it behind him.

"What are you going to do about that?" Tam nodded to the mound.

"Let it marinate for a bit and then stew it up for dinner, of course," Matthias answered with a shrug. He ignored Tam's shudder of revulsion as he led the way through the marsh to the woods and the Faery Hill.

Chapter 3

"How's she doing?" John asked, leaning against the door frame of Jessie's office.

"Not great," Jessie sighed and pushed her silver curls out of her face. "I got her to drink enough catnip, lavender, and chamomile tea to sedate a small elephant, and she's at least willing to consider coming up with a game plan instead of tearing the world apart to the core."

"That's... good," John hedged. "Where is she now?"

"In the garden. She has to tell her brother what happened. That's the really scary part," Jessie said with a little laugh that had a hysterical edge to it.

"Someone's scarier than a pissed-off Greta?" John tried, but he couldn't keep the doubtful tone out of his voice. For an earth witch, the bearer of the element of healing and creation and defense, Greta was one of the most bloodthirsty people he had ever met with a famously short temper and no patience whatsoever.

"Oh, yeah. Stefan's an air witch. When the original cabal targeted their family and killed their mother and sister, he perfected using air as a form of biological warfare. He sucked it out of people's lungs and watched them suffocate, or he used the air in their bodies to crush their organs. He is the monster under the bed of bad witches everywhere. If he gets to this cult before we do, there's no telling what will happen."

"Is that a bad thing?"

John returned Jessie's surprised stare and crossed his arms. After all, as a man of the law he was usually the voice of reason and temperance in their community. Werewolves, however, lived and died by the pack, and pack meant family. Like it or not, his pack now included a couple of witches and witch apprentices, a Matagot, a pair of vampire brothers, and a handful of the fae.

"Not if we get Stephanie out first and get Vitorio's word that there won't be any retaliation against the witches. He's the vampire sire and still heads the Vampiric Council when he doesn't teach night classes on graphic design."

John paused, taking in the incongruity of that statement. "When he does what now?"

"He loves teaching," Jessie shrugged. "He's never been able to just sit back and amass wealth and prestige and do nothing with his free time. He's a scholar and artist at heart."

"Is Stefan likely to act before you get Stephanie out and talk to Vitorio?"

Jessie considered the question for a moment.

"Probably not," she admitted. "He's pretty calculating. Not in a cold way or anything like that. He used to be a politician, he's owned businesses, and he's a natural leader. Yeah, you're right. I'm probably worried about nothing."

John smiled. It was nice that they had reached the point in their relationship where Jessie could read between his lines. He sprawled on the battered sofa in front of her dilapidated desk that looked like it was about to fall into a pile of kindling on the floor. Jessie swore by duct tape and spellwork when it came to keeping her comfortable and perfectly broken-in furniture alive.

"What's Vitorio like?"

"He looks like a portly robber baron," she grinned. "He's a little older than Mikael and Nicky, but not by much. He did turn them though. They all came from somewhere around ancient Greece at the end of the Helladic period."

"They're Greek?" John couldn't hide his surprise. The brothers didn't have an accent to speak of, and a vampire's natural pallor hid any identifying skin tones, but he had assumed they came from somewhere in Eastern Europe.

"Yeah. You have to remember that for those of us who are either immortal or live abnormally long lives, we had to constantly remake our identities. I don't think they even remember their birth names. After all, they are close to three thousand years old. Vitorio's last identity change was to some kind of Spanish minor nobility. He renamed himself Don Vitorio Peligroso Santos Vida, which is ridiculous and why most of us call him Vito for short. It'll make sense when you meet him."

"How did he hide his identity if he was nobility?" All of the supernatural backstories made John's head hurt even though he himself had to remake his own identity from time to time. After all, he still remembered the Revolutionary War.

"Well, true to a vampire's nature, it's a little convoluted," Jessie said. "He took in an orphan and raised the boy. When the boy came of age, he was given the choice to be turned or remain human. The kid chose to be turned, and Vitorio took a step back and went into hiding until the villagers forgot about him. He did that a couple of more times until he had enough minions to keep up the charade for centuries, mostly by being very hands-off landowners."

"Were Mikael and Nicky part of that?" John couldn't contain his curiosity.

"No, they were turned before Vitorio decided to play his little nobility game. It happened because of something embarrassing."

She grinned again, remembering when Nicky recounted the story in the most dramatically embellished fashion possible until Mikael stormed, scowling, out of the room.

"Vito was a commoner. The brothers were part of a royal procession traveling through Vito's village at the time. Mikael was a viscount and an advisor to a king, and Nicky was the king's eyes and ears among his court as well as a military advisor and part time assassin. Nicky cut himself sharpening a sword, and Vito couldn't contain his bloodlust. He was still a very young vampire at that point and had no one to teach him or any kind of rule book to work with. Mikael tried to fight Vito off of Nicky, but Vito was stronger and got Mikael instead. He felt really, really bad about it and offered to turn Nicky too."

"This is fascinating," John leaned forward. "So how did Vitorio become a vampire?"

"The story goes that one of the great Celtic dragons somehow made his way to Greece where he was attacked and badly wounded. Vito found him and saved his life. In return, the dragon used his blood to grant Vito the gift of immortality, but, as is par for any of the ancient guardians, the dragon didn't really understand the consequences of his actions because he had never taken the time to truly study human anatomy. So instead of being an immortal human, Vitorio became a vampire.”

“I thought dragons were reptiles. Where does the bat part of being a vampire come in?” John asked in surprise.

“They are partially reptilian, but they’re also mammalian, amphibian, and piscine. That means fishlike, in case you didn’t know.”

“I did know that. Were-creature, remember?” John shot her an amused smile.

“Well, I don’t know what’s common knowledge and what’s not,” Jessie retorted. “Anyway, magical beings can’t be defined using classifications from the natural scientific order humans created. They just have characteristics similar to creatures we already know, and the closest mammalian traits a dragon carries are those of a bat: the wings, claws, and sense of hearing. I’ve heard that some have fur, but I’ve never gotten to see a dragon up close in its true form. Greta has though. After I left the Witch Council, she was appointed to the same Celtic dragon who sired Vito as her asset in research and acquisitions. They became good friends over time.”

“How does that work?” John sat up, fascinated. “Surely people would have noticed a dragon walking around.”

“They can shift into a human form,” Jessie explained. “They travel among us all the time, and we never know it. Anyway, I don’t know how this dragon got his blood to bind to Vitorio’s. A dragon’s magic goes way beyond anything that can be found on our plane of existence. But the end result was immortality, superhuman strength, abilities like being able to turn into a bat and fly at night, and a need to survive on blood."

"You called the dragon one of the guardians. Is that different from being fae or cryptid?" John asked. He knew Jessie should probably check on Greta, but he didn't want the discussion to end. He ate up stuff like this.

Jessie hesitated before answering.

"We don't know if the guardians are fae or cryptid or something else altogether. They were some of the first beings made in the universe, and they're responsible for maintaining the balance of good and evil. Rupert called the gargoyles guardians too, which makes sense when you think about it. No one knows how old they are, and they're always present at the cusp of any event large enough to upset the balance. I think that's one of the reasons why Warsaw was targeted instead of anyone else Nicky cared about."

John steepled his fingers and looked across the desk at Jessie.

"That makes sense. I always wondered why he was the target when they hadn't dated that long, and, not to belittle how much Nicky fell in love with him, it's not like anyone knew how serious it was. Attacking you or Mikael or Greta would have been a more strategic choice."

Jessie nodded. She remembered the last words from Brigitte, the unfortunate banshee who the cabal turned into a necromancer just before she tried to kill Jessie and Greta and frame John:

"If it looks like you, a cryptid leader in the community, killed two ancient witches, then the talks will be stalled long enough for the ones behind this to take power. I do not know what they did

with your friends or the White Lady. After what they did to the gargoyle, I didn't want to know anymore. I just did what I was told and hoped they would kill me too."

It was a last-ditch effort after the cabal's original plan fell through. On the surface, the cabal's scheme should have brought the Alliance's talks to a screeching halt. A human vampire groupie named Marshall, who chose to go by the unfortunate moniker Morticient, was bespelled with a talisman that granted invisibility– and contained a potent love spell that caused him to become obsessed with Nicky. He was supposed to kill Nicky's lover, causing Nicky to kill Marshall in retaliation at Jessie's bar.

Robin the Puck had also been under a mind-control spell that Brigitte, using stolen magic from one of the most powerful witches in existence, placed on him to force him to drive up the conflict and destroy fae and witch relations. The whole plan was a set-up to create the impression that witches, cryptids, humans, and the fae couldn't coexist.

However, the witches behind the plan had not taken into account the self-control a vampire as old as Nicky possessed or that Jessie would be able to recreate Warsaw's murder with Charlie's help and learn the truth. Now Astrid, who had allowed the cabal to take advantage of her youth and hubris in exchange for power and prestige, was in a wormwood cell at the Witch Council. The rest of the newly formed cabal remained in the shadows, waiting for another chance to try to undermine the Alliance and seize control of the Witch Council.

"I should go check on Greta," Jessie pushed her chair out from behind the desk and came to her feet. She circled the desk to perch on John's lap and nestle into the crook of his shoulder first.

"I really did not want to have to deal with this bullshit again," she sighed.

"I know," he murmured and planted a kiss on her temple before standing up and dumping her on the sofa. "Go and see about Greta. I'm going to check in at the station and just make sure nothing weird is going on around here. Well, weirder than usual anyway."

"Uh-huh. And then what are you doing?" she fixed him with an accusing glare.

"Kicking someone's ass at foosball," he grinned and ran out the door before she could hit him with a throw pillow.

Chapter 4

The sky was a map of stars, and a Cheshire Cat smile of a moon hung low over the trees as Greta hid in the garden out of sight from the bar patrons' openly curious stares. She sat on the cold ground at the edge of the pond with her knees pulled to her chest and arms wrapped around her body. Her fists were clenched, the knuckles white. Jessie shivered as she stepped out of the bar's warmth and into the frosty mid-December night, but Greta was unbothered by the cold. Her eyes were still black. That wasn't good.

"Honey, let's get you inside," Jessie knelt by her friend's side and hugged Greta's shoulders. "We can call Stefan together."

"We already spoke," Greta's voice still had that chillingly dreamy quality that meant she had completely disassociated and moved her emotions into a small corner of her mind. At this point, she was, for all intents and purposes, numb from pain.

"You did? When?"

"I called him after we got here. He's on his way."

Jessie paused, startled. It wasn't that she had to be part of every decision, but Stefan and Greta together were a nearly unstoppable and legendary team of vengeance. A picture began to form in Jessie's mind of what the two of them would do to Stephanie's kidnappers, and it was not pretty. It was also exactly what the cabal needed to prove that witches and cryptids couldn't peacefully coexist, thus disrupting the Alliance.

"Greta, sweetie, come with me to the Library. Let's talk about this and what you plan to do."

"I know exactly what we're going to do," Greta turned to look her friend full in the face. "We're going to Vito and having a little chat with him. We're going to get him to convince the Vampiric Counsel to openly sanction Stephanie's rescue and our revenge, and this time I get to destroy Robert and end the cult. And then we're going after the cabal, and we're annihilating them too."

"Oh. Okay, well that was easier than I thought it would be," Jessie was a little taken aback.

Greta gave a soft snort.

"Yeah, well, that's because it's Stefan's idea. This is a setup, another attempt to make it look like we can't all get along. I know you know it. I can see it in your face."

She turned back to the pond, and slowly the black drained from her eyes.

"I'm going to need you, Jessie. I don't know if I can do this without losing control."

"Yes, you can. I'm here, and so are the rest of us. Just tell me what to do."

"Help me find Draig. He can track Robert and find the cult, probably better than the Vampiric Council can."

"You don't know where he is?" Jessie asked in surprised. The Witch Council did not like it when their consultants disappeared.

Dragons didn't feel a need to name themselves, and Draig figured the Welsh word for "dragon" worked as well as anything else. He usually preferred his human form– probably because he was less likely to be pestered by ridiculous knights trying to make a name for themselves. He hated having to kill people for any reason other than food.

He and Greta had worked well together for years. His alignment to air and the insight and clarity that brought to the table perfectly dovetailed with her earth magic. Celtic dragons were aligned with elements like witches, but their meanings were a little different.

"No, I haven't talked to him in a while," Greta admitted. "We sort of drifted apart in the 70's when my research became more focused on ancient witch relics as opposed to creature based magical artifacts. But he sired Vito, and he can find any vampire through the blood."

"Like by calling to the vampire, or does he actually need the blood?"

"Calling. He knows the existence of every vampire in the world, although it can be a little hard to narrow them down sometimes."

"How does he keep all of them straight without going crazy?" Jessie marveled.

"He's millennia old and a magical being," Greta shrugged. "A dragon's brain works in completely different ways from ours."

"What time will Stefan get here?" Jessie asked, shivering. It was great and all that Greta didn't mind the cold, but Jessie certainly did.

"Now," a baritone voice answered from behind them.

They turned toward the tall witch standing in the light from the bar. Stefan looked every inch the community leader and stellar businessman he was with neatly trimmed gray hair that matched his mustache and goatee, a lean physique, and a perfectly tailored, navy blue suit. Greta's shaggy pixie cuts and perpetual jeans and tank tops unless she had to dress up for Council business were a stark contrast.

Stefan crossed the ground between them in long strides and knelt down to sling his arm over his sister's shoulder.

"Thanks for coming." Greta hugged him around the waist.

"Of course. Stephanie is my niece too," he reminded her. "Hey, Jess. Come on, let's go inside so you can tell me everything. Greta, how are you not freezing? Where's your coat?"

"I'm not cold. I'm too... I don't know. Upset? Angry? Anyway, yeah, we can go in."

"Hi, Stefan," Jessie gave him a little wave. "I'm glad you're here. I was about to test using fire magic to create internal combustion so I could feel my toes."

Greta didn't rise to the bait, and Jessie tried to hide her worry. That should have at least earned her an eye roll.

"Let's go to our Library," Jessie climbed to her feet and gave Greta a hand up before she pushed past them to lead the way. They ignored the glances and whispers from the bar and headed straight for Jessie's office, followed by Mikael, Nicky, and John. Mikael and Nicky shook Stefan's hand, and Jessie introduced him to John before opening the portal in the wall.

Once they were through, Jessie heated up a pot of Earl Grey tea and passed a cup to Stefan while he settled on the sofa where Lucy and Spot vied for his lap. Greta called him the cat whisperer– cats flocked to him no matter where he went.

"I want to reach out to Isabel and Vito," Greta didn't mince words. "I want Vito to sanction an attack on Robert and the cult for Stephanie's rescue and make it public knowledge."

Mikael nodded in agreement.

"Smart. That way we can eradicate them and give the appearance of witches and vampires working together against a common threat."

"Exactly," Stefan said.

Greta moved to stand in front of the huge windows along one wall that overlooked a mountain range glistening under moonlight. Unlike the moon outside the bar, this one was full. She wrapped her arms around her middle and stared unseeing out the windows. Jessie felt a pang. She wanted to fix this so badly, and there was nothing she could do at the moment.

"Can you guys get in touch with Vito?" Greta asked without turning around.

"We can. Jessica, if you could be so kind as to let me back into your office, I'm afraid my phone does not have Cassie's magic touch and won't work from here."

As he spoke, Mikael pushed off from the wall where he leaned in order to avoid getting cat hair on his Armani suit. He had twisted his hair up into a knot. He hated the term "man bun". Jessie and Nicky used it as much as possible.

"Cassie's touch?" Stefan looked from Mikael to Jessie.

"Yeah, she's a human who figured out how to rewire electronics to work around our electromagnetic fields. Somehow she also got our phones to work in this plane. She was able to do it for the local fae court too."

"That's... impressive," Stefan absently scratched at his short, grizzled goatee. Jessie could see the wheels turning.

"No. Hands off. She's mine," Jessie firmly nipped that in the bud.

"What? I didn't say anything." Stefan had the innocent act down almost as well as Greta and Jessie did.

"You didn't have to. I saw you thinking it. Nicky, stand here and keep the portal open for Mikael," Jessie said.

After she had the vampire situated, she walked to a panel in the wall next to the windows and opened it into a beautiful room.

Isabel sat in her Witch Council office at a gorgeous antique writing desk under an ornate, stained glass skylight. A barn owl perched on a stand next to a pretty little cabinet overflowing with bobbins of yarn and knitting needles. Isabel looked up in surprise as Jessie, Greta, and Stefan walked through the open portal and cocked her head to the side, her birdlike expression enhanced by large brown eyes set in a fine-boned face.

"Well, hello! To what do I owe this unexpected pleasure?"

"Hey, Isabel. You remember Stefan, don't you?"

Isabel's warm smile lit up the room.

"Of course!" She hurried from around her desk to grasp his hand. "How are you? It's been a while! I caught your lecture on the importance of security, awareness, and discretion for witches in the age of social media. Very true! I constantly battle this with my own staff."

"We can never be too careful," Stefan returned the smile.

"Does anyone want some tea? And what, exactly, are you doing here?"

Isabel never lost her pleasant expression, but she had known Jessie their entire lives. They were born at the same time in the same little Scottish village lost to memory centuries ago, and she knew Jessie would never show up unannounced without a very good reason.

Jessie and Greta exchanged glances.

"Do you remember the dangerous vampire cult that tried to turn witches?" Jessie asked.

Isabel stiffened and dropped her tea pot. Stefan saved it with a puff of air.

"You can't be serious," Isabel stared from one to the other.

"They're back, and they kidnapped Greta and Stefan's niece," Jessie told her. "We're going to Vitorio and asking him to sanction a rescue and the elimination of the cult while we're at it. I thought you should know."

"We would appreciate it if you also sanctioned a rescue at the very least as well," Stefan added. "We want the public to see witches and vampires working together to abolish a dangerous threat."

"Of course, but the Council has to vote to approve it. It can't just be my call," Isabel said.

"Do you think they will?" Greta asked. "We know the cabal has at least one spy on the Council, and I believe they tipped off Robert about Stephanie."

"They would be stupid not to. Even if the cabal told Robert about your niece, he is a wild card and dangerous to every witch. And it's also possible that this was a strategic move to eliminate Robert and his followers. You're too smart and politically savvy to go after this cult without talking to Vito and me first, and now both Councils can openly authorize any actions you must take that lead to the cult's destruction. You could be doing someone's dirty work for all we know. Regardless, the clear and present danger cannot be ignored."

"I didn't think about it as us being put in the position to clean up someone's mess," Greta admitted.

"I'll call an emergency session right now," Isabel said. "Meanwhile get to Vito as soon as you can and then let me know what he says."

"I'm pretty sure he'll try to lead the charge," Jessie said with a wry smile. "He would have destroyed Robert and his followers way back when they first attacked witches if they hadn't gone to ground so well."

"Yes, my guess is Robert found sanctuary through the cabal. They probably gave him witches to experiment on to keep him happy," Isabel scowled.

"I wouldn't be surprised," Jessie agreed. "Then the cabal set a trap for us using Stephanie as bait. Either Robert is wiped out or we are, but either way, it's a win for the cabal."

"Yes," Isabel sighed. "I take back my offer of tea. Time is of the utmost importance. You need to talk to Vito now and then report back to me immediately."

"Yes ma'am," Jessie gave a mock salute.

They exchanged quick hugs before Jessie led Greta and Stefan back through the portal and into the Library. The trio looked at each other.

"Do you know how long it will take Mikael to set up this meeting with Vito?" Stefan asked.

"Within the hour, I imagine," Jessie replied.

"Good. Keep me posted on that, and I'm going to start digging around online and through my networks to figure out where Robert might have taken Stephanie."

"Sounds good," Greta nodded. She hugged her brother good-bye before he stepped through his portal to his own Library. Jessie caught a glimpse of pine shelves and well made leather furniture before the portal closed behind him.

Greta dropped onto the sofa and put her head in her hands.

"I guess I knew they would show up again one day, but I was not prepared for it," she said. Her own experience had been a harrowing nightmare that she never wanted to relive, much less see forced on someone she loved.

"I know, honey," Jessie sat next to her friend and pulled Greta into her arms. "They will pay. I promise you."

"I know."

Chapter 5

It wasn't hard for Isabel and Vito to convince their respective Councils to hold a conclave in order to sanction Stephanie's rescue and the cult's capture. The assembly took place at the Witch Council session hall, a formal and intimidating space where hooded witches met in a shadowed chamber lined with balconies and deep red velvet cushioned chairs.

Grandiose wormwood carvings and frescoes decorated the walls in an attempt to dampen the Council members' magical abilities. The sessions were known to get a little heated, and the wormwood was added after a number of witches were set on fire in the middle of a debate.

The conclave lasted three nights. On the first night, Greta and Stefan were allowed to plead their case. On the second night, Robert was given the chance to place a rebuttal. If he didn't show up, then the councils assigned a proxy to speak on his behalf. They also might call the siblings back for further questioning. The third night was open to debates.

Isabel and Riza, their fire witch friend and head of the Witch Council's security team, kept Jessie and Greta up to date as best they could. Riza's long, iron gray hair and dark eyes spoke to her Cuban heritage. She was a skilled warrior and had proven invaluable when Jessie and her friends rescued the ogres from exile on another world.

"Almost all members of both Councils are willing to endorse a rescue attempt, several witches and vampires even going so far as to call for Robert's outright death rather than just capturing him," Isabel told them at the end of the first night.

She had switched out her heavy Council leader robes for a pair of jeans and a sweater with a unicorn on the front. It wasn't often she could dress down, but she took the opportunity where she could. She was curled up in one of the armchairs that flanked the Library's huge stone fireplace, Lucy firmly snuggled down in her lap, and a cup of rosemary and orange zest tea cradled in her delicate hands. Her large brown eyes were shadowed with dark circles, and exhaustion drew at her delicate face.

"Mmm, this is good," she smiled. Her shoulders relaxed as some of the tension went out of them.

"You said 'almost'," Greta looked up from her spot on the sofa where she had been curled up like a ball ever since she arrived from the conclave. Her body was as tense as a coiled spring, and she still had on the now very wrinkled tailored, forest green linen pants suit she had worn to present her case.

"I'll do background checks into the dissenters," Riza said from the armchair on the other side of the fireplace.

She sipped an ale, and her dark eyes looked as weary as Isabel's, although her athletic, fighter's build remained as alert as ever. She wore a black and gray ceremonial suit befitting her rank that made Jessie think of a grayscale version of Napoleon's oft-painted red, white, and blue uniform.

"What are their arguments?" Jessie asked.

She sat on the floor in front of Greta and waved a feathered cat wand for Ace and Lemur. She and Nicky attended the conclave as members of the audience, but the session hall had been cleared of everyone except the Witch and Vampiric Councils after Greta and Stefan presented their case.

"The biggest one is that the humans, fae, and other cryptids will think we just revert to martial law and vigilantism whenever we want. Obviously what this cult did and is threatening to do is atrocious, but if we just take them out, then what's to stop us from wiping out any group for any reason? If the Vampiric Council refuses to sanction this, then the Witch Council may not have enough votes to go through with it."

"If the Vampiric Council doesn't sanction it, do you think they'll retaliate if you take out Robert and possibly the cult anyway? You have a closer relationship with the vampires than pretty much any of the rest of us," Isabel asked.

"No," Jessie said. "But I think they'll turn it into a 'witches do whatever they want' thing, and that's where we have to be really careful. I know Vito, Mikael, and Nicky are completely on board though. Nicky's not on the Council, but he can still influence votes, and Vito's vote counts for a third of the majority."

"What's your back up plan if they don't sanction it?" Riza asked. They all knew that Greta and Stefan were getting Stephanie back with or without the Council's blessing, and they all knew that Jessie would be right by Greta's side, no matter what.

"Don't worry about that," Greta said at the same time Jessie said,"Plausible deniability is a hell of a thing."

"Do you know what she has planned?" Isabel stared at Jessie.

"Nope. And I don't want to know until it's time to act. Then I'll do whatever she needs me to do."

"Fair enough," Riza shrugged. "The dissenters proposed that the Council sanction the rescue but instead of slaughtering the cult, we try a therapy and deprogramming route."

"That's the Vampiric Council's call," Jessie said with a snort. "Maybe we should see how many are left first."

"No, they're right," Greta said.

They all stared at her in shock.

"I'm sorry, what?" Isabel asked when she recovered enough to speak.

"Look, we know who's the power behind the cult. And he absolutely needs to be eliminated. But you have to remember that Robert took people, callously turned them, and then forced them to act against their vampiric nature just so he could create an army. Maybe if the cultists get help from vampires who care and want to teach them, then they can live the rest of their lives with some sense of belonging and normalcy. At the very least they deserve a chance to know what it feels like to be a real vampire or be given a true vampiric death on their terms."

Riza and Isabel looked at each other before Riza lifted her glass in Greta's direction with a nod.

"Well, I guess that's the argument we'll present to the Vampiric Council tomorrow night then," she said. "After the rebuttal, if there is one, Isabel can call on you to speak. If the Councils hear it from you, then the idea of deprogramming and rehabilitation will carry more weight."

"I'll be there," Greta promised.

She hugged her knees tighter to her chest. Jessie got up and made a cup of chocolate mint tea, passing it to Greta before resuming her spot on the floor with the cats.

"Do the dissenters have any cabal ties that you know of?" she asked

"No," Riza replied. "So far their arguments align with their political and personal ideologies. Personally I think you were right that the cabal had used Robert in the past and realized that he and his cult need to go, so they instigated the kidnapping to force you to do their dirty work."

"Maybe look at the people who agree with the decision and see if that tracks," Jessie suggested.

"I can, but since the whole ideology of the cabal seems to be world domination, I don't know that agreeing to wipe out a subset of another species will turn up anything suspicious," Riza pointed out.

"Yeah, this is basically the perfect way to mask their agenda," Isabel agreed. "Have you reached out to Emma yet?"

"No, why?" Jessie was startled by the question.

"To warn her to keep an eye out. We don't know for sure that the cult came out of the woodwork and took Stephanie as their first victim in centuries. The solitary practitioners make pretty good targets too."

Jessie and Greta exchanged a glance. Their friend Emma helped maintain the community of solitary practitioners that included the hedge, hearth, and hood witches in eastern Atlanta along with the transitory witches who migrated up and down the East Coast. The solitaries kept to themselves and distrusted the Council– and for good reason. Most of them had born the brunt of the Council's McCarthy-like tactics of hunting down and persecuting anyone who was different after the end of the first cabal war.

Jessie and Greta had earned the solitaries' gratitude and respect by defending them as much as possible and working with Emma to insulate the community from the Council's prying eyes. Isabel was right. Emma needed to know about the threat to her people.

"I didn't really think about that," Jessie admitted. "I'll call her tomorrow."

"Good," Isabel nodded. "We'll ask our connections in law enforcement if there's any way to monitor the human homeless and transient populations as well, although I fear that may be a lost cause."

"Thanks for keeping us in the loop," Jessie said as Riza and Isabel finished their drinks and stood up to leave.

"Of course. This is important to us as your friends and as witches," Riza said with a hug. Greta didn't move. Riza, Isabel, and Jessie shot each other a worried look over her head.

The next night Jessie paced the bar until Jared and Caroline made her go to her office to get her out from underfoot. She hadn't been allowed to attend the conclave, and the later it grew, the more worried she became.

"Hey, I have something for you," John walked into her office and tossed his hat on the battered sofa opposite her desk. He was still in uniform and had circles under his eyes. He had pulled every law enforcement string he had to start a forensic work up on the letter and the man buried in front of Matthias' cottage– or what was left of him. Matthias had not been too happy to give up his dinner.

"What?" Jessie asked. She tucked herself into his arms and raised her face for a kiss.

"The man was a druggie out of the French Quarter in New Orleans. Had some petty priors, mostly theft, breaking and entering, and possession. He fell in with some vampire about two weeks before he showed up at Matthias' house. The last anyone heard from him, he was talking about being turned after he did some kind of really important job for the vampires."

"And I guess no one knows who the vampire is," Jessie sighed.

"No, but we have a description. Pretty, blonde, a European accent of some kind. I'll run it by Mikael and Nicky when they come back."

"What else?"

"I got a buddy of mine at the Georgia Bureau of Investigation to run the letter. The paper is old, like from the 1940's. They're doing chromatography on some residue they found, which could help them narrow down where it came from."

"Tell him to look at places underground," Jessie suggested. "Robert likes to hide in tunnels. My guess is that he hid the cult somewhere in New Orleans if that's where the guy came from."

"Good to know. How's Greta holding up?"

"Barely holding it together," Jessie sighed. She burrowed her head in his chest and breathed in his warm, comforting scent.

"We'll get her through this," he said into her hair. She couldn't help but smile that he accepted that he was as much part of making Greta whole again as she was.

Her phone rang, breaking them out of their moment of peace, and she tensed when she saw Nicky's name on the screen.

"They must have wrapped up."

She pushed away from John and answered the phone.

"Hey, what happened?" she asked.

"We'll tell you when we get there. Vito is coming with us. We need to be discreet, and we need a quiet place to talk."

"Can we use the Library?"

"It's preferable if you're okay with that. We'll fly in through the office."

"I'll open the window," she said and hung up.

Half an hour later, three silver-haired bats flew into the office and followed Jessie through the portal to the Library where Greta was back in a ball on the sofa. The black silk shirt dress she'd worn to the conclave that night fared about as well as the linen pants suit. Mikael sat down next to her and pulled her into his arms. The fact that he didn't once mention the cat hair getting on his charcoal gray Dior suit spoke to the gravity of the situation.

Vito looked exactly the way Jessie described him. He had an imposing stature with a handsome, heavy jowled face and hooded eyes that were a startling light green color. With his Mediterranean good looks and the dashing twinkle in his eyes, John could, indeed, see him as a robber baron, lording it over his court while counting his ill-gotten riches. Vito owned several islands and chateaus around the world, and he employed his own tailor and cobbler who were paid millions for his wardrobe of surprisingly practical suits and Italian leather shoes.

Despite his standing as the vampire sire, he was very down to earth and practical. His love for materialistic things was as strong as the next vampire's, but he saw beauty and joy in the mundane as much as in the luxurious. Unlike his offspring, his strength did not wane in daylight– he was powerful day and night. He was also an accomplished artist who welcomed the digital age with open arms and went so far as to teach night classes on design at a small college outside of the Atlanta area.

He shook John's hand after they were introduced and greeted Jessie with a kiss on both cheeks before kneeling in front of Greta and clasping her hand in both of his.

"My dear, we will resolve this one way or the other," he said in a voice that still held a touch of an ancient Greek accent. "If our Councils do not agree to let us work together, then rest assured that the vampires will wipe out this blight and return your niece to you unharmed."

"I know, but I want to do it," Greta said in a small voice.

Vito's lips twitched.

"Yes, well, how about we keep one for you to beat up?"

"Can you keep three so Stefan and Stephanie get one too?" Jessie asked.

"Whatever makes my two favorite witches happy," Vito said with a little sigh of resignation.

"They make vampires look like pacifists. You learn to live with it," Mikael told him.

"Speaking of, where is Stefan?" Jessie asked.

"He went back to his Library to follow up on some leads. He has his own network of aides working on this," Greta said.

"How did it go tonight?" John asked.

Vito pushed back to his feet with a ponderous sigh. Jessie opened a cabinet under the old writing desk in the corner and pulled out a bottle of Palo Cortado sherry and a set of glasses. Mikael raised his eyebrows but didn't say anything at this surprising addition to the Library.

"Just because I don't drink doesn't mean I don't keep a very good wine cellar," Jessie said as Nicky gave an outraged gasp. She poured glasses for John and the vampires and used her fire magic to heat water for tea.

"Not surprisingly, no one showed up to speak on Robert's behalf. So, after reviewing Greta's and Stefan's testimony, I believe the Councils will agree to the cult's eradication, especially since you insist on a deprogramming option for its members," Vito said. He swirled the sherry in his glass and took a deep sniff. "My compliments, Jessica. This is quite a treat."

"Thank you," Jessie smiled.

"Like I told Isabel, I know not everyone is to blame for this. I think that the cultists who can be deprogrammed and learn how to embrace their nature should be given that chance. But Robert and his closest advisors absolutely know what they're doing. I want them destroyed," Greta said.

"As they should and will be," Vito agreed.

"What else?" Jessie asked. They didn't need to have this discussion in private unless there was more to the story.

"We think we narrowed down the location of the cult," Vito said.

"New Orleans?" John asked with a raised eyebrow and slight twist to his lips. He didn't get to show off very often, but he enjoyed it when the opportunity presented itself. Vito stopped, surprised.

"Why, yes. But how did you know?"

"Oh, you know. Pulled a few strings here and there," John's nonchalant shrug was a work of art as he told the vampires what he learned so far.

"I'm going to get my buddy who works for the FBI to get in touch with their field office in New Orleans and start looking for activity in basements or crypts," he finished with a little nod to Jessie. "Does anyone have anything on the vamp who gave the guy the letter?"

"No," Mikael said. "All we know so far is that she came from somewhere in Europe, probably London. She did not introduce herself to the local coven, which, while not mandatory, is expected as a matter of courtesy."

"And no one recognized her?" Jessie asked with a small degree of skepticism. New Orleans, more than any other city in the Americas, logged vampiric activity with the utmost attention to detail. The high level of tourists looking for thrills made such tracking a necessity.

"No, which we found equally difficult to believe," Vito said. "She went out of her way to achieve secrecy, which is not part of the vampiric nature. Perhaps I should pay a little visit to New Orleans myself."

"Be careful," Greta looked up. "They will try to take you out. It would be the pinnacle of their achievements and cement their power."

"I will not allow them to harm me," Vito reassured her with a warm smile. "I have many resources up my sleeve. I have been around for a very long time, and it is pretty difficult to kill me."

"We found him in pieces on an island once humming to himself and looking at the sky," Nicky said with a shudder. "Mikael found his head and right leg, I found his torso and left arm, and together we found his other arm and leg. We had to get a gypsy to sew him back together."

"And you could never tell," Vito beamed.

"Wait, what?" John almost dropped his glass when he tried to put it on the end table and missed.

"Oh, I think that was the time my gang of robbers decided to cut me out of their profits. Literally. They were quite surprised when I walked in on their little *fête* the following night. I believe one even went so far as to urinate in his trousers."

John stared at him and then at Jessie, who shrugged as if to say, "Vampires, what are you going to do?"

"At any rate, it is imperative that we get eyes on any jails, halfway houses, and homeless shelters in New Orleans. The inhabitants of such establishments are more vulnerable and easy targets," Vito continued. "We also can't rule out other cities or routes."

Jessie shot a glance at Greta who remained curled up in Mikael's arms. The vampire may be asexual, but he loved his friends and family fiercely, especially Greta. She was like his sister, and he would do anything for her.

"What now?" John asked.

"Well, Sir Wolf, now we wait for the verdict tomorrow night. We should go ahead and get our plans firmly in place since it seems likely that both Councils will move ahead on the sanction. It is imperative that we do this with the utmost discretion, or we could send unpleasant ripples throughout the fae and human communities, not to mention the remainder of the cryptids," Vito warned.

"I doubt the fae will offer any opposition," Nicky pointed out. "If this cult decided that hybrid witchpires are possible, imagine what they could come up with for the fae– and Robert most likely looks at humans as mere fodder for his armies."

"The important thing is to make sure humans believe that they are not looked at as 'mere fodder'," Vito reminded his offspring. "They still have powers that rival ours, and they outnumber us thousands to one."

"We all talked about how this could be a way for us to do the cabal's dirty work for them and get rid of this cult," Jessie said. "But it also may be a way for the rest of the world to get rid of us."

They paused to consider that gloomy possibility. She was right– if anything went wrong, then this would be a perfect opportunity to paint their little group as a bunch of vigilante, hot-headed, out-of-control rebels set against the new world order.

"Then we absolutely move forward with deprogramming," Greta declared. "I will not let Robert or the cabal manipulate us anymore. We outmaneuver them this time. End of discussion."

"You heard her," Vito said with a sweeping bow in Greta's direction. "Lady Witches, I take my leave of you this fine evening. But rest assured, this is far from over. I will return tomorrow eve with tidings from the joint Council sessions."

"Can you locate Draig?" Greta asked. "He can help us find Robert."

"I will do my best," Vito said with another shallow bow.

"Here, I'll let you out," Jessie unwound herself from the floor and cat toys to open the Library portal and office window. Vito kissed her hand and Greta's before shifting back into a silver haired bat and whisking himself out of the building.

"I hate waiting," John muttered as he poured himself another glass of sherry.

"Same," Nicky agreed, taking the bottle. "You don't mind if we finish this off, do you? Since you don't drink and all."

Jessie cracked a smile despite herself. His look of angelic innocence was too much to resist.

"Fine, but you're buying the next one!"

Chapter 6

"Careful, watch your aim! It's imperative that you focus and stay calm," Jessie tried to keep the tension out of her voice. It was early the next afternoon, and, despite her nocturnal tendencies, she was determined to make Christopher get some solid training in before the bar opened for business.

Jessie had promised Mara to take him on as an apprentice when the Tuatha de Danann Duchess granted the young witch her protection after she helped rescue him from a rich human teenager named Zach. Zach alarmingly thought that humans could siphon a witch's magic and relentlessly tormented Christopher, trying to access the power he so covetously sought.

Luckily, Mara took Chris under her wing; an act which included wiping Zach's memory and unceremoniously dumping him on a well manicured street in one of Atlanta's most prestigious neighborhoods– a neighborhood that he called home. His family's wealth and access to power still gave Jessie chills. As Greta pointed out, the idea of stealing a witch's magic came from somewhere, and it probably hadn't originated in the drug clouded mind of a spoiled teenager.

Caroline sat at the bar to support her brother. Like all witch twins, they were opposites in almost every way down to Chris' unruly jet black hair and dark eyes set in a face so pale that it was almost snow-white. Where her element was water, his was fire. She was outgoing and fearless, he wanted nothing to do with crowds and social gatherings.

When he first came to Jessie, he was afraid of his own shadow. He had been bullied at school and exploited by other witches, and it took several weeks under Jessie's tutelage before he believed that she might actually want to help him learn and grow.

Now he smiled and joked around with Jared, Cassie, Charlie, and the bar regulars. All in all, it was nice to see him start to feel comfortable in his own skin, even if he was still afraid of his fire magic.

He flinched and barely corrected his course before the white hot fireball he shot from his fingertips could burn down half the building.

"I think maybe we should stop," he said. His adam's apple bobbed, and his hair stuck to his sweaty forehead.

"No, we're not," Jessie said in an even tone. She refused to back down.

"I know you can do this," Caroline encouraged him. He shot a doubting glance her way before he squared his shoulders and lifted his chin as he prepared to try again.

Up until now, Jessie had let Chris stick to controlled fire bursts against an old, out of the way, stack of bricks in the garden where the pond and lack of anything really flammable made him feel safe. But it was time to ditch the training wheels and get his power under control.

Twins were born into the witching world once every hundred years, and their magical powers were unparalleled. Even as an apprentice, Caroline was almost as strong as Jessie, and she and Chris would be virtually unstoppable by the time they finished their training. As one half of the most powerful pair of witches in this century, Chris needed to learn how to listen to and accept his magic. Years of trying to stifle his talent only blocked his growth, leaving him vulnerable and afraid.

"You're not going to hurt anything," Caroline assured him. "Jess and I won't let you, but you have to learn. Or do you want the cabal to come after you too? Do you really think they'll let you get away with refusing to use your power just because you're scared?"

Jessie silently watched the twins. If Caroline couldn't get through to Christopher, then no one could. He had to master his considerable power. Jessie didn't want to think about the consequences if he didn't.

"Shouldn't we have a full-fledged water witch here?" Chris asked, slanting a dubious glance at his sister. "I get that you're trying to help, Care, but how can you stop me if I set the bar on fire?"

Caroline and Jessie exchanged a glance.

"Throw a fireball at me," Jessie said.

"What?" He stared at her in disbelief.

"Come on, just do it."

He opened his mouth to argue, but she cut him off.

"As your teacher, I command you."

An ancient order, and with the weight of her own impressive magic behind it and with his stunted magical growth, he couldn't resist. The fireball blossomed in his hands and was halfway between them when it suddenly snuffed out of existence. He stared in shock at the sudden wet spot on the floor.

"What–"

"You forget that I'm your other half and that I trained a lot longer than you have," Caroline couldn't keep the smug note out of her voice. "Not to brag, but according to Jessie, being a twin makes me as strong as a full fledged witch."

"And I control fire, even as powerful as yours. It was never going to reach me, with or without Caroline here," Jessie added. "You're not fast enough— yet. With training and confidence in your power though, you will be one day."

"Oh…" Chris stared at both of them in wonder.

Then his hands blossomed with dancing white and blue flames, and he laughed, and it was pure joy that made Jessie's heart sing as much as it made tears fill her bright blue eyes. Caroline ran to her brother and hugged him fiercely to her, the flames dancing along her skin but never quite touching.

"Now do you feel better about letting your magic out?" Jessie asked.

"Yes," he ducked his head with a sheepish, shy grin.

"You should also know that I had this bar cured and blessed a hundred times over by dragon flame. No one can set it on fire, no matter how hard they try," Greta said from where she watched at the entrance to the hallway. "You need to not just learn how to control your magic, you need to learn how to embrace it and let it be part of you. It's alive within you, and it needs you as much as you need it."

She gave the flaming twins a wide berth as she made her way to Jessie's side where she curled up on a bar stool by her best friend. They wrapped their arms around each other and watched Chris and Caroline for a moment longer.

"How are you holding up?" Jessie asked.

"Not great. I gave Stefan everything John found out from the GBI so far. He has some connections too, so I figured maybe it would help."

"Smart move," Jessie said. "Okay, enough hugging, everyone. Let's get back to the drills. The goal is not only for you to hit the target but for you to learn to control your magic enough to just put a hole in the target without setting it on fire."

"It would be easier if the target wasn't paper," Chris objected, looking at the silhouette on the opposite wall. Jessie had batted her eyelashes at John a couple of times until he showed up with a stack of paper targets from the sheriff office's gun range.

"That's the whole point," Jessie laughed. "We spent the last month and a half blasting bricks, but not everything you come up against will be made of clay. Now you need to learn focus and self-control."

"Fine," Chris said with a dramatic eye roll followed by another shy grin.

This was the most Jessie had seen him come out of his shell since they rescued him from Zach. Even Greta got into the spirit of training. She moved them all outside and flung mudballs at Chris for him to blast out of the air. It went much more smoothly after he figured out how to aim at a moving target. Caroline eyed his shirt when they were done.

"I can get that clean for you if you want," she offered.

"No, I'll do it." He looked down at himself and chuckled. "Thanks, Greta. That really helped a lot."

"Any time," she smiled back.

Jessie followed Greta inside, leaving the twins to lounge by the small pond in the herb garden and soak up the December sun.

"Did you talk to Emma yet?" Greta asked as she pulled herself onto a barstool.

"I left a message, but I haven't heard back. She's not exactly a morning person, so I figure it will be another hour or so—"

She stopped when her phone rang.

"Speak of the devil, hey Emma. Hang on, let me put you on speaker. Greta's here too."

"Hey, ladies. How's it going? How's Chris?" Emma's perky voice came through the speaker. She was even tinier than Jessie and Isabel, not quite five feet tall, with the personality of a lioness. She was plump with a pleasant face and dancing blue eyes framed by ash gray ringlets that belied her sharp intellect and foul mouth— and love of pipes.

She also was the reason why Chris was still alive. The hedge, hearth, and hood witches along with the rest of the solo practitioners had been some of the first to feel the wrath of the Council's Inquisition after the cabal was defeated. Now they kept to themselves and offered a haven to refugees and runaways alike. It had taken a lot of convincing to get Emma to bring Chris to them. She took her role as protector and guardian over those who had nothing very seriously.

"Thriving," Jessie didn't try to hide the note of pride in her voice. "We had a breakthrough today. He's not as scared of his magic anymore. He even started to learn how to focus it."

"That's awesome," Emma cried. Jessie heard clapping through the phone and smiled as she pictured her friend jumping up and down.

"He owes it to you, which is partly why we're calling," Greta said. Something in her voice made Emma pause.

"What's going on?" she asked.

"Greta's niece was kidnapped by a vampire cult, and they demanded that Greta surrender herself to them."

"What?" Emma exploded. "Where are they? Do I need to kill somebody?"

"No, I get to do it," Greta said.

"We ran into them a long time ago," Jessie cut in. "They believe that they can turn a witch into a vampire and create and control the ultimate magical being."

"But that's not possible," Emma protested. "The magics will conflict with each other, and the witch will die. And I'm pretty sure there are some scary magical fae who would like to contest that claim."

"Exactly," Jessie said.

"Wait a minute, was that when all of those covens turned up dead and no one could figure out what happened to them? They looked like they had been obliterated."

"Same guys," Greta said. "They're led by a real piece of work named Robert."

"Shit..." Emma's voice trailed off. It was one of maybe three times Jessie had ever heard Emma become speechless.

"Robert is fixated on Greta and convinced that she is their answer to world domination, and now he has her niece."

"Why Greta? I mean, not to say you're not special, honey, but why you?"

"I accidentally healed a new vampire through her transition while Jessie and I were holed up in a tavern in Paris during a plague. Wrong place wrong time kind of thing," Greta replied.

Emma was quiet for a moment longer.

"What can I do? Obviously we're going to help. We're not going to sit here and let some fucking vampire use witches as a science experiment."

Jessie grinned despite herself.

"Yeah, I don't think any of us are. We're waiting for the Witch and Vampire Councils to sanction a rescue because the big thing right now is maintaining the Alliance. We don't want humans, fae, or the rest of the cryptids to think that we operate by some kind of vigilante justice. But we need to know if you have anyone missing. If Robert's back to focusing on Greta, then maybe he has already started to experiment on other witches."

"It's more than that," Greta added. "You have to make sure that the transient and solitary practitioners know they could be targeted. Their natures make it hard to miss them if they disappear, and that makes them the most vulnerable. We don't know yet if Robert is working with the new cabal or if we're being played by the cabal to get rid of a liability, but I seriously doubt that after this much time Robert suddenly wants to get his hands on me again of his own volition. Maybe someone convinced him that he used the wrong ritual before or told him he's strong enough now. Whatever the reason he came back, you need to get eyes on your people and keep them where you can see them."

"Understood," Emma said. All levity left her voice, leaving a brisk, cold tone. She would die to save the ones she protected. Jessie hoped it wouldn't come down to that.

"How are Frank and the dogs?" Jessie asked.

"They're fine. Frank's getting ready to open another restaurant, and the dogs are adorable assholes as always. How's John?"

They chatted a little more before Jessie hung up. Yes, time was of the essence, but as she grew older, she cherished the moments of connection she got with the people she loved and took them where she could.

"Who's next on our call list?" Greta asked.

"Madame Blanche. I want to check on Rupert," Jessie said and searched through her phone for Madame Blanche's number.

"Bonjour, Jessica! How are you this evening?" Madame Blanche's elegant Parisian accented voice flowed into the room. She had been born Charlotte de Valois, the illegitimate daughter of King Charles VII in France, and was considered by many to be the original Dame Blanche, or White Lady.

"Hello, I'm well. Greta's here with me," Jessie smiled.

"Bonjour," Greta waved at the phone even though no one but Jessie could see her.

"To what do I owe the pleasure?" Madame Blanche asked.

Jessie and Greta exchanged a quick glance.

"We want to see how Rupert's doing." Jessie said, as casually as she could. She had no doubt Rupert was somewhere close by and could hear everything.

"There is much improvement," Madame Blanche replied slowly.

"I sense a 'but'," Greta said.

"*Oui*," Madame Blanche sighed. "I will never tell him what to do, of course, but I sense a darkness that has not been present for a long time. As you know, the Matagot are, as you say, chaotic neutral. For one to go down a rabbit hole to the bleaker places of the mind would be a terrible thing."

"Well, he went through a terrible ordeal," Jessie pointed out. "Do you think that he would heal faster if he were here and fighting for a cause he believed in, or would he give in to the dark side of the force?"

"How many gaming and movie references can we fit into one conversation?" Greta muttered. Jessie and Madame Blanche ignored her.

"Is a fight necessary at this time?" Madame Blanche was startled.

"Unfortunately it looks that way," Jessie said before filling the White Lady in on the cult.

There was silence on the other end and then a burst of short, astonished laughter.

"Surely you jest," Madame Blanche exclaimed. "No one can be that idiotic!"

"Well, Robert did not come through his transformation into vampiric life very well," Jessie explained. "He had been a monk when he was alive. He's extremely good looking, which, unfortunately, was his downfall. He drew the attention of a greedy vampire obsessed with beautiful things and beautiful people. The vampire turned him against his will, and Robert's vampiric nature went to war with his vow of poverty and love for the church."

"He would have been ripe pickings for lies from a master manipulator," Greta chimed in. "We think that someone in the cabal put this idea into his head and convinced him that he was doing God's work."

"If you are, indeed, correct, then you realize this means that you can't rule out the possibility that vampires are involved in the cabal as well," Madame Blanche pointed out. "A witch would not have been able to manipulate a vampire nearly as well as another vampire. And after all, if the cabal encompassed witches and the fae, then why not vampires too? Out of the cryptids they are the most power hungry. It is quite literally in their blood."

Jessie should have been surprised by the revelation, but she wasn't.

"Do you think Rupert would be safe in this kind of fight?" Jessie couldn't keep the worry out of her voice.

The giant black Matagot who preferred the shape of a cat and spent his days shedding on the bar when he slept in the sunspots that streamed through the stained cut glass windows had quickly become a dear friend to all of them and a deeply valued ally. But Jessie would never put her friends' lives or health on the line– no matter how important the cause.

"I do not know. Only he can tell us. I have to trust that he will choose wisely and that we will do what we can to keep him safe."

Jessie was glad Madame Blanche included herself in that directive. The last time someone trusted Jessie with their charge's safekeeping, Jared had to kill his uncle to save Jessie's life. His mother still had not forgiven Jessie, no matter how much Jared told Sharon that she was being irrational.

"There is only one way to find out," said the deep, gravelly voice behind them. Jessie and Greta whirled around to see Rupert sitting majestically on the floor, grooming his whiskers with a paw.

"I suppose he made up his mind for us," Madame Blanche could not keep the resigned note out of her voice. "Bonne chance, mes amis. Rupert, be mindful of your needs and health. I am here if you need me."

"Of course," Rupert sniffed. "All shall be well. Now. What's this I hear about a kidnapping?"

Chapter 7

They gathered in the Library again that night to await the Councils' verdicts. John sat in one of the armchairs with Jessie curled up in his lap while Greta paced in circles around the furniture. Her tension was so high that the cats avoided her, choosing to hide under the sofa or behind the old desk in the corner instead. Only Lucy remained unperturbed. Not even Greta's obvious anxiety could dislodge the tiny calico from the back of the other armchair where she basked in the fire's cheerful warmth.

Nicky leaned against a set of shelves, and Mikael stared out of the floor to ceiling length windows that overlooked the moonlit mountain range. The range did not show up on any of Earth's maps. He had never asked where the witches chose to put their Library or if the beautiful landscape even existed on any plane of existence. Some things, he had decided a long time ago, were better left unanswered.

LaSalle waited on the sofa. His never-ending goblet was absent. Instead, a wicked looking battle axe rested on the floor by his feet. Rupert sat in front of the fire like an immovable statue and watched Greta with his emerald green eyes. He finally broke the weighted silence.

"Is there any idea how long these things take? I think I detect a groove forming in the carpet under Greta's feet."

"They have to come to a resolution by dawn," Jessie said. "If they can't reach an agreement, then they leave the outcome to chance."

"What do you mean?" John was startled. "Like they draw the decision out of a hat?"

"Something like that," Greta said with a short, mirthless bark of a laugh.

"It is highly unlikely that will be necessary," Mikael turned away from the window and gently stopped Greta in her tracks. "Greta, love, you are making us dizzy. Let's get you some tea instead."

"That's a great idea," Jessie uncurled herself from John's lap and went to the little table littered with boxes and tins of tea, a collection of mismatched mugs, and Greta's dented cherry red tea kettle. She used her fire magic to heat the kettle and poured them both a cup of sage and peppermint tea.

"Vito and Isabel said that both Councils agree that the cult must be stopped," Mikael told them once Greta sat down next to LaSalle. "Now they have to decide on a method. Vito thinks that Greta's insistence on deprogramming is the key to presenting this as an united front to the humans, the fae, and the rest of the cryptid world. It's politically the best solution for all parties involved."

"Except the cult," John wryly pointed out.

"Except the cult," Nicky agreed. "But at least the bulk of the members will be given a chance to live as vampires are meant to live or find their true death."

Jessie and Greta jumped when Jessie's phone rang. She almost dropped her mug trying to dig it out of her back pocket.

"Hey, Jess, some guy is here looking for you. He says his name is Vito," Jared's voice came through the line. "Is he really the vampire sire? I thought he would look more, I don't know, scary and less like a college professor."

"He *is* a college professor, and trust me, he can be plenty scary when he needs to be. Tell him to come to my office and I'll open the Library," Jessie replied. "Vito's here. I'm going to let him in."

"I love how she states the obvious as though all of us lack superb hearing," Rupert remarked to no one in particular.

"I can send you back to Madame Blanche," Jessie threatened.

Rupert sniffed and began to groom a front paw.

"You mean you can try," he corrected her.

"Hello, hello! Greetings!" Vito beamed as he came through the door. He was very cheerful, which boded well.

"What did they say?" Greta jumped up from the couch and began to pace again.

"Has she been doing that all night?" Vito asked Nicky as John groaned and buried his face in his hands.

"It's a witch thing. You get used to it," Nicky replied with a straight face.

"Greta, my dear, if you could find it in your heart to stand still for a moment, I would appreciate it if you could please summon your brother. I believe he will want to be part of this discussion," Vito said with a shallow bow as he accepted the glass of port Jessie offered him and then turned to face Rupert and LaSalle. "You must be the famous Matagot and Nain Rouge I've heard so much about. It is a pleasure to make your acquaintance."

Greta shot him a glare, which he ignored with equanimity. She pulled her phone from the small bag on the coffee table and sent a text. After a moment, her phone buzzed back. Relief made her shoulders sag as she read Stefan's message.

"He's on his way," she said as she pushed a knothole on one of the wall panels, opening a portal into their library. Stefan stepped through wearing a bespoke navy blue suit complete with an embroidered waistcoat. He had a glass of wine in one hand.

"You're awfully dressed up," LaSalle raised a bushy eyebrow after Greta introduced her brother to Vito and Rupert.

"Fundraiser," Stefan grimaced. "I hate those things. Didn't realize I brought the wine glass. I should probably take it back after this."

"I thought you got out of politics?" Jessie asked. She resumed her perch on John's lap and gestured to the opposite arm chair. Stefan put his wine on the end table, sank into the chair, and coaxed Lucy into his lap. Unlike Mikael, he had no qualms about covering himself with cat hair. And, unlike Mikael, he could also whisk the cat hair off of his clothes with a wave of his hand and a puff of air.

"Yes and no. I always keep my finger on the government pulse, and besides, I figured it wouldn't hurt to use some of my law enforcement and agency connections to see if we can get anything out of John's information. Thanks for that, by the way. That was a huge step forward," he nodded to John.

"Anything for my pack," John replied. That drew a pleased smile to Stefan's face.

"What did you find out?" Greta asked. Now that her brother was there, she calmed down and returned to a corner of the sofa where she curled into a ball, hugging a throw pillow to her chest.

"Nothing yet, *liebchen*," he said. "It's still early, but I promise that you will be the first to know."

"Vito, what did the Councils decide?" Jessie asked.

"They agreed to sanction action against Robert. Greta and Stefan, you may proceed with your plan for Stephanie's recovery. The cult members are to be captured, if possible, rather than intentionally killed and turned over to the Vampiric Council immediately for deprogramming at our hands. Unofficially, if Robert doesn't make it, no one will cry themselves to sleep."

"Who added the line about 'intentionally killed'," Nicky grinned.

"That would be Isabel, the ever adroit diplomat," Vito gave an answering smirk.

"We can do that," Greta said. She sat up straight, crossed her legs at the knee, and turned to her brother. "No one can die or be hurt unless we have exhausted all other options for a peaceful resolution. Even then, casualties and injuries must be kept to a minimum. We need to make sure that only companions we trust implicitly accompany us on this mission to avoid the possibility of an unfortunate accident. In addition, we need our vampire allies so that they can help us reach out to the unfortunates who were brought into this cult with no knowledge or understanding of what they have become."

"Of course," Stefan replied with a politician's smooth grace. "I never had any intention of this rescue going otherwise."

"Wait, what?" LaSalle's jaw dropped. Even Rupert stopped his fastidious grooming to stare at Greta in shock.

"Plausible deniability is a hell of a thing," Jessie murmured into her tea.

This was a side of Greta that their friends hadn't yet seen. They knew her to be impetuous, fierce, and sometimes bloodthirsty, but they forgot that she was also a diplomatic representative for the Witch Council and could navigate and manipulate politics almost as well as her brother.

By taking this approach, she presented herself and her brother as sympathetic to the poor cultists who were brought into this against their will– and she made sure that no one who accompanied them on the rescue mission might "accidentally" kill one or more cultists and frame Greta or any of her friends for the murder. She also made sure that if someone did have to die– like Robert– only her most trusted allies would be along for the ride.

"LaSalle," Greta continued as if there had been no interruption. "We need to let our fae allies know about our plans. Can you set up a meeting with Robin and Mara?"

"Sure, I mean, yes, but are you really just going to sit there and do nothing for your family's honor?" The little dwarf's beard quivered in outrage.

"LaSalle," Jessie interrupted. "Just trust her and do it."

"Fine, but we're going to have a discussion about this later," he snapped and popped out of sight with a thunderous glare. Only a trusted fae could portal in and out of their Library without the witches' aid, and he was their most trusted ally of all of the faery folk.

"This is quite fascinating," Rupert murmured. His unblinking emerald gaze never left Greta's face. "I suppose next you wish for me to enlighten Madame Blanche?"

"If you don't mind," Greta returned his stare. He inclined his head and left through the portal Jessie opened for him to her office.

"And I shall return to the Vampiric Council to let them know your course of action," Vito bowed. He handed his empty glass to Jessie and gave her a gentle hug and kiss on the cheek as he followed Rupert.

LaSalle popped back into the Library, only now his goblet was clutched in his hand.

"Mara said the Puck is on some errand for Oberon, but she'll be able to see you tomorrow."

"What else did she say?" Jessie grinned.

"That I needed to mind my own business and trust you and if I didn't know you better by now, then I should be ashamed of myself," he scowled.

"To be fair, I sometimes tend to overreact," Greta admitted.

"Sometimes?" Jessie stared at her friend.

"Is that sometimes like 'I think I'll bury half of the cabal in the ground and leave them'?" Nicky asked.

"What?" Stefan looked between them, startled.

"Never mind," Greta hastily cut them off. "We need a solid plan, and we need to come up with it soon. Obviously Robert dies, and I get to do it, but we really do have to try to save as many of the others as we can."

"That's my girl," LaSalle beamed and chugged his beer.

"Any word on Draig?" Stefan leaned back in the chair.

"Shit, I forgot to ask Vito if he heard anything yet," Greta admitted in chagrin.

"I'll ask him," Mikael said. "Jessica, if you would please let me back into your office?"

"Of course."

"Without him, I don't know if we can pull this off. There are a lot of them and not a lot of us," Greta said.

"How many of them are there?" John asked.

"When they captured me before, there were probably two hundred of them. We destroyed most of them, thanks to the little fact that Robert had starved his recruits because he believed that consuming blood was too 'vampiric' and therefore evil. Didn't stop him from feeding whenever he felt the need though."

"Naturally," Jessie rolled her eyes

"When a vampire does not feed, they enter a state similar to mummification," Nicky explained to John. "It makes us rather flammable as they found out when Jessie here unleashed her fire magic on them."

"I helped," Stefan winced as Lucy made biscuits in his lap.

"Yes, you fanned the flames," Jessie said. "You get a gold star. We have to assume that Robert learned his lesson and is keeping his new recruits fairly well fed."

"I don't think a cultist could bespell the guy who brought me the note if she didn't feed on a regular basis," Greta agreed. "And besides, the point is to capture and deprogram, not annihilate. Even if our hands weren't tied by the councils, I want to give the cultists a choice. They haven't had that right yet."

"Did you give them one before?" LaSalle asked. It wasn't an accusation.

"I was unconscious. Jessie and Stefan didn't have time to ask my opinion," Greta replied. "That's one of the things we would like to avoid this time around."

"I hate that there's a 'this time'," Jessie scowled and jumped as her phone rang, startling them all. "Hang on, it's Emma. Hey, Emma. You're on speaker. Stefan, Nicky, Mikael–"

"Yeah, yeah, there are other people there, I don't care. Jessie, listen to me. I did what you asked. A lot of my people are missing. Not just transients, either. I mean, they're missing too, but we have a sort of migration that takes place from Boston to Miami, and not even half of them passed through here."

"How did you miss that?" Stefan asked. Again, it wasn't an accusation. He knew as well as anyone that if Emma's sharp mind missed a huge segment of migratory witches, then something bad happened.

"I don't know," she admitted.

"Can you reach out to your counterparts in the rest of the cities? Clearly a spell or glamour is in place, and it seems that Jessie's questions raised your awareness and broke it. Perhaps you can do the same for others."

"I'll try," she said before they heard a loud crash in the background. "Hey, what are you doing here? Who are– Jessica! Help me!"

And then the phone went dead.

Chapter 8

Jessie launched herself off of John's lap and through a hastily sketched portal that let them out in front of Emma's shattered door. Greta and Stefan were right on her heels. A curtain of darkness blocked the normally cheerful red paint and Pittsburgh Steelers welcome mat, but beyond it they heard a scream and a wet, meaty thump.

"Greta, open the earth," Stefan commanded.

Greta jerked the earth out from under the cloaking spell, disrupting it enough that Stefan could send a blast of sharp wind and rip the veil apart. Jessie darted through the doorway. Flames danced on her fingertips, and she honed them to an arrow's point as she ran from room to room until she saw the hulking figure towering over a huddled heap on the floor, balanced on one foot and ready to stomp down with the other.

He turned toward the sound of her shout, and she barely had time to see an ugly, snarled face before she shot the fire arrows into his chest. He burst into flame and went down with a thud, missing Emma's comatose body by inches.

Greta dropped to her knees by their friend as John shot past her in wolf form and up the dark stairs, snarling as he went. Nicky stayed by Greta's side while LaSalle searched the rest of the ground floor.

"She's in really bad shape," Greta looked up at Jessie with worry-filled eyes. Emma wasn't moving. One eye was purple and swollen shut, and livid finger prints striped her throat.

One of her arms bent at an unnatural angle, and blood seeped from her nose and mouth.

"Can you heal her?" Jessie asked.

"I'm sure as hell going to try. Find Frank and tell him to get one of the hearth or hood witch healers over here. Stefan, I need soil from her garden. I need the earth that loves her to help me."

Hood and hearth witches, especially hood witches, were also known for their healing. If Frank could get someone to help them, then Emma stood a fighting chance. And every witch in hiding would lay down their life for Emma— just like she would lay down hers for theirs.

Jessie pulled out her phone and started to head for the front porch as she looked for Frank's number. Stefan disappeared through the back door to Emma's wild garden and Greta began to work, coaxing the minerals and elements that made up Emma's bones to knit back together. Jessie was so caught up in her search, that she didn't realize someone was right in front of her until she walked straight into Sharon Daniels, Jared's mother, and a witch who definitely did not count Jessie among her favorite people.

No, it hadn't been Jessie's fault that Jared had to kill his uncle to save her life, but Sharon had to see the shattered innocence and hurt in her child's eyes every day since. His teacher, the one who was supposed to protect him, had let him down, and Sharon could not forgive Jessie for that.

Right behind Sharon, Jessie saw Frank run toward the house as fast as he could, his face blanched with fear.

"Emma! I felt pain! Where is she?"

"Greta's with her. It's my fault. I asked her if she knew whether any witches were missing, and I must have broken some kind of spell because all of a sudden she figured out that a lot more are missing than anyone even realized, and then someone broke in and attacked her," Jessie managed to get out before scalding tears rolled down her cheeks.

Sharon firmly, but surprisingly gently, moved Jessie out of her way.

"We've got this," she said. "Frank, get me some water from Emma's pond. Jessica, where is she?"

"Inside with Greta," Jessie sniffled. "On the floor in the back room."

"Is anything else in the house?"

"John and LaSalle are looking, but I don't think so."

"Okay, go find me some boneset. And Jessie– blow your nose," Sharon ordered before she tied up her gray locs and strode through the door, disappearing into the darkness beyond. Frank followed, clutching a flask of pond water to his chest.

Stefan joined Jessie in the garden where she plucked the boneset from the ground. He had already delivered a pot of soil to his sister and looked unsettled.

"Do you need a hand?" He asked.

"Here, take this to Sharon. I'm going to pick some more," Jessie thrust an armful of the plant at him, not caring about the mud she splattered on his suit. He wisely chose not to mention it.

It took three armloads before Sharon was satisfied. Jessie and Stefan huddled against the wall watching Sharon and Greta work. Nicky stayed by Greta's side, and Frank sat by

Emma's head and stroked her hair, begging her to be okay. John and LaSalle finally joined the little group.

"The rest of the house is clean," John told them.

"I didn't see any other signs of entry besides the front door," LaSalle added.

"LaSalle, I want you to go back to Mara and tell her what happened here. Tell her and Robin that we think a master spell was placed to mask the cult's activities and we're not certain that they only targeted witches. There are plenty of isolated fae who make as good a target if not better," Jessie said.

"Understood," LaSalle nodded. A grim, angry undercurrent ran through his voice. After all, the Nain Rouge were such fae, as were the Fir Darrig like Matthias.

"You might want to reach out to your chief," Stefan suggested. "And any others you know who prefer to remain out of sight of the Courts."

"Aye, true. Tam and Matthias are already on the lookout as well. They started digging around after that man showed up on Matthias' doorstep. Watch your backs, and I'll meet you at the bar," LaSalle warned before he popped out of sight.

"Jessie, look," John whispered.

Emma groaned and opened her eyes.

"Emma," Frank cried and collapsed by his wife, wrapping her in his arms.

"Jess?" Emma's eyes searched the room. Her voice was hoarse, but her face was clear.

"I'm here," Jessie said past the lump in her throat. She forced herself to smile through her tears of relief.

"Thank the Goddess," Emma sighed. "I knew you'd come."

"Did you recognize the one who attacked you?" Stefan asked.

"No. He was some thug. He cast something that paralyzed me."

"And then beat you even though you couldn't defend yourself," Sharon snarled. "Some big man he was. Where is he?"

"There," Jessie pointed at the smoldering mass on the floor.

"Damn it, Jessie. Next time leave the face intact so we can at least try to identify him."

"Can we not have a next time?" Emma groaned.

"Here, let's get you up," Frank finally pulled himself together enough to help Emma sit up.

"Be careful," Greta warned. "You're probably going to need to walk with a cane for a while, and you have to take it easy. We did a damn good job if I dare say so myself, but your body still needs to rest."

"And you need to find a safe house," Jessie added.

"We can stay in our Library. It has enough provisions for a week or two. Where are the dogs?" Emma looked around in alarm.

"They're upstairs under the bed," John told her. "I explained that it was safe, but they wouldn't come out."

"That sounds about right," Emma chuckled and then winced. Frank steadied her against his chest and buried his face in her hair.

"Jessie, I don't know what's going on, but it's really bad. Sharon, call everyone together. I have to let them know what happened and how many of our own are missing. We've got to reach out to the other witches in hiding too."

"Won't that put them in the crosshairs like it did you?" Nicky asked.

"Maybe," Emma said. "But if we can spread the word fast enough, then we might overwhelm whoever is responsible."

"They can't send a thug after every witch on the Eastern Seaboard," Sharon agreed. "I'll get the word out, Emma. Frank, get her to your Library and make sure she lays down and rests. Jessica, a word before you go please."

Jessie followed Sharon out the front door, ignoring the concerned faces that watched them.

Sharon stopped once they were outside and turned to Jessie, arms crossed across her chest.

"Look, I'm always going to be upset by what Jared had to do. And as his teacher, you do bear some responsibility. No, let me finish. This is hard enough," she held up one hand as Jessie started to interrupt.

"But maybe it wasn't your fault. And maybe I should have paid more attention to his projects too. And maybe we both should have been more aware that he's precocious, driven, ambitious, and creative."

She stopped and looked at the ground. Jessie waited.

"I guess what I'm saying is that a lot of really bad stuff is going on right now, and we're right back in the thick of it, you and me. I choose to focus my energy on stopping this new cabal and protecting the people I care about instead of holding a grudge over a decision my adult son made."

"Does that mean we can be friends again?" Jessie asked in a small voice.

Sharon held her stern frown for a second longer before she gave a warm chuckle and held out her arms.

"Yes, you idiot."

Chapter 9

"**I** knew Mom would come around," Jared said with some satisfaction.

The bar was closed, and the apprentices, Tug, and Rupert joined them in the Library. Jared sat at one end of the sofa with Ace on one side and Aleister on the other, and Greta curled up at the other end with Lucy in her lap. Caroline lounged in one of the arm chairs by the fire with Cassie at her feet, and Christopher sat in the other with Spot in his lap and a look of intense concentration on his face. Tug leaned against a row of shelves, flanked by LaSalle and Rupert. Stefan had gone back to his fundraiser with a promise to return when it wrapped up.

John stood by Jessie with an arm wrapped around her shoulders, watching Chris.

"Christopher, what are you doing?" he asked.

"If I focus, I can heat up my lap just enough that it makes Spot happy," he said with a smile.

"That's a far cry from being afraid to burn the bar down," Jessie said.

"This is different. I'm not attacking anyone. I'm just using my body heat and making it a little warmer," he objected.

"That's what fire magic is," Jessie explained. "You have natural heat. You just use it to do whatever you want it to do."

"Oh," he looked startled and then thoughtful.

"Where are the vampires?" LaSalle asked.

"Mikael and Vito are looking for Draig, and Nicky went to get Renard," Greta said.

"Are you certain that the Fox is the best option for a diplomatic mission?" Doubt colored Rupert's voice

"He's not my first choice," Greta admitted. "But it goes back to who we can trust. Mikael and Nicky were there the first time all of this happened, and our friendship is well known. They'll be accused of being too close and having an agenda. Vito can't do it because he's the Sire and head of the Vampiric Council. He has to look neutral. Out of all the vampires we know, Renard is the only one I trust to act in our best interests."

"He can do it," Jessie added. "He may chafe a bit, but he can be as diplomatic as Stefan when he needs to be. Besides, if he, with his reputation, can get Stephanie out with little to no bloodshed, then it proves that we do not intend to resort to vigilante justice."

"If you say so," Rupert murmured.

Renard was a wild card. Formerly a Visigoth chieftain named Hathus, he had enlisted Mikael and Nicky's aid to save his village from the Roman army centuries ago. He felt that he owed them a debt he could never repay, which was why he proved himself to be a staunch ally when Greta and Jessie asked him to help find Warsaw's killer.

He also ruthlessly toyed with vampire groupies, often leaving them drained almost to the point of death when he tired of their fawning, and he treated humans in general with a modicum of contempt despite his love for all of the luxuries that only came about due to humanity's ingenuity.

The silence grew, its heaviness weighing on Jessie and Greta until Jessie felt like her skin was going to crawl off of her body. Just as Greta opened her mouth to announce that she really hated waiting, Jessie's phone rang.

"Let us through," Nicky said and hung up.

"Friends! Do not fear, all will be well! The Fox has arrived," Renard's booming voice scared the cats as he leapt through the portal. Nicky followed behind, not trying to hide his grin.

Despite his lack of physical beauty, which was exacerbated by a nose that had been broken and reset too many times, the Fox had an animal magnetism and flair for fashion that drew eyes wherever he went. Tonight he was dressed in an exquisite slim fit, single-breasted pearl gray linen suit over a deep crimson silk shirt, his wild strawberry blonde mane twisted up in a messy bun.

"Renard," LaSalle roared. "Good to see you, old friend! Have a drink!"

"You *will* clean the rug this time," Jessie threatened as she watched the goblet swing through the air in an alarming arc.

The last time Renard came through, she had found trails of beer throughout much of the bar and Library. She could not understand why the two of them felt a need to wave the goblet around so much while they bellowed old drinking songs, much to the amusement– and some wincing at the more off key notes– of the bar's patrons.

"I would never dream of bespoiling your fine rugs, Madame Witch," Renard said with a flourishing bow and wink. "Despite the fact that they seem to have lost any semblance of nap or color years ago."

Then he swung Jessie and Greta into bone cracking hugs before he took a long pull from the goblet and handed it back to LaSalle.

"Tell me everything. I need to know what we're up against this time."

He listened as Jessie and Greta talked, his face grim.

"You're certain we can't kill a few of them? Just to teach them a lesson?" He asked when they finished. Greta ignored Rupert's scoff.

"We can't kill anyone except Robert, and he's mine," she said firmly. "We need to offer the cultists a chance to live as normal a life as possible, and we have to turn Robert's advisors or lieutenants or whatever he calls them over to the Vampiric Council where they will stand trial."

"It's the only way to show humans, the fae, and the rest of the cryptids that witches and vampires will not take the law into their own hands," Jessie added.

"I understand that, but I hoped I could have a little fun," Renard sighed.

"Now if someone gets away and tries to evade justice and maybe disappears for, oh, I don't know, all eternity, then I doubt anyone will notice," John gave the vampire an angelic smile.

"And if there's a fight and someone has to die out of self-defense," Greta added. "But no one else!"

"There's going to be a lot of self-defense," LaSalle muttered to Tug who grinned in reply.

"What is our plan now?" Renard asked.

"Tomorrow I'll meet with Mara," Jessie said. "I want to make sure she and Oberon are aware of the situation and see if they know about any missing fae."

"Matthias and Tam are digging up information on the more remote fae for us. The high fae won't know where to look," LaSalle told her.

"I should hear from my contacts within the FBI soon. They are also looking into some leads," John added.

"So we still don't know where these miscreants are hiding like the vermin they are?" Renard scowled.

"No, and I want to take them by surprise," Greta tried to hide the worry in her voice. "If we have to meet them on their terms, it's not going to be so easy."

"I agree," Renard said. He pulled her back into a hug. "You two are as dear to me as any sister. We will see this through to the end. I give you my word."

"Thank you," Greta said with a kiss on his bearded cheek.

"I shall speak with my brothers and enlist the aid of the ogrekin," Tug rumbled. "We can assist you if a battle proves imminent, and we can protect the fae and witches who are often overlooked."

Jessie enjoyed the flummoxed look on Renard's face.

"Ogres are smart," she smirked as she let Tug and Rupert through the portal.

"Obviously," he rolled his eyes, annoyed. He hated being caught off guard.

"Everyone be extra alert," Jessie looked at her apprentices. "Do not go anywhere alone, do not trust anyone, and keep your guard up. If you see someone you think you know, make sure they are who they say they are. Ask them something only they would know."

"Caroline and Chris, that goes double for you," Greta added. "Everyone keep your wards up too."

After the sobered apprentices and Cassie filed out of the Library, the witches, vampires, and John looked at each other.

"What now?" Nicky asked.

"How do you feel about foosball?" John looked at the vampires with a raised eyebrow.

"A friendly game would be a nice way to end the night," Renard brightened up. "Perhaps with a good ale to take the edge off?"

"Oh, you are in for a treat," John's grin was feral as he led the way to the bar, Jessie's beer taps, and Renard's certain doom.

Chapter 10

"I don't care. That was uncalled for."

Greta paused at the doorway to the bar and eyed the scene between Jessie, who scowled in front of the foosball table, and John, who, for lack of a better term, pouted on a bar stool. LaSalle stood nearby, grinning and leaning on his axe. The goblet rested on the bar next to him.

"Is this because he started to wolf out last night when he beat Renard?" Greta asked.

"Yes. There's friendly competition, and then there's… wolfing out," Jessie snapped.

"I can't help it if I'm a little competitive. And it's not like I hurt anyone!" John protested.

"Still don't care."

"Fine," John heaved a pained sigh before walking over to her and giving her a kiss on the temple. "I should have an answer from my FBI buddy about the New Orleans connections within the hour. He called me this morning and said he had news."

"Good or bad?" Greta asked.

"He didn't say, but trust me, you'll be the first to know."

"Fine. Greta and I are going to go see Mara. John, I love you, do not do that again. I'll be back as soon as I can," Jessie gave John a kiss on the cheek and started to head to the Library.

"Where are you going? The parking lot's that way," LaSalle jerked a thumb toward the door.

"We're not going to drive," Jessie replied.

"You're just going to port into the fae realm?" LaSalle sounded shocked.

"No, I'm porting into the fae parking lot. We have a lot to do and not a lot of time to do it, so I'm going to Mara in the most direct way possible. If you find that offensive, then suck it."

"Well… I suppose that's fine," he said, but he still looked disquieted.

"Just wait here. I'll be back," Jessie stifled an annoyed sigh, and she and Greta walked down the hall to the office, leaving him to mutter, "Well I never!" in their wake.

The thin wintery sunlight sifted through the bare trees as they stepped into the parking lot of a decrepit cathedral on the outskirts of town. Surrounded by menacing, thorn laden rose bushes and a jagged wrought iron fence, the building looked like it would blow over in a stiff breeze. The Fae had their own ways of deterring unwanted visitors– including dropping a fake, rotted roof on a trespasser's head.

Annie waited for them with an amused smile.

"Mara felt the ripples in the ether when your portal began to open," she explained in response to Jessie's questioning look. "Honestly, we always wondered why you and Greta don't just do that every time you visit."

"I thought it would be rude," Jessie admitted. "Apparently LaSalle feels the same way. He was very offended."

"From anyone else it would be," Annie acknowledged. "From you two though? You're family, Jessie. You're always welcome here no matter how you choose to enter."

"I appreciate that, Annie," Jessie smiled at the little brownie.

"Just once I'd like to visit the Court for a night of dancing and light refreshments," Greta remarked as they walked across the parking lot.

"I know. It seems like it's been nothing but trouble lately," Jessie agreed.

"That's because it has been nothing but trouble lately," Annie gave a little shake of her head. The little brownie, decked out in her neat apron over a plain blue dress and sturdy shoes, lead them to the cathedral's steps. Neither of them commented on the lack of a page. Dain, the beloved Tuatha de Danann orphan Mara had fostered, would be very difficult to replace.

The battles with the cabal had claimed many casualties over the centuries, but some hit home more than others. Dain had been like a son to Mara, a close friend to Jared, and well liked by everyone who knew him. When he took a poisoned dart meant for Mara, his death had all but destroyed her.

Annie led them through the cathedral's heavy stone doors, where the illusions that created the impression of a weathered, decaying building fell away to reveal a beautiful stone hall hidden from the public's eyes.

The hall's walls were adorned with wood and stone that interlaced in a beautiful, shifting fresco, courtesy of the resident wood nymphs. All around them were depictions of Dain– Dain being presented at court, Dain taking his first post as a page and anxiously looking up at the beautiful Tuatha de Danann Duchess for approval, Dain practicing archery, and countless other images until they reached the one Jessie dreaded the most: Dain throwing himself against Mara to save her life. Greta made a small pained sound, and Jessie reached for her hand, squeezing to comfort them both.

"Her Grace is outside at the bier. She spends much of her time there when she is not handling affairs of state and such," Annie told them. Her grave expression was a far cry from her normal cheer.

"I appreciate it, Annie," Jessie said. "We know the way."

"Aye, I imagine that you do. This is a sad business, girls. Very sad," Annie said with a sigh that seemed to come all the way up from her little toes.

Jessie and Greta followed the emerald green runner trimmed with sky blue threads, the Court's colors, to a small wooden door tucked into an alcove that opened out on the gardens. The gardens were lush with herbs and flowers always in bloom no matter what season it was in the outside world.

The witches skirted the herb garden where Brigette the Banshee sought solace before the cabal's manipulations forced her to meet an untimely end at Nicky's hand. They walked past the tower where Robin almost died from iron poisoning while they fought to save him. The Fae had been marked by the cabal almost as much as witches, but nothing could have incentivized Mara to wholeheartedly join her forces to theirs like the loss of her adopted child.

She waited for them in Dain's bier where he would lie for a year and a day before finally being laid to rest in his own hill. He looked as beautiful and pure as the day Jessie met him, for the fae did not decay.

"Jessica, Greta, I appreciate that you're willing to visit me out here. I know it's not ideal for some," Mara said as she rose from a cushioned seat to greet them with outstretched hands. Her waist-length, plum-colored hair rippled down her back, and her emerald green eyes were deep with sorrow.

"Of course," Jessie said. She had to reach on her tiptoes to give Mara a kiss on the cheek.

"How are you holding up?" Greta asked, giving Mara a warm hug.

"As well as can be expected," Mara replied. "I miss him. But what about you? Is there any word from the kidnappers? Do you know where to go?"

"No, but the Witch and Vampire Councils sanctioned action as long as we agree to their terms."

"So LaSalle said," Mara said with a wry smile. "He was very put out that you did not intend to go in, what's the expression? Guns blazing, I believe."

"That's the one," Greta smirked before her smile faded. "Mara, we need to talk to you about this cult. They're picking off transitory witches. Our hedge witch contact in Atlanta, Emma, was under a spell that Jessie broke when she started asking too many questions. Because of that, Emma realized that a lot of witches are missing. When she tried to warn us, someone brutally attacked her. It took two of us to put her back together."

"We were never sure that the cult only targeted witches, and now we know the fae are involved in the cabal. If someone cast spells capable of confusing every hedge witch from Boston to Miami–” Jessie began.

“Then it’s possible they are doing the same for transitory and lesser fae,” Mara finished.

“Do you have any way of putting together a census?” Jessie asked.

Mara laughed, and her laugh had an edge of near hysteria.

“I might as well look for a pin in a haystack of needles,” she said, running her fingers through her long hair and pacing back and forth. “What you’re asking is impossible, which makes it all the more likely that such an event is taking place. No one would even have to cast a spell on us. The Seelie court rules and tries to pretend the Unseelie court does not exist and vice versa. The high fae act as guardians and rulers, but we have never known the breadth or depth of our subjects. Look at how easy it was for the cabal to pick off the doom-called fae to become their necromancers.”

“That’s what I was afraid of,” Jessie shook her head.

“Do you really think this cult would target the fae? I thought their aspirations were reserved for the witches.”

“We don’t know. If Robert kept trying and failing with witches and now has confirmation that the fae, creatures of pure magic, are in the world, then why wouldn’t he turn to fae creatures no one would miss? And if those fae don’t know what the cult did to witches, then it probably won’t be that hard to convince them to join up, especially if they believe that they’ll become all-powerful. Look how easy it was for the cabal to convince willing volunteers to be turned into necromancers.”

"Okay, so how do we let the fae know what Robert and his vampires are trying to do and how dangerous they are?" Greta asked. She perched on the stone bench by Dain's bier and pulled her knees to her chest. "Is there some way Oberon can get word to his subjects?"

"We don't have anything in place for something like that," Mara had the grace to look embarrassed. "The Courts deal with the high fae and leave the lesser ones to fend for themselves. We were always that way. It's only recently that courts like my own began to welcome all kinds."

"Fae prejudice," Greta grimaced. "Got it. Well, what about a phone tree?"

Mara looked lost.

"A what?"

"Before the internet and email, whenever someone needed to get a message out in schools or small towns, there was a phone tree," Jessie explained. "Someone called two people, and those people called two more people, and so on. That's a good idea."

"LaSalle said that Tam and Matthias started looking into fae they know might go missing," Greta reminded Jessie. "Mara, can Annie help them?"

Mara looked up at the sky, deep in thought.

"Yes, she can tap into the hobgoblin and brownie network. I'll reach out to the Courts in Louisiana and Mississippi too," she said. "Because their communities are much more varied, they don't have quite the same prejudices as the rest of us. They should know if anyone has gone missing or if any strange vampires passed through. They're also better situated to warn the lesser fae in their demesnes and thus spread word throughout the kingdom."

"That would help," Jessie said.

"What else do you need me to do?" Mara asked.

"Nothing unless you feel like beating the crap out of someone when we find the cult," Jessie said.

"I thought you were going for a peaceful resolution," Mara raised an eyebrow.

"We will not voluntarily kill any cultists and will attempt deprogramming," Greta corrected rather primly. "Robert and the cabal are fair game. Just do what you can to reach out to the fae."

"I will," Mara rose to her feet. "Well, my friends, it seems we have our work cut out for us. I fear you must cut your visit short, for time is of the essence. But one day soon we will meet for simpler and better reasons. Like tea! Tea is good."

"And those little cakes Annie makes," Jessie added wistfully.

"And her cookies," Greta agreed.

Mara led them back to the parking lot. When Jessie turned to hug her, the gardens had vanished behind winter slumbering trees and snarls of briars.

"Safe travels," Mara said. "Stay in touch, and I'll do the same. I will send word as soon as I hear from the Gulf Courts."

"And we'll send word as soon as we get any news," Greta promised.

They were quiet as Jessie opened her portal.

"Do you think she's still alive?" Greta finally broke the silence in a small voice.

"For their sake, she had better be."

Chapter 11

John and Stefan were already waiting in Jessie's office when she and Greta opened the Library portal to come back into the bar.

"We got some news," John said. He pushed off from the wall where he leaned, tension in every line of his body.

"What's going on?" Jessie asked as she waved them into the Library.

"The New Orleans FBI field office found something on Esplanade just outside the French Quarter," Stefan told her. "There's an old building with a basement door that sits right below street level. The local fortune tellers call it the Doorway to Hell. Someone reported a bad smell coming from it, and the police found dozens of corpses that looked like they were turned inside out. The remains are humanoid, but the FBI isn't sure yet whether or not they're witches. I tried to reach out to a hedge witch I know down there, but thanks to Emma's warnings, the entire solitary practitioner district is on lock down. Which is a good thing."

"The remains were anywhere from a few weeks to several months old," John added. "A spell had been placed on the room so no one would smell the decomp, but it finally wore off. The FBI found similar crime scenes in Philly, New York, and Boston. Right now they're treating it as scenes of domestic terrorism. I don't understand– how can a group of vampires subdue entire covens like that?"

"Solitary practitioners don't belong to covens," Greta explained. "And covens can be as small as two people or as large as thirteen. Technically Jessie, Isabel, and I are a coven, although we don't practice together very often. But with that many bodies across that time frame, my guess is that your FBI buddies found a dumping ground rather than the actual murder site."

She started to pace. For once no one made fun of her. They all felt her anxious frustration.

"And if they look in any of the other cities along the solitary witches' migration path, they'll probably find the same thing," Jessie added.

"But you realize this means a witch has to be helping the vampires because vamps can't cast anything other than glamour and shapeshifting," Greta pointed out.

"I guess that answers the question as to whether or not the cabal is involved," Stefan said.

"We always suspected they were," Jessie snapped, her voice rising. She was tired of the cabal nipping at their heels. "How else could Emma have been placed under a spell that made her overlook the fact that more than half of her witches were missing at the same time Robert and his cult show back up?"

"It's good to have confirmation," John reminded her as he pulled her into a gentle hug.

"I know," she said.

Her anger drained away, leaving her feeling weary. Her shoulders slumped, and she relaxed against his solid warmth until her phone rang, startling them all.

"It's Caroline," she said with a frown. "Hey, Caroline, what's up?"

"Someone's on the bar phone for John," Caroline said. "He says he's from the FBI."

John was already at the entrance of the portal with Jessie right on his heels. Greta and Stefan were close behind, but John outpaced them as he strode to the bar and snatched the phone out of Caroline's waiting grip. Charlie hovered nearby, and Jared and Chris stopped polishing glassware long enough to shoot them worried glances.

"John here," he said. "Yeah, hey. What? Are you sure? And you haven't found anything else? Okay. Yeah. Call me back at this number if you can't reach my cell. Better yet, hang on. I'm going to give you another back-up number."

He rattled off Jessie's cell from memory and then hung up, turning to face the others with a dark scowl.

"They found two more mass graves, one outside of Richmond and one in the North Carolina mountains close to the Georgia border. Same thing, all of a sudden the smell was there, they checked it out, and they found the sites full of bodies ranging anywhere from a week to several months into decomp."

"Fuck," Greta sank onto a barstool. "What are we going to do?"

"First things first," Jessie went into what John affectionately called "fix it" mode. "We need to confirm that these are vampire kills and vampires were present."

"How? Mikael and Nicky are too close to us," Greta objected. "We can't risk them being accused of bias."

"Renard isn't," Charlie pointed out. "And you can send LaSalle with him. That way if there's trouble, LaSalle can open a fae portal and get the two of them out of there."

John and Stefan exchanged a glance.

"That could work," Stefan said. "How do we get hold of Renard?"

"I'll call him." Greta slid off her bar stool and fished her phone out of her back pocket. It took three tries before he answered.

"Greta, my love, I adore you, but why are you calling me in the middle of the day?"

"Because we need you," she replied.

"I'm on my way," he said before he hung up on her.

"Wouldn't it have been faster to open a portal?" Christopher asked.

"I have to know exactly where he is so I don't open the portal in the wrong place, like inside a wall or in midair. I'm sure he's somewhere close by," Greta assured him before she dialed LaSalle's number.

"Lass, do you know what time it is?" he snarled after the fourth time she called.

"Yes, yes, I know, middle of the afternoon, already heard about it from Renard, but we need you."

"Fine. I suppose I need to pick up the vampire."

"I don't know," Greta admitted. "He hung up on me."

"I'll take care of it," LaSalle said before the line disconnected.

Sure enough, about five minutes later the two of them stumbled through a dark fae portal. LaSalle didn't bother to hide a yawn.

"Now then, what is so important that you had to get us out of bed?"

"We need you to check out a possible dump site that Robert might have used to dispose of his failed experiments," Jessie said with distaste. "John and Stefan both heard from their friends in the FBI that six mass graves contained by stasis spells were uncovered."

"Vampires lack that type of magic," Renard frowned.

"We know that, but we need to see if they were present. If they were, then that probably confirms that Robert is working with the cabal."

"Or the fae," LaSalle said.

Greta and Jessie stared at him in surprise.

"What? Most fae can pull off something like that. It just depends on how long the graves were concealed," he pointed out with a shrug. "And we already know some fae are involved with the cabal."

Jessie and her friends discovered that little gem of information when Jared stumbled upon the ogrekin, banished to another world to get them away from Oberon and leave the fae vulnerable to attack. Only a faery monarch had the power to cast a spell of glamour across the entire ogre race and make them forget they had once been Oberon's elite honor guard, standing by his side for millennia. And only a faery monarch could make Oberon and the rest of Faerie believe ogres had been extinct for hundreds of years. The realization that a fae with that kind of strength and power was part of the cabal was chilling.

"I don't know why that didn't occur to me. Can you tell if fae magic was used?" Jessie asked.

"Aye," he said, his voice grim. "Where do we need to go?"

"The North Carolina site is closer, so go there," John grabbed a bar napkin and jotted down a phone number. "This is how you can get in touch with my FBI contact. He'll take you to the grave. He's a wolf too, and I trust him. And guys, we know a lot of migratory solitary witches are missing. You saw what happened to Emma when she started to ask questions, so be careful. If you see any sign of danger that you can't handle, get out of there."

"How do you think I lived this long?" Renard sounded offended.

"Just come on," LaSalle rolled his eyes and pulled Renard back into a rip in the air. Jessie caught a glimpse of a forge glowing in a dark cave before the opening sealed behind them as if it had never existed.

Happy hour came and went. Stefan returned to his Library, eager to keep digging through any information on Robert and the cult's activities he could find. Rupert stood by Tug's side at the front door, and Mikael and Nicky had rejoined them by the time Renard's call came through.

"The FBI just finished processing the gravesite," he said when Jessie answered the phone, not bothering to hide her tone of relief.

"What did you find?"

"I hate to say this, but I think you had better come take a look. I'm going to send you a picture so you have a visual point of reference for a portal."

"You sound awfully subdued. Are you okay?"

"No. Just get here."

"Library. Now," Jessie told her anxious friends before spinning on her heel and hurrying down the hall. She had never heard Renard sound like that.

"What happened?" Mikael asked once they were through the Library portal.

"I don't know," she said. "Renard wants us to come meet him. He's sending a picture of the site."

Her phone chimed as Renard's picture of a clearing in some woods came through along with latitude and longitude coordinates.

"Looks like it's off of the Nantahala River," John said after he pulled the coordinates up on his phone.

"I think perhaps Nicodemus and I should remain behind," Mikael said. "You were right to be concerned about our involvement, and arriving with you would defeat the purpose of appearing to be impartial."

"I guess you're right," Jessie sighed. "I don't like it though."

"Neither do we," Nicky said. He perched on the back of the sofa and scratched Ace behind the ears. Jessie sometimes wondered if he looked at the cats and saw a trace of his lover in their infinite gazes.

"I shall remain with Tug and then report your findings to Madame Blanche upon your return," Rupert informed them.

"Good call," Greta said. "Come on. Let's get this over with."

Chapter 12

The site they ported to should have been beautiful in the December twilight. It should have been a riparian masterpiece of nature with tall sycamores and pines gracing the riverbank as it drifted merrily over huge rocks with swirling eddies.

But it wasn't beautiful, not at all. Even though law enforcement had removed the bodies, the smells of blood and offal still filled the air with their putrid stink. Jessie had to clench her teeth against the bile that rose in her throat. Greta retched beside her, and a low growl came from John's throat. The dead had been tortured so badly that the pain, despair, and fear of their passing hung in the air like a miasma.

Above it all, one thought hit Jessie with enough force to stop her in her tracks. If they hadn't found Greta in time all those years ago, Greta would have been like one of those poor corpses, just a mutilated carcass in an unmarked grave.

"Hey, look at me," Greta took Jessie's shoulders in her hands and forced her best friend to look away from the gravesite and into Greta's face. "I'm right here. They didn't get me. You stopped them. We're going to be okay."

Jessie bit her lip and looked at Greta with tears in her bright blue eyes.

"But what if they did?

"But they didn't, and we're going to stop them again."

"I'm glad we all agree," Robin spoke up from behind them. Jessie and Greta both jumped.

"Robin! When did you get here?" John asked.

"LaSalle called me in after he detected the presence of the fae so I could report back to Oberon. I am sorry that my erstwhile brethren chose to participate in this crime against nature, although I sense that they were part of the concealment rather than the act itself. Their horror and revulsion underscores their magic. I would be quite surprised if any of them made an appearance and tried to challenge us."

"Well, that's something at least," Jessie said. "This is bad enough without having to take on the fae too."

LaSalle and Renard, who had kept the FBI agents left behind company, walked over to join them.

"Sorry you had to be stuck here all afternoon. Do you want me to send you back?" Jessie asked. "Mikael and Nicky are waiting in the Library."

"That would be most appreciated," Renard flashed her a grateful smile. "The scent of blood is overwhelming. I wouldn't be surprised if Robert's recruits lost control at some point. If you could be so kind as to let me through to the bar, I think I would like to be around the living for a while."

"I'll stick around," LaSalle said. "This place is disturbing, and I don't want you three to have to deal with it alone."

"Thank you both for coming out here today," Greta told them. "Renard, come on. I'll port you."

John introduced himself to the FBI agents, who shook his hand and then strode away, men one step and wolves the next. He walked back to join Jessie just as Greta returned.

"They're members of a pack within the FBI, like my contact who gave us the intel," he explained. "We have half an hour to check things out. They just ask that we don't disturb or contaminate the site."

"That's nice of them," Jessie remarked before John frowned.

"I can smell the older levels of decomposition. Did they say how long they think the bodies were here?"

"Your buddy said that the ones at the bottom of the pile were at least three months old," LaSalle told him.

"That's about when the cabal sent Astrid after us," Greta said. "They probably used Robert to start getting rid of the solitary practitioners around the same time."

"Picking off your enemies one by one is sneakier than an all out war," Jessie agreed. "Less casualties, less attention, get rid of most of the opposition and then come out in the open when there isn't anyone left to stand up to you."

"The fae cannot maintain concealment spells of this magnitude without the spell caster remaining present at the scene. How can a witch accomplish such a thing?" Robin asked.

"They would have used a talisman," Jessie explained. "It could be anything. They just needed it to hold enough magic to power the spell for three months."

"Look for something nearby that feels magical," Greta ordered. "It probably doesn't have any power left in it, but there will be a residue that doesn't belong."

"But if it's supposed to hide this site then wouldn't it be invisible?" John asked.

"No, it has to be touched by someone or something that's also invisible for that to work. Remember the bracelet Marshall had on when he killed Warsaw? When he triggered its power, it became invisible because it was in contact with him. In this case, they would have had to put it in the grave with the bodies."

"Which is too risky when you think about the amount of corpses that were in there," Jessie added. "The talisman would have to fill the site from the bottom up with its magic in order to hide everything. That much power would completely drain a witch. It's a lot safer to just hide the surface."

"So probably a large rock or tree then." Robin looked around with a sigh. There were rocks everywhere, along with stumps and logs.

"Not a tree," Greta told him. "A talisman has to be an inorganic object."

"A rock is my first guess," Jessie added.

"Or an old necklace," John said.

They turned to look at him. He stood still, carefully holding an old, ornate locket at the end of a stick.

"It was buried in the leaves at the base of the tree, it reeks of magic, and it definitely does not belong here."

Jessie bent to peer at the necklace.

"I think you're right. We need to put this somewhere safe until we can get it to Isabel and Riza."

"Here, let me do it," Greta said.

They all moved back as she knelt at the edge of the river and scooped up a handful of mud. Whispering softly, she formed a small pot that Jessie baked with her fire magic until it was completely solid. John gingerly lowered the locket in the pot, and Greta sealed it.

"That should hold it," Greta said, looking at the little pot with satisfaction.

"I agree. I must thank you for tying up that particular loose end for us so neatly."

John swore, and they jumped back. Five witches wearing deeply cowled hooded cloaks that hid their faces appeared behind them in the woods.

"Robin, get Stefan," Jessie ordered before calling her fire magic arrows to her fingertips.

The Puck blinked out of sight as Greta snarled, eyes glowing green.

"No, wait–" the witch started to raise his hand to try to stop them, but Greta, with a clawing motion and guttural scream of rage, ripped open the ground under his feet and dropped him into a hole. Muscadine vines erupted out of the earth and wrapped two more witches from head to toe, pulling them off the ground to dangle upside down nearly twenty feet in the air. John, in wolf form, and LaSalle, who plucked his battle axe out of thin air, pinned the last two witches to the ground.

"We're here to parlay," one of the dangling witches gasped. "You're choking us."

"Hang on, I know that voice," Jessie's eyes narrowed. "Greta, bring them down, but don't release them yet. I want to hear this 'parlay'."

Greta loosened the vines enough for the witches to speak and lowered them until they were still upside down about eight feet off the ground. Jessie shot her best friend a slightly exasperated glance. Greta beamed back.

"What do you want?" Jessie demanded.

"We seek a truce while we work to solve our mutual problem."

"You mean Robert and his cult," Stefan walked out from between the trees. He paused long enough to lean over the edge of the pit and give the witch cowering at the bottom a nasty smile. The witch shrank back against the side and whimpered.

"Well, yes. All right, look, I know you have no reason to trust us, but it's hard to talk to you like this. Can we at least be right side up?"

Greta and Stefan looked at each other. Jessie pinched the bridge of her nose.

"Greta, turn them right side up, but don't let them go."

Muttering something about not being allowed to have any fun– which Jessie ignored– Greta waved her hand and righted the two dangling witches.

"But we still get to keep ours, right?" LaSalle called. He had taken the pragmatic approach and clubbed his witch over the head with the handle of his axe, rendering her un-conscious.

"Yeah, you're good," Jessie called back.

John's tongue lolled out from where he lay on his witch, who was too terrified to move.

"Find your mistress yet, crone?" Jessie didn't try to hide her scorn.

The witch gave a wordless snarl of hate and rage.

"Your time will come, Jennet, no matter how much you hide among these mongrels and unworthy dead!"

"I notice she didn't insult the fae," Greta remarked.

"Probably worried about pissing off her overlords," Jessie agreed. "Although I'm curious about the 'unworthy dead' part."

"Was there a point to keeping them alive? I don't believe the agreement with the Council included egomaniacal witch traitors," Stefan asked.

"I suppose it wouldn't hurt to hear what they have to say," Jessie said.

A small sigh of relief wafted up from the pit.

"Well, get on with it before I turn these two loose on you," Jessie waved at Greta and Stefan. "They're pissed, and it's mostly your fault, so I don't think anyone will mind if you disappear."

"Our compatriots will destroy you," the second dangling witch spoke, but her words rang hollow.

"Quiet, you fool," hissed the first one.

"I'd listen to her," Greta said, oh so sweetly. "Forests are particular friends of mine. No one is going to interrupt us right now, no one will hear you scream, and no one will ever find your bodies when we're done with you."

The witch went very still.

"We discovered the cult's existence when one of our novices combed the Council archives looking for weapons we could use against you," the first witch said.

"Was that before or after you sicced Astrid on us?" Jessie folded her arms across her chest and raised her eyebrows.

"After. When I appeared to you in your garden, I was sent to determine the extent of your injuries. While we didn't expect Astrid to eradicate you and your companions, we had hoped that you would at least be neutralized to some degree. To see you and your apprentices whole was... surprising."

"You're being awfully forthcoming right now," Stefan raised his eyebrows and crossed his arms as he leaned against a tree.

"Our mutual problem is too dangerous for me to be coy any longer. I must be frank," the witch said. Her voice had lost its haughty sneer. Now she just sounded tired.

"We have certain... allies who wish to stop the Alliance negotiations for their own reasons. They helped us find the cult. We told Robert that we could help him capture you and that we had a talisman that would let him turn you into the witch and vampire hybrid he so desperately sought," the second witch said with a nod to Greta. "Of course no such thing exists. The talisman we gave him was designed to locate its wearer's target. We thought he would come after you, not kidnap your family or attack the solitary practitioners along the entire eastern seaboard."

"Not yet anyway," muttered the witch in the pit.

"So if you and your 'allies', who, let me guess, are vampires, didn't plan on making the solitary practitioners some of your collateral, why was your talisman at the grave?" Jessie demanded.

"Once we realized what Robert was doing, it was too late," the first witch admitted. "We tried to conceal the evidence long enough to reason with him and hide our involvement, but it became clear that he would not stop."

"If he tried it out on this many witches and it failed, then surely he knows by now that it won't work on me," Greta said, pointing to the grave behind her.

"He has no intention of turning you anymore," the first witch said with a dry, humorless laugh. "Robert now believes that he was made into a vampire to carry out God's will by cleansing the world of witches, cryptids, the fae, and any vampires who embrace their true nature. As for you, he plans to hold your friends and families hostage to force you to heal his initiates through the turning process so he can create new vampires more quickly."

"This is the most ridiculous thing I have ever heard," LaSalle said, "And that's saying something."

"Not every witch in these graves belongs to the solitary ones," the second witch cried out. "When our representatives did not return to us, we discovered the cult's duplicity. Further attempts to reason with Robert resulted in more deaths of our fellow witches."

"If you expect sympathy from us, you are sorely mistaken," Stefan snarled. "You sent a vampiric cult after *your own kind* and are surprised that Robert turned on you? Clearly whoever did your little archival research expedition didn't take the time to read the whole story because ever since Robert was turned, he has looked for a way to spread across the world like a disease and wipe out all other races. His belief that he is God's instrument? He had it from the beginning."

"Why do you think he was obsessed with me?" Greta added. "He thought I would become his ultimate weapon."

"Not to mention the sheer hypocrisy. You hide behind the young, inexperienced witches you send out to be cannon fodder in every fight and shed crocodile tears because some of your compatriots are at the bottom of this pile?" Jessie scoffed. "See, what I think is that you don't care about your 'friends' at all. Your higher ups, including the fae and vampires who helped you– and don't think I didn't notice that you haven't denied that, by the way– realized they might be exposed and are scrambling for damage control. You can go fuck yourselves."

"If you're not willing to work with us, then we can at least agree to stay out of each other's way until this threat is ended," the second witch said.

Jessie, Greta, and Stefan exchanged a glance.

"They dragged your niece into this," Jessie told the other two. "It's your call."

The siblings looked at each other for a long moment before Greta turned away and pulled out her phone.

"We will agree not to hunt you down until this situation is resolved, but we do not promise to avoid any attempts at retaliation should your cabal get in our way," Stefan said.

"John, LaSalle, come on. We're going home," Jessie said.

As soon as John stood up, his witch vanished through a portal, leaving her friends behind.

"Wait, you coward," the second dangling witch yelled in frustration. Jessie laughed as the witch in the pit, suddenly realizing escape was, in fact, an option, disappeared through his own portal.

"Let us down," the first witch pleaded.

"Oh, you'll get down all right. Just as soon as Riza gets here," Greta said with a nasty grin as she finished her text to the Witch Council's ecstatic head of security and put her phone back in her pocket.

"But you promised!" The second witch wailed.

"It doesn't count as hunting you down if we already trapped you," Stefan pointed out. "Ladies, shall we?"

Jessie opened their Library portal and followed her friends through, leaving the frantically struggling witches behind. She glanced back before the portal closed in time to see Riza and a cadre of Council guards step into the clearing, and she smiled. At least something went in their favor.

Chapter 13

"What will happen to the witches?" Cassie asked. She looked up from her laptop where she configured a point of sale system for Annie's Brownie Cleaning Services. Some fae may long for the good old days, but the brownies had no problem adapting to technology. LaSalle had left to tell Mara about the grave sites.

"They'll be held in wormwood cells like Astrid," Jessie replied.

"Why couldn't they escape from the vines?" Cassie frowned. "Were they weaker than Greta?"

"I imbued the vines with earth magic to make them impervious to a magical attack," Greta explained. "The witches probably could have freed themselves eventually. As Jessie is about to explain, it's possible to undo another witch's spell if you have enough time."

Jessie turned to her apprentices who huddled over the vessel Greta had made to hold the talisman. The bar was closed one night a week, and she liked to use the time to make sure her charges got some supervised practice. The the tiny urn made the perfect opportunity.

"Okay, now concentrate. Find the workings Greta and I used to build the vessel. Can you feel how it fits together?"

"Yes," Jared said immediately, to no one's surprise.

"I can if I trace the water Greta used to make the mud," Caroline said, her brow furrowed.

"I can feel the fire, but not the magic," Chris admitted. He looked crestfallen, and Jessie gave him an encouraging smile.

"You're still learning. Feeling the fire is a pretty good step," she said. "Now, three elements went into the making of this, earth, fire, and water. To take it apart, you're going to convince the elements to listen to you and work for you."

"But there's no air," Jared objected.

"You're not using air. Jared, you talk to the earth, Caroline, you get the fire, and Chris, you take the water. You all know how to talk to and work with your core elements, but sometimes you need to convince other elements to help you too. Your opposite elements are the hardest to work with, so you're going to start with them today."

"Wouldn't it be easier to handle elements adjacent to ours?" Chris objected.

"Yes, and you're welcome to go out in the garden and strike up a conversation with the earth if you think it will help get water to listen to you more quickly."

"Is that how you took apart that spell in the bathroom? You know, the one that covered up Warsaw's murder?" Charlie's question was punctuated with a belch.

After she discovered him floating around her bar as an undead patron, Jessie had devised a spell using a beer mug to transport anything it contained— which was usually beer— to the spirit world so Charlie wouldn't have to be deprived of everything he enjoyed in life. She didn't count leaving the TV on for him during football season as a pleasure. To her, being a Falcons fan felt like another form of torture.

"Sort of. While elements fuel our magic, that doesn't mean that our spells always have to come from nature. The cloaking spell we found in the bathroom wasn't made with elemental magic, so I could take it apart with my crystals and the power of the bar. We can also take advantage of traits our elements represent to make things work. For instance, fire purifies, so it's easy for me to dismantle contaminated magic or counter magic used for harm."

"Whereas I have an easier time with magic that performs healing, growth, shielding, and emotional connection," Greta added from where she stood by one of the walls.

"Is that why you're whispering to the building?" Charlie raised an insubstantial eyebrow.

"I convinced the wood in the walls to block any eavesdroppers. We kept the listening spells the cabal placed around here active, but I like to be very selective in what they actually pick up."

"Smart," Cassie said over her laptop.

"Ha, take that!" came an exultant shout from across the room punctuated by the sound of cracking stone.

"Jonathon Ezekiel Rossford and Hathus Renard Fox!" Jessie shouted. Everyone froze.

"What?" John tried to look innocent. It came out slightly garbled around a set of fangs that protruded under glowing yellow eyes.

John and Renard, who didn't actually have a middle name for Jessie to use when he was in trouble, which didn't stop her from making something up, had decided to play foosball while Jessie worked with her apprentices. Renard understandably needed to blow off steam, but even the vampire's speed was no match for a very competitive werewolf.

"You are not allowed to play any more until you can learn to play nicely with others!"

"But–" John protested, the fangs retreating.

"It was just a friendly game," Renard added, failing miserably to hide one little stone statue's shattered body with his foot.

"You broke them!" Jared rushed to pick up the pieces of the statue.

"No! Go sit down!" Jessie snapped as she pointed at the front door with one hand on her hip.

"Fine," Renard scowled. He and John stormed outside where they glowered on the porch.

"Little harsh on them, weren't you?" Greta asked mildly.

"They have to learn! What if they had been playing against a human?"

"A human would never have gotten that far against either of them," Cassie pointed out.

"I have got to find a way to make these guys indestructible," Jared sighed mournfully. He finished scooping up the remains of his tiny statues. One little stone arm waved feebly at its maker before it went limp.

"Why do I feel that I missed something both ridiculous and tragic?" Rupert's raspy voice greeted them from the doorway. "And does it have anything to do with why our good sheriff and visiting vampire are sulking like scolded children?"

"Yes. They can't play with the foosball table any more until they learn to act like adults," Jessie glared at the front door and the porch beyond.

Rupert blinked at her.

"This bar never fails to astonish and amuse me," he chuckled. "What did I miss?"

"Oh, not much. Just the cabal asking us for help," Greta said.

It wasn't often that they could render Rupert speechless. Jessie let Greta enjoy the moment before filling him in on the showdown in the woods.

"Knowing that vampires are involved with the cabal makes sense," he remarked, grooming one front paw. "It also confirms that the cabal is more about elitist control than attempting to keep witches at the forefront of power."

"True," Jessie agreed. "Although we figured that part out when we discovered that some of the fae helped exile the ogres."

"And what of your hedge witch friend?" Rupert asked.

"Mom said that Emma's doing a lot better and should be completely mobile in a week or two. The guy who attacked her did a lot of internal damage, so it's taking more time to heal. She and Frank are just going to lay low in their Library for now," Jared reported. "What are our next steps?"

"Good question," Riza said as she walked through her portal. "Caroline, can I have a beer?"

"Of course," Caroline hurried back around the bar and grabbed a glass with a toss of her blonde ponytail over one shoulder.

Riza pulled her dark gray mane up into a bun and rubbed her eyes. She looked exhausted.

"Thanks for that little present earlier. They're languishing nicely in our cells. Do we have any word on the rest of the solitary practitioners?" Riza asked before downing her beer in one gulp. Caroline silently set another in front of the older witch.

"According to my mom, all of the solitary practitioners around here went into hiding," Jared said. "They should be safe until this is over."

"They're not going to fight with us?" Rupert put his ears back.

"Why should they?" Jessie asked. "The Council has never supported them, and they make easy targets."

"Plus a lot of them are very young or don't have the resources to really build up their knowledge and defenses like we did," Greta pointed to Jessie and herself.

"If you remember, we almost didn't make it when Astrid attacked us. Tug helped us win that battle," Jessie reminded the still sulky Matagot. "And we are much more battle ready than most of the solitaries."

"Some of the more trustworthy council members offered to set up safe houses for anyone who wants to use them," Riza said. "I wish I could say that Jessie and Greta are wrong about the way the Council tends to treat solitary practitioners, but, sadly, they're not. A couple of us are trying to change that though."

She pushed her empty glass away and shook her head at Caroline's raised eyebrow.

"I'll let Mom know, but don't hold your breath," Jared told her. "Mom doesn't talk too much about what it was like after the last uprising, but she was thrown in one of the Council's camps they set up for known friends or family of cabalists. And the solitaries already trust the Council about as far as they can throw the collective bunch of members."

Jared's uncle had joined the cabal, and his family paid the price for his betrayal, something Sharon would not forget for the rest of her life. While Jessie regretted that Jared was the one who had to kill his uncle, she had to admit that she was not sorry to see Theo die.

"That's what I figured, but it's worth a shot," Riza said. "Do we know if there are any other sites like this one?"

"At least five more that we know of," Jessie said. "John and Stefan both have contacts who are keeping them posted."

"I imagine it's more than that," Greta said. "If the other sites are about the same size as the one we saw today, then they aren't nearly big enough for all the missing migratory witches."

"So do we keep looking or let human law enforcement take over?" Riza asked.

They all glanced at each other as John and Renard rejoined them. John's wolf abilities and Renard's vampire ears had let them hear everything.

"I think that if the Witch Council wants to prove their worth to the solitary practitioners then they should take over the investigation side by side with the FBI," John said.

"I agree," Jessie nodded. "We need to focus on Robert and getting Stephanie back, and we need to let Vito and the

Vampire Council know that vampires are working with the cabal."

"Why am I not surprised?" Riza heaved a sigh. "Is anyone not working with the cabal?"

"Pretty sure werewolves aren't," John gave her a bright smile.

"Speaking of Vito," Greta muttered as her phone rang. "Hey, Vito, I'm going to put you on speaker."

"We come bearing good news, Madame Witch. We will arrive shortly," his jovial voice boomed from the phone.

"Well, that's a nice change," Jessie exclaimed. "The bar's closed, but you can come in through the front door. Is it okay if Riza hears this?"

"Of course. We wish for the Witch Council to stay apprised of all developments," Vito said before hanging up on them.

"Maybe I will have that third beer after all," Riza said. Caroline grinned and grabbed another glass while Greta sent her brother a quick text.

"Did you find Draig?" Greta demanded as soon as Vito walked through the door, Mikael and Nicky close on his heels. Stefan had joined them and sat by Riza nursing his own beer.

Vito chuckled and pulled her into a side hug.

"I thought Earth is slow moving and patient," he teased.

"The earth is. Greta definitely is not," Jessie laughed.

"Yes, my dear. We located our erstwhile dragon. He has agreed to assist us, but he was quite surprised to discover how prolific vampires became. It will take time to weed through the myriad of sire lines to discover Robert's."

"How long?" Greta asked. She didn't try to hide the anxiety in her voice.

"As long as it takes. I wish I could give you more hope than that."

"It's better than nothing," Riza pointed out.

But before Greta could respond, they were all startled by a loud pealing sound.

"Why are the wards going off?" Jessie looked at Greta in alarm.

Their friends and family could come and go, but the wards let the witches know when a stranger stepped foot on the property– which wasn't supposed to happen. The building had a persuasion spell on it that encouraged anyone who might want to stop by to go elsewhere when the bar was closed.

"I don't know," Greta answered.

"Someone's at the door," John snarled, eyes glowing yellow. He and Renard leapt for the door at the same time, but when they opened it, no one was there.

"What's that?" Cassie pointed. A small box sat on the porch in front of the door.

"I smell blood," Renard hissed.

"Jessie–" Greta couldn't hide the fear in her voice.

"Stay here," Jessie ordered as she moved to John's side. They stared at the box.

"I don't sense any spells on the box, but there's one inside," she said.

"Well, here goes nothing," John said. He bent down and gingerly scooped the box up, pausing to give one last scan across the parking lot before he shut and locked the door.

"Whoever delivered this cloaked themselves well," Jessie said.

"Or moved very quickly," Mikael pointed out.

"What is it? Why did Renard smell blood?" Greta's voice raised, sharpened by an almost hysterical edge.

"Honey, wait. Let me see," Jessie said as soothingly as she could manage. The last thing they needed was a panicked Greta losing control right now, but Jessie knew a small box that smelled of blood and spells could be nothing but bad.

"Can we help?" Caroline asked, coming around the bar. She reached for Chris, probably remembering on some level what it felt like to think he might be lost to them.

"Yeah, grab a glass of water. Jared, go in my office and look in the desk drawer for my pouch of crystals."

Her apprentices rushed to get the things she needed while Greta and Stefan stood frozen, waiting. Neither asked to help. A witch's ability to maintain their self-control was vital, and despite their ages, Greta and Stefan had never quite been able to keep it together when family was on the line.

"Here you go," Jared handed the bag to Jessie who took it while keeping a sharp eye on Greta. Riza and John moved to Greta's side, and the vampires flanked Stefan. Greta and Stefan were strong. Very strong. If the box's contents were as bad as Jessie thought they were, she really didn't know if they would be able to restrain the siblings.

"Thanks, Jared. Caroline, I want you to reach in the bag and grab a crystal by feel. You want something that can cleanse and contain. Don't think too hard about it— trust your instincts. I'll do the same, and then we're going to build a fire and water containment unit designed to purify whatever comes out of this thing when we open it. Don't worry that water extinguishes fire. I'm going to keep my magic just slightly enough away from yours that they can coexist without canceling out. Understand?"

"Sure," Caroline said without a hint of irony as she reached into the bag.

"Okay, here we go," Jessie took a deep breath and reached for her apprentice's magic. She used the threads of Caroline's water power to intertwine with fire into a type of basket. It only took a few seconds for Caroline to catch on and join her.

The box popped open with surprising ease, and when it did, the vampires recoiled. The scent of fresh blood rushed out, and Caroline gasped and started to back away.

"Don't lose your concentration," Jessie snapped and grabbed Caroline by the wrist.

"Jessie, is that..."

"Yeah. It is," Jessie turned to Greta, pleading in her bright blue eyes.

"Greta, honey, I really need you to stay calm. It's bad, but it's not as bad as it could be."

"What is it? Let me see!" Greta pushed past Riza and snatched the box out of Jessie's hand.

She went white when she looked inside at the bloody finger laying on a velvet pillow at the bottom. Written in blood on the side was a message:

Your niece is quite delicious. I hope you don't find her in time so we can enjoy the rest. You have until Yule to recover what's left.

Your master,

Robert

Chapter 14

"Fuck, stop him!" Riza shouted at the vampires, but they were too late. Stefan disappeared in a pop of displaced air.

Jessie didn't have time to dwell on that little problem because when Greta screamed in pure, unadulterated rage, the entire building shook. The glassware and bottles behind the bar crashed to the floor, and tables cracked while chairs splintered. Greta had been barely keeping herself together since she first got the note at Matthias' hut, and this was the last straw.

"Greta, stop! You're going to bring this place down!" Jessie shouted. "Riza, help me!"

"I'm going to get Isabel," Riza ran through her portal and vanished from sight.

"What should we do?" Jared shouted over the noise of rending wood as the doors blew off the hinges.

"Get somewhere safe," Jessie yelled back. "She's too strong for you. Grab Cassie and go to the garden and hide."

Greta howled with mindless fury. The vampires lunged forward and tried to grab her, but she ripped the floor open and started to drop them into a gaping pit.

"Greta, *no!*" Isabel's voice cracked through the chaos as she used her air magic to whisk the vampires to safety.

"This is very bad," Vito gasped. "I had no idea she could do that."

"Yeah, burying people in the ground is one of her favorite things," Nicky couldn't keep the wry note out of his voice. "I don't know what we thought we could do to stop her."

"It was worth a try," Mikael said. "But perhaps we should let the witches work?"

"Yes, let's go protect the apprentices," Renard ran for the door. "John, come on. You can't help here. It's best to let them handle it."

"You know what, I think you're right," John ducked as a table leg flew past his head and beat a hasty retreat into the garden with the vampires. Rupert hissed and vanished through his own portal right before a table crashed to the ground where he had been sitting.

Every time Jessie, Isabel, or Riza tried to get close, Greta flung floorboards, furniture, and clods of earth at them. She ripped the paneling off the walls and the door off its hinges. Jessie and Riza used controlled bursts of fire on the wood, but they couldn't risk baking the earth and giving Greta more deadly missiles to play with.

"Just had to make a bar out of an element she can control, didn't you," Riza shouted to Jessie.

"Well, I'd like to see you come up with a building material that doesn't come from the earth," Jessie yelled back. "We need to try to contain her until she calms down. I don't have a way to stop her without hurting her."

"No shit," Riza snapped. "How do you plan to do that? We need a water witch and another earth witch to make a containment box, and none of us can exactly leave right now."

Jessie was at a loss. When a witch lost control like this, they were on par with a natural disaster. Greta could level the entire town if she didn't stop. But with Stefan gone and probably on his own rampage, there was no one else left who could talk Greta down.

"If we surround her in a fireball, maybe some of what she's throwing will recoil back on her and, I don't know, knock her out?" Jessie called out.

"You have terrible ideas, you know that right?" Riza yelled back.

"Shut up and help me!"

With Isabel pulling oxygen out of the air to fuel their fire, the fireball containment unit worked– mostly. Riza swore when a fire hardened clod of earth struck her on the arm, drawing blood as it glanced off her bicep.

"Greta, sweetie, I love you, but I do not love this behavior. I need you to stop it, please," Jessie yelled into the fire.

"She's not a child," Riza gasped as the effort to contain Greta's rage started to take its toll.

"Well, she's not acting like an adult right now either," Jessie snapped, exasperated. "Greta, please! You're destroying our home– my home and our safe haven. I need you to stop, now! Don't make me hurt you!"

"Jessie, we don't have a choice," Isabel called out. "We have to take her down. You can do it or I can, but one of us has to do something."

"I know, I just... Okay."

Jessie gritted her teeth and focused. She pulled her magic out of the fireball surrounding Greta and created a white hot arrow. With one gesture, she sent the arrow flying at her best friend and tried not to wince at Greta's screams of pain as the arrow grew until it wrapped itself around and around Greta's body. The arrow of purification would draw Greta's rage out of her spirit and into itself until it burned up, but it could also incinerate Greta herself if Jessie lost even an iota of control. Already Jessie could see blistering burns on Greta's arms and legs where the fire left its mark. This would be a bitch to heal.

But it worked. As Greta's screams shifted more from rage to pain, the arrow burned brighter and brighter until it vanished into ash. Jessie rushed to Greta's side as her best friend collapsed to the floor, crying with deep, anguished sobs.

"Go get Ivan and Caroline," Jessie said to Riza and Isabel as she pulled Greta into a fiercely protective hug and did what she could to draw the heat out of Greta's burns. "She needs water healing."

"On it," Riza jumped through her portal while Isabel rushed out to the garden where the apprentices, vampires, Cassie, and John huddled in the December night trying to stay warm around a small fire that floated in the air over Christopher's hand.

"Is it safe?" Jessie heard Jared ask through what was left of the door.

"Yes, just watch your step," Isabel replied.

They carefully stepped around the debris as they filed back into the building and Riza and Ivan came through Riza's portal. Ivan gave a slow whistle as he looked around.

"When you told me Greta lost her shit, I didn't imagine it would look quite like this," he said.

"Yeah, well, it does. Jessie needs you to help heal her. We had to use fire to take her down," Riza gestured to where Jessie sat on the floor, still cradling a sobbing Greta.

"Caroline, I need a vessel of water, lavender, jojoba oil, bandages, and a mortar and pestle, and then you and I will handle this," Ivan ordered.

He knelt next to Jessie and touched Greta's arm.

"These burns are nasty. She may have some lasting nerve damage," he looked up at Jessie.

"I know. I had to use a purification arrow to draw out her rage," she told him.

"Ouch. Well, I think we can fix her up. Caroline, you sit here," he said as he took the water from his student. He had been Jessie's first choice to take on Caroline's water magic training, and he was a good teacher.

Ivan showed Caroline how to draw the moisture from the lavender before grinding it into a powder, soaking it in the oil, and accelerating the extraction process. They applied the oil to the burns with a gentle touch before soaking the bandages in water from the garden and wrapping them around Greta's injuries. Then Ivan walked Caroline through the spell to draw out the rest of the heat and speed up the healing process.

"Lavender is one of the best agents for a severe burn," Ivan told them. "She'll have some lingering effects, but she should be completely healed in a few weeks."

"Why did Jessie have to burn her so badly?" Jared asked. He sat on the only unbroken stool where he watched from a safe distance.

"When a witch loses control it takes an act of equally powerful magic to stop them. Ideally, we would have contained her using air, fire, earth, and water to form a type of magical force field until she raged herself out, but we didn't have a full fledged water witch or another earth witch handy," Isabel explained. She had taken on the role of his teacher for his air magic, and this was a lesson she'd hoped he wouldn't have to learn yet. "Either Jessie had to use the purification arrow, or I was going to have to suffocate her until she lost consciousness. Suffocation is a lot more dangerous since there's a risk of brain damage, which is almost impossible to heal."

"We use nature to fuel our magic. Older witches like Greta, Jessie, and Isabel are powerful enough to be as destructive as a natural disaster," Riza added.

"Why doesn't the cabal use that to their advantage?" Christopher asked. "It seems like they could do a lot of damage if they wanted to."

"The only way to reach that point is to lose all control over your emotions," Jessie told him. "It's like going berserk. You don't know who you are or what you're doing anymore. You can't unleash that kind of chaotic magic while remaining self-aware, so the cabal would risk losing everything they're trying to gain."

"I guess that makes sense," Chris shook his head. "Have you ever lost control like that?"

"We all have," Ivan said with a sad look in his stormy blue-gray eyes. "Not everyone can be brought back to themselves in one piece. There is a hidden sanatorium for witches whose bodies survived but whose minds and powers did not."

Chris blanched, and Cassie drew him in for a comforting hug.

"There's a big difference between losing control because you're trying to learn without a teacher and losing control because you're out of your mind," Riza told him. "Don't be afraid of your power, Christopher. It's part of you, and you're more dangerous if you don't master it."

"I'm not that afraid anymore. Well, not much anyway," he said.

Greta's sobs died down, but she didn't move.

"Mikael, help me get her in the Library," Jessie said. Mikael knelt by Greta's side and gently lifted her in a bridal carry. The small group trailed after Jessie down the hallway to the office where Riza stopped.

"I'm going to head back if that's okay with you. You might want to hold onto this though. Maybe the vampires can get something off of it," she discreetly handed Jessie the box.

Vito cocked his head to one side, eyes narrowing.

"That's actually a good idea, Mistress Witch. The stasis spell they used to keep the finger fresh also preserved the blood. If Robert drank from this, then there is a chance that Draig can use it to narrow his search."

"Take it then. See what you can find," Jessie thrust the box at the vampire. "I just want to get it away from Greta. Riza, you and Isabel should take the talisman we found at the gravesite and see what you can get out of it. It's around here somewhere."

"I grabbed it when you told us to run," Jared pulled the little pot out of his jacket pocket and passed it to Riza. "Chris, Caroline, and I almost got it open."

"Good job," Riza said. "I can get it the rest of the way. Jess, I'll let you know what I find out."

"Same," Jessie gave Riza a quick hug before Riza squared her shoulders and disappeared through her portal.

"A finger in a box. How cliche," Renard snorted when Mikael had Greta safely through the Library's barrier and out of ear shot.

"It could be worse," John shrugged. "It could have been her head."

Chapter 15

"Did you even sleep?" Jared asked Jessie, who stumbled through the door of the bar with a gaping yawn late the next morning. He and Chris had come in early to clean and try to repair as much of the shattered remains of the bar and its furniture as they could. Jessie had no idea how they would be able to open for business that night. The building was in shambles.

"I did not," she admitted. She had kept Greta at her house, waking up every time Greta so much as twitched and only surrendering her best friend to Isabel's care when Isabel showed up at dawn.

"How is Greta?" Rupert appeared in the bar and paused mid-stretch to look around and take in the destruction.

"Hopefully she's still asleep. Isabel came to get her this morning."

Rupert shook his head and jumped onto the bar top.

"At least we know the bar is stable." Chris walked past with an armful of splintered chairs and table legs. He paused long enough to scratch Rupert under the chin and was rewarded with a deep rumble of a purr.

"Sending Greta her niece's finger seems... unwise of the cult," Rupert said as he began to groom his back toes.

"Yeah, no shit," Jared agreed. He passed the Matagot with a box of glassware John had dug out of storage the night before to replace the pieces Greta destroyed.

"You seem to be handling this well," Rupert eyed Christopher. "I thought you were concerned with excessive displays of magic."

"Oh, I'm terrified, and if anyone ever did something like that to Caroline or any of you then I honestly don't know what I would do. But running away isn't getting me anywhere, so I might as well learn how to control my magic and hope that I don't set half the world on fire," Chris shrugged.

Jessie paused in surprise. This was a very pragmatic approach from the student who was terrified of his own glowing shadow. Chris caught her expression and gave her a lopsided smile.

"I know what you're thinking, but watching Greta lose it like that was enlightening. If I'm supposed to be a lot stronger than she is, then I might cause a volcanic eruption and wipe out a small country. You're right. I need to learn and not run."

"Well, at least one good thing came from all of this," Cassie said as she rose from the floor under the bar where she installed a new modified router. Greta's tantrum had destroyed all of Cassie's hard work, although Jessie suspected Cassie didn't mind too much. The catastrophe gave Cassie the chance to install much needed new hardware and upgrade the bar's system after weeks of hounding Jessie to let her make the changes.

"Okay, Jessie, you should be back online. I'm going to go help Caroline. John gave her the key to the storage unit last night, and we're going to see what we can bring over here to replace some of this damaged stuff."

"Thanks, Cass," Jessie said. She hugged her friend with a grateful smile before Cassie ran out the door.

"Where do you keep disappearing to?" Jared asked Rupert.

"Here and there," Rupert said, curling up on the bar and covering his face with one paw and the tip of his tail. Jared's eyes narrowed.

"Let it go," Jessie touched Jared's arm. "He'll tell us when he's ready."

"But he doesn't even care about what's going on," Jared didn't bother lowering his voice.

"He does. Trust me, let it go," Jessie didn't hide the warning in her voice this time.

A Matagot was a creature of chaos, treating others as they were treated, and pushing Rupert's buttons while he was in his current state would not end well for anyone. Rupert had survived the near extinction of his species once only to learn that the cabal still had access to the compounds that could penetrate his bulletproof coat. The discovery was a shock even the unflappable Matagot couldn't bear.

"Oh, good, you're up," John came through the front door. "I got coffee for you."

"Why do you look so cheerful?" Jessie complained.

"I slept. It felt great," he grinned at her before pulling her close and kissing the top of her head. "Seriously though, how is she?"

"Isabel took over this morning so I could get some sleep. Which I did not do. I'm about to check in," Jessie said. She snatched the coffee out of John's hand and chugged half of the scalding container.

"Mmm. The Nagas' cafe?"

"Of course. I know better than to show up here with anything else."

"What else did you bring?" she batted her eyelashes at him.

"Why would you think I brought anything else?"

"Because you wouldn't show up here empty handed after the night we had."

"I brought coffee! Doesn't that count as not being empty handed?" John protested.

"Nope. Gimme," Jessie started patting down his pockets.

"Please just give her whatever pastry you brought so we can stop watching this," Jared groaned.

"I don't know, I kind of like seeing Jessie happy and all," Charlie floated into the room. "Better than last night, that's for damn sure. I had a moment there of worrying what would happen to me if the whole building came down."

"Oh, I didn't think about that," Jared paused.

"Yeah, we're all kind of invested in this bar now," Chris said. He emerged from under the bartop covered in dust and splinters and huffed at a lock of black hair that dangled over his eyes.

"When Greta wakes up she's going to feel horrible about everything that happened," Jessie turned back to her friends with a warm apple danish clutched in her hands. "Let her apologize and don't say 'it's okay' or 'I understand' because it's not okay and you don't understand. Accept her apology, hug her if you feel like it, and move on."

"Very wise of you, Jennet. By the way, did you know your wards are still down?"

Jessie didn't even blink at the apparition that appeared on the porch just outside the door.

"Then why don't you just come on in?" she asked in a voice as sweet as honeyed poison.

The hooded figure paused and then took a step backward.

"I'm quite comfortable here, thank you," she said.

"Who's Jennet?" Jessie heard Chris whisper.

"The name Jessie was born with," Jared whispered back. "Apparently witches had to remake their identities to keep from getting caught way back in the olden days."

"So are we supposed to be impressed that this witch knows Jessie's old name?"

"Nope."

John slung an arm around Jessie's shoulders.

"Isn't that our little friend from the gravesite?" he asked as he sipped his coffee. "I thought she was being held at the Council."

"Sure is. I imagine it's quite painful to project herself here from the Council's wormwood cells. What do you want, Crone?" Jessie asked through a mouthful of danish. She wasn't about to let a perfectly good pastry go to waste because the stupid cabal had to show up right at that moment.

The figure twitched in annoyance.

"I have a message for you."

"Aw, look at you playing messenger now! Did you really screw up so much that your precious cabal has no other use for you?"

Jared snickered, and Jessie didn't bother hiding her own grin. The crone snarled and jerked forward until her toes were on the threshold. Her hood fell back, revealing a pretty, thin face with a long, aristocratic nose, wide, thin lips, and pale blue eyes. Her ash colored hair was pulled back in a fishtail braid over one shoulder. She looked like she was trying to recreate a gray-haired Disney's Elsa.

"Watch it, Zelda. You're showing yourself," Jessie's tone was cool.

"As if that matters anymore," Zelda snapped. "You have bigger problems, as do we. I know about your little package. My compatriots received something similar with the remains of one of our own along with a message. You have until Yule to surrender Greta or the world will be bathed in the blood of witches."

"Yeah, we know about the Yule part," Charlie said from his spot by the bar. "Don't suppose they told you where she's supposed to go, did they? They neglected to mention that when they sent us their note."

"All we know is that they're somewhere in the mountains between here and Kentucky."

"That narrows it down," John muttered.

"Okay, you can go now. And make sure to tell your masters what a good little witch you were too, delivering that message all by yourself," Jessie taunted with a wave of her hand. They could hear Zelda's shrieks of rage echo on the wind as her shade vanished in the cool December air.

"All joking aside, we have to figure out where they are and stop them before this gets any worse," John said. "Yule starts on the solstice, right? That's two days from now."

"Yes," Jessie said. "That's not a lot of time."

"I agree," Rupert sat up and began licking his front paw so he could groom his ears. "Contrary to what seems to be popular opinion, I am quite concerned for Greta's well-being. And I would hate to see her level a mountain range or plunge a city into the ocean."

"Sorry, Rupert," Jared said. "It just seems like you're not really here anymore. Not just physically, but mentally too. I'm worried about you and Greta and everyone."

Rupert stared at Jared with his emerald gaze before jumping off the bar and padding over to the young witch. He almost knocked Jared over with an affectionate head butt.

"I'll try to do better. Knowing you care... helps."

"I know Caroline would let you sleep on the bar as much as you want if it means you'll be here with us," Chris added.

Rupert gave his raspy, huffing chuckle.

"As if she ever stopped me."

"Knock knock," Vito said from the doorway where he stood with Renard behind him. "I have news that will most likely make Greta feel better. Is she here?"

"No, she's with Isabel," Jessie told him. "Please tell me you have a lead on the box."

"I do indeed," Vito replied.

"Then let's go to the Library. Greta's with Isabel, and it'll be easier to reach the two of them from there," Jessie said, shoving the last of the danish in her mouth and turning on her heel.

Chapter 16

The others hurried to catch up with Jessie as she opened the Library portal. She wasn't surprised to see Isabel already there sitting next to Greta on the old sofa. Lucy was ensconced in Greta's lap, hissing at any other cats who dared to draw near. Jessie ran to Greta, who collapsed in her friend's arms.

"I'm so sorry–" Greta began, but Jessie cut her off.

"No, stop. I don't know that any of us would have reacted any differently if we were in your shoes, and you've had to stop me before too. We love each other. It's what we do."

"I know. It doesn't make me feel better about it. Is the bar okay?"

"It will be," Jessie hedged. "We just have a lot of work to do on it."

"I'll do what I can," Greta declared with a lift of her chin.

"I thought we were supposed to let her apologize," Christopher whispered to Jared as they hoisted themselves on top of a low set of shelves.

"Jessie doesn't count," Jared whispered back.

"Perhaps you would like to hear my news first," Vito interrupted. He gingerly tested one of the armchairs before sinking into it. "Don't roll your eyes at me. Your furniture has seen better days. We have a lead."

"What is it?" Greta demanded, coiling like a taut spring on the sofa.

"Draig was able to trace the blood. Robert is in Tennessee outside of a small town called Butler, close to the North Carolina border."

"Why does that sound familiar?" John furrowed his brow.

"According to legend, Butler was built to replace Old Butler around 1948," Vito replied. "Old Butler was so infested with vampires that the Tennessee Valley Authority had to flood it, so the TVA built the Watauga Dam."

"Was it really a legend?" Jared asked.

"Who's to say?" Vito shrugged. "The TVA told the public that they needed to provide northeastern Tennessee with electricity. I suppose it depends on which story you want to believe."

"Assuming the vampire angle is real, was it Robert or someone else?" Jessie asked.

"We don't know," Vito admitted. "While vampires did, in fact, run rampant through much of the Smoky Mountains, we can't know for certain if the original Old Butler coven was Robert's. When the rumors reached our ears, we chose not to get involved in the TVA's decision. In those days, it was vital that we remain hidden and secret, and whoever was in charge of the Old Butler coven did not seem to care whether or not they exposed us to the world."

"I figured the Parisian labyrinths would be more Robert's style," Chris said.

"True, young witch, but he has too much hubris to return to the site of such a humiliating defeat," Vito chuckled. "After all, that was where he learned the folly of coming up against our Jessica when Greta's life was on the line."

"Did you lose control too?" Chris asked, eyes wide.

"Almost," Jessie admitted. "If Greta hadn't woken up when she did, I probably would have burned Paris out from the bottom up."

"What do we do now?" Greta asked. She still sounded exhausted.

"You have to rest," Jessie told her in no uncertain terms. "Not to make you feel worse, but you probably drained your magic. You'll have to go with us, so you need to power up. I will put you in a Council cell if I have to, but you're going to have a lot of tea and sleep."

"Yes ma'am," Greta said in a small voice as she burrowed into a chenille blanket and pulled it around her head like a hood. "See? I'm resting. I even have a cat."

Lucy immediately dove under the blanket, and in seconds all they heard was her thunderous purr. Jessie smiled despite herself.

"Very good. Okay. We need to find Stefan, get more info on Butler, and figure out who's going."

"And finish the bar," Jared added.

"And finish the bar," Jessie agreed.

"Has anyone heard from Stefan?" Renard asked. He lounged in the other armchair, long legs outstretched and crossed at the ankle.

"I'm calling him now," Jessie said. "Stefan, hey. I'm putting you on speaker. How are you holding up?"

"I've been better," he sounded as exhausted as his sister.

"Yeah, I bet. We have news. Do you have enough energy to port here?"

"Yes, but that's about all I can do. I'll meet you in your office. Getting through your Library's wards may be too much for me right now."

"Okay," Jessie said and hung up. "Be right back."

She stepped into her office as Stefan came through his own portal. He was dressed as immaculately as ever, but he had a grayish cast to his skin and bags under his eyes.

He paused and looked around at the cracked floorboards and shattered windows.

"Greta?"

"Yeah. She's in the Library. I had to burn her pretty badly, so don't freak out when you see her."

He winced, and a flash of guilt shadowed his eyes.

"I'm sorry. I should have been here–"

"Why? So we would have to deal with two ancient rampaging witches? Don't take this the wrong way, but leaving when you did probably saved our lives and this building. We're creatures of nature, Stefan. You're one of the best of us, but that means you feel as strongly as I do or Greta does. Wanting to protect her and loving her enough to get out when you know you can't are the same thing."

"I know. You're right. Still... you said you have news?"

"Come on," Jessie said with a gentle smile.

Jessie led Stefan back through the portal to the Library where everyone kindly chose to ignore his obvious discomfort. He sat down next to Greta who handed him another blanket, scooped up Aleister and dropped the cat in his lap, and put her head on his shoulder.

"Okay, here's where we're at. Draig tracked the vampires to Butler, Tennessee. It's about five hours from here right on the North Carolina and Tennessee border," Jessie said.

"I can reach out to my government contacts to get some good aerial shots so we can form portals," Stefan offered.

"That would be smart," John nodded. "I'll contact the Pisgah Forest pack and see if they can help us in any way. Seanan is already on stand by to step in for pack matters here."

"I know she's your second in command with the pack, but what about the sheriff's department?" Jared asked.

"He's right," Jessie said. "It's one thing when we know we're only going to be gone for an hour at most, but this could take a few days."

John's brow furrowed in consternation as he stared at her.

"Look, I don't like it any more than you do, but if it makes you feel any better, I was doing this since before you were born," Jessie said as she moved to his side and wrapped her arms around his waist, looking up at him.

"See, that just means you're old. You need someone to watch out for you in your dotage."

"Hey," Greta and Isabel protested in unison.

"Don't forget, we'll all be by her side," Rupert reminded the sheriff.

"And if you already reached out to the packs there, then we should have backup," Greta said.

"That's true," John said as he wrapped his arms around Jessie and rested his chin on the top of her head. "But I have a better idea. We go as a team and finish this in one night. If we fail, then I promise you can send me back here through a portal."

"I can live with that. If Rupert goes with us then we need to see if one of Tug's brothers can double as security here," Jessie said. "I don't want Caroline, Jared, and Chris left unguarded."

"Some of my pack will be here too," John pointed out.

"Yes, but the pack won't have a battle trained witch to help with the cabal, and they fight dirty."

"Battle trained witches or the cabal?" Vito asked.

"Both," Jessie replied.

"I can help there," Isabel spoke up. "Nothing says trusted Council guards like Riza can't hang out here while you're gone. Unofficially, of course."

"Of course. Feel better now?" John smiled down at Jessie.

"I guess," she said.

"You and Greta need to rest for at least a day," Isabel informed Stefan. "You're too weak right now for a fight. You can stay in your Libraries or we can find space in the Council, but you're not going home or anywhere Robert's people can find you."

Everyone knew better than to argue with her when she put her foot down.

"Yes ma'am," Greta said again. Isabel smiled and leaned forward so she could pat Greta on the head.

"Good witch. And that gives us time to get our ducks in a row."

"There really isn't a lot on Butler," Jared looked up from his phone with a frown. "But there is a museum we can check out."

"That would look a little suspicious, wouldn't it?" Jessie asked. "I'm pretty sure the cabal fed all of our descriptions to the cult if they didn't already have them."

"It wouldn't seem quite as odd if a vampire groupie looked around though," Renard said with a mischievous grin.

"Who– oh, no." Jessie groaned. "Please tell me you did not keep in touch with that vampie Belladonna or whatever it was she called herself who was obsessed with Morticent."

"Far be it from me to let a resource go to waste," Renard replied as he folded his hands in his lap and recrossed his legs.

"He's right," Jared admitted. "She's annoying as all hell, but no one at the museum would look twice at her, especially if she asks about the vampire legend."

"Just don't tell Nicky that she's part of this," Greta shook her head. "After all, her buddy did kill his boyfriend."

"How could I forget?" Jessie grimly. "I don't want her to be part of it at all."

"She won't remember a thing," Renard assured her. "I'll make sure to wipe her memory."

Vito looked at them with a slightly baffled expression on his face.

"Sometimes I think that it would be nice to spend more time with my children. Then I am privy to conversations like this that remind me why I stopped."

Jessie laughed despite herself.

"It's just that the vampire fan club is quite a thing around here," she explained. "It's mostly Nicky's fault. He loves the attention too much to stop encouraging them. But one of them, a guy named Marshall who chose to call himself Morticent, killed Warsaw. Belladonna was Morticent's closest friend as far as we know. Renard took advantage of her obsession with vampires to try to get information on Morticent and the talisman he used to hide in the bar's bathroom and ambush Warsaw."

"When can you take her to Butler?" Greta asked Renard.

"I'll fly us there before dawn so she can go in the morning," Renard said.

Rupert jumped with a startled yowl as LaSalle ported in next to him.

"Sorry about that," LaSalle grinned. "Probably should have warned someone I would be doing that this afternoon. Good to see you, friend."

"I'm sure I'll feel the same as soon as I recover," Rupert half-heartedly grumbled.

"Oh, good. LaSalle, you're here. You can help Jared and Christopher with the bar until Cassie and Caroline get back from the storage unit. Greta and Stefan, you are not to move a muscle. Got it?" Jessie fixed the siblings with her best glare.

"We're not moving!" Greta protested.

"I don't have the energy to fight off the cats," Stefan added.

Even Sunny had come out of hiding and squeezed himself next to Aleister on Stefan's lap. Stefan was also sandwiched between Lemur and Spot with Ace draped behind his head. Lucy's purrs continued to drift out from Greta's blanket.

"Stefan, would you rather go back to your Library? I can help you get the portal open."

"Yes, I think I would rest better there," he said. He squirmed out from the protesting cats and followed Jessie to her office where she helped him open his portal and made sure he was safely through and resting before going back into the Library.

LaSalle turned to Jessie.

"Jess, Mara wants you to check in. Nothing serious, she just wants to see how you're doing with everything."

He gave the goblet a vague swing on the last bit.

"Can I call her? Or do I have to go there?"

"Sure, you can call her. It's not like she would get any kind of comfort from a friendly face while she sits vigil all alone in the cold garden."

Jessie scowled at the Nain Rouge.

"You're worse than a Southern grandmother, you know that?"

"I learned from the best grandmothers in the world. You gonna go or what?"

Jessie was saved from answering when her phone rang and Annie's number popped up on the caller ID. LaSalle looked at John as Jessie turned away to answer the call.

"Just how bad is the bar?"

John gave a low whistle and shook his head.

"Let's just say this might take a while. But I hear that the Nain Rouge are great with tools!"

LaSalle glared at John for a long moment, bushy eyebrows beetled over his red eyes and then gave up, leading his way out the door.

"I have got to get new friends," he muttered under his breath and then was gone.

Chapter 17

"I t's probably not on your radar, but since I began the Court's Yule preparations, I figured it wouldn't hurt to find out if you want me to decorate your bar this year too?" Annie asked

Jessie shook her head even though Annie couldn't see her. The little brownie loved technology, including the magical device that let her call everyone she knew and chat at any time. Truth be told, Jessie didn't mind it so much. Sometimes it was nice to stop and catch up with an old friend.

"We have to put the building back together first. The cult sent us Stephanie's finger in a box, and Greta lost control."

Jessie could almost hear Annie's frown in her voice.

"That's not good. Here, I'll let you talk to Mara, and I'll see you soon."

Jessie heard a rustle and the murmur of low voices before Mara's voice came through the line, albeit with a bit more distaste than Annie. Mara was not as keen on all of the new gadgets that had found their way into her court.

"Jessie? Can you hear me?"

"Yes, very well. You don't have to shout," Jessie winced and held the phone away from her ear.

"Oh, sorry. How's this?"

"Much better," Jessie smiled.

"Excellent. Now, tell me what happened with Greta and the bar. I gleaned some of it through your conversation with

Annie, who, by the way, speaks for me on the security and maintenance of this Court. Just in case it ever comes up."

Jessie's smile broadened into a grin.

"I figured Annie was your seneschal. I didn't want to ask though."

"While some question placing a brownie in such a role, I can't imagine a more suitable assignment," Mara replied. "I don't trust anyone as much as I do her, and her advice is always practical and sound."

"I would put her in charge of my bar in a heartbeat if it were possible," Jessie agreed.

"What about Charlie?"

"What about him?" Jessie tried to make the leap.

"Well, he's there all the time out of necessity, he needs to feel useful, and he used to manage a farm. So you know he can handle a bar. He already does most of your legwork, does he not?"

"Huh. That's true," Jessie thought for a moment. "Plus putting him in different situations might make it possible for him to keep testing the boundaries of what a ghost can do. And then I can also pay him by putting money into a trust for his family."

"See? It works out for everyone," Mara smiled. "Now enough chit chat. Tell me what happened with Greta and the bar."

Jessie filled Mara in on the night before from the time the box appeared until Zelda's visit that morning along with Draig's information about Butler.

Mara was quiet for a moment when Jessie finished her story.

"And you know this Zelda?"

"We were apprentices together. She hated me from the beginning. When Isabel and I joined the Council, my teacher was delighted to take on my training. Zelda had been her only student up until that point, and while she wasn't a bad student, her powers were never as strong as mine," Jessie explained.

It wasn't a boast. Her nimble mind had always been able to easily grasp and unravel the mysteries of magic, and she surpassed Zelda after only a year and a half of studying under their teacher. Zelda never caught up even though her training began long before Jessie's, a fact that had rankled her to no end. After Zelda attacked Jessie out of jealousy and spite, the Council banned Zelda from taking on a student of her own.

"How was she able to project herself if she's held at the Council?" Mara asked.

"She's not as strong as I am, but she's older. Her age and training alone give her a higher resistance to the wormwood cells than someone like Astrid. Projection is very painful for her, but she can still do it. And the cabal isn't about to let her off the hook just because she was captured."

"Well, I have some news from the Gulf Courts. Nothing that will really come as a surprise, but I wanted to let you know all the same."

"Fae are missing?"

"Fae are missing."

"Sometimes I hate being right," Jessie sighed.

"I know, dear friend. Me too."

"Can we try to track them down somehow? Or send one of us to talk to the Courts? We have to find them before it's too late."

"Not to sound harsh or cold, but it probably is already too late," Mara reminded her. "And you need to get your plan together, stop worrying about problems outside of your own, and focus on rescuing Stephanie. Time is running out. Every time the cabal tries to outmaneuver you, they distract you and spread you and your resources thin. That's how they keep you from getting ahead in all of this."

"You're right," Jessie admitted. "We're sending someone to Butler to check out the museum in the morning. If all goes well, we'll be there tomorrow night."

"I wish you could take Robin," Mara said. "He's perfect for reconnaissance missions, but Oberon has him tracking the fae who were present at the graves."

"We'll have LaSalle," Jessie assured her friend. "And I'm pretty sure Matthias and Tam will be in yelling distance."

"I'm sure they will," Mara agreed. "Those two have made quite a name for themselves among the lesser fae. They give me hope that maybe the higher and lesser fae can bridge this gap after all."

"Getting rid of terms like 'higher' and 'lesser' would be a good start," Jessie pointed out.

"And what of Rupert?" Mara asked, concern lacing her voice.

"He's... okay," Jessie hedged. "I'd be lying if I said Madame Blanche and I aren't worried. I wish he would stay behind for this fight, but I don't have a way to suggest that without insulting his honor."

"No, I suppose you don't. Well, I hope for the best. Maybe he won't be in as much danger since the cabal agreed to stay out of your way."

"Our cease-fire only lasts until Robert is vanquished," Jessie frowned. "For all we know, they'll have us get rid of him and then attack us while we're down."

Mara grew quiet and then cleared her throat.

"Well, now that we got the pleasantries out of the way, I'm afraid I have more bad news."

"Those were pleasantries?" Jessie stared at Isabel, who gave up all pretense of not listening to the conversation. Greta had fallen asleep almost as soon as the others left the Library, and Isabel sat curled up in the armchair, sipping tea and stroking Ace, who was upside down in her lap.

"What could you possibly have found out that's worse than what we're dealing with already?"

"The humans are more involved than we thought," Mara's voice was grim. "After we dumped that Zach kid back at his home, I had a satyr who is loyal to me keep an eye on Zach's family estate. There were a number of suspicious comings and goings, including creatures who reeked of magic as well as some of the elves who had fled Oberon's court."

"What do you mean, 'reeked of magic'?" Jessie frowned.

"Satyrs have a nose for magic," Mara explained. "It's one of the ways they can find nymphs so well. Call it a gift from Pan, that old goat."

She said this last bit fondly before sobering.

"I don't know if the ones he sensed were just witches or if vampires walked among them, but they weren't fae."

"Does it matter anymore who they were? We know they're all in bed together," Jessie scowled.

"What do we know about Zach's family other than they're rich?" Mara asked.

"Nothing," Jessie admitted. She raked her fingers through her curls in frustration. "I meant to dig into it, but there was always something more important to do. I shouldn't have put it off, especially since he kept going on and on to Christopher about that bizarre idea that humans can siphon magic from witches."

"It may not be that bizarre after all," Mara said. "I don't know a lot about humans, but I thought it odd that one would spend this much time and effort amassing a fortune only to throw it behind a half-baked scheme that has no proof of its validity."

"Unless they're glamoured," Jessie reminded her. "We know some pretty high level fae are involved in the cabal. It's not a stretch that they bent a mortal's mind to their will."

"True," Mara admitted. "But I went to Oberon with my discovery. He enlisted the aid of one he trusts to infiltrate the renegade fae's ranks. Zach's father is, indeed, bankrolling the cabal in exchange for a promise of magical powers."

"But why? Surely the vampires and fae who joined have their own wealth?"

"Why spend your own money when you can find someone else willing to give you all of theirs? Especially someone who has none of your weaknesses and access to technology," Mara pointed out. "I think we need to bump this up on our priority lists. We need to learn who this family is, how much power they have in the human world, and if there is any validity to the promise the cabal made to them."

"Agreed. As soon as we get Stephanie back from Robert, I want to look into this. I can get John or Stefan to use their contacts to check out the family. But I need to go join the others. We don't have a lot of time to prepare for the rescue, and we still have to try to fix the bar before the general public realizes that the building is holding itself together with splinters and luck."

Mara gave a tinkling laugh. Jessie was glad to hear it. Mara had not laughed or smiled often since she lost her adopted son.

"Be well, Jessica. Please reach out if you need assistance. I will do what I can.

"You always do," Jessie's voice was gentle. "I'll visit more when we get back. Promise."

"I know," Mara replied "Good fighting!"

The line went dead, leaving Jessie to stare at the phone before looking up to meet Isabel's worried gaze.

"Well. This just really went to shit," she said. "What do we do now?"

Chapter 18

"**H**ave some more tea for starters."

"I love you," Jessie said as Isabel passed her a cup.

"My own blend," Isabel told her. "I make it out of apples I get at the Apple Festival in Ellijay every year."

"I need more of this in my life," Jessie took a sip, feeling some of the tension leave her shoulders.

Isabel set her own cup on the side table and leaned forward.

"When you told me Zach was obsessed with Chris' magic, I figured it was human hubris. You know, the rich, entitled kid wants what he can't have and is going to get it come hell or high water. Why on earth would the fae think it's a good idea to let humans have access to that kind of power?"

"We don't know for sure it's real," Jessie reminded her. "It could be fae glamor and empty promises like the one the cabal made to Robert to get him interested in Greta again."

"Yes, but do you really believe a human family with that kind of money and power wouldn't ask for proof?"

"Can a human become a necromancer?" Jessie asked with a frown.

"In theory they shouldn't be able to since they can't do magic, but I don't know if anyone ever tried."

"Maybe they're about to," Jessie raised her eyebrows at Isabel and took another sip of tea. "If humans who can control our weaknesses get our powers too, they will be unstoppable."

"Not quite," Isabel cautioned. "They will be powerful, but they won't know what they're doing."

"The ogre's old world is sounding better and better," Jessie said with a small sigh.

"Let's hold off on that," Isabel said. "We need to know how much the cabal is in bed with the humans first and if it's even working as a cohesive unit, which doesn't seem to be the case most of the time. Do you think there were any fae in that mass grave you found?"

"Who knows?" Jessie shrugged. "Robin is trying to track down the fae he sensed at the sites, so maybe he can get some answers if he finds them. Mara said we need to stop worrying about the small details though and get our plan of action together. We have to bring Stephanie home so we can put Robert and his cult behind us and start focusing on this new threat."

"She's right, of course. So what now?" Isabel asked as she studied her oldest friend. "You need rest too, you know. You look terrible.

"I know, but we've got to get back on track."

"Go see how they're doing with the bar," Isabel rose to her feet. "Let me know what Renard and the vampie find out tomorrow. It's too bad he can't take Cassie. I trust her impressions much more than that vampire-obsessed girl."

"Me too," Jessie grimaced. "But if the cabal knows what Cassie looks like, then Robert probably does too."

"Speaking of, she and Caroline should be back by now. I had Ivan show Caroline how to make the healing and sleeping draught I used on Greta, so you can keep Greta out for a while. Just promise me that you'll get some rest before you go after the cult."

"I promise," Jessie said as she hugged Isabel. "I'm not going in this half-assed. Three quarters assed maybe, but no less than that."

Isabel laughed as she stepped through her portal into her beautiful office at the Council. A barred owl slept on the perch next to her ornately carved desk.

"Take this," she plucked a feather from the owl's tail and winced at his ear shattering screech. "Shh, it's okay. I'll give you a nice, fat rat later to make up for it."

Jessie wrinkled her nose at that, but Isabel ignored her.

"This feather will let me find you if you need me. You only get one shot with it, so use it wisely."

"Thanks, Isabel." Jessie hugged Isabel as she took the feather and squared her shoulders. She cast Greta one last worried look before hurrying through the door to her office.

Which was immaculate. Her furniture looked sturdier than it had decades. Was that a new frame on the sofa? What happened to the patches that kept the stuffing in place? Where was the duct tape that held her desk together? And were those actual *nails*? What happened to the wood that had been too split to drive anything bigger than a thumbtack into it?

She stared around in shock before launching herself through the doorway and into the hall beyond. The hallway was perfect. The floorboards lay flat and varnished with no trace of the destruction from the night before, and the oak paneling on the walls gleamed golden in the soft light from the new sconces mounted on the walls.

"What the–" she managed to get out as she ran into the main room and almost collided with John, who huddled against the wall along with her apprentices, Cassie, Rupert, LaSalle, and Renard. There was nowhere else to stand because the bar was packed with at least a dozen ogres, all sporting woodworking tools.

"So apparently we forgot that ogres are the best builders in the world," John said in a dazed voice.

Jessie couldn't answer. She was too busy staring around in shock. The ogres had removed every ding, scratch, and splinter in the building.

"I don't think this place ever looked this good," she said in awe. The closest ogre beamed with pride.

"We owe you a debt we can never repay. When Elisian came to us and beseeched our aid, we could hardly deny his honorable request."

"Elisian?" Jessie heard Cassie whisper.

"Tug's real name," Jared answered.

"Oh, right."

"This is incredible," Jessie told the ogre. "You don't know how much this means to me. To us."

"It's the very least we could do, Madame Witch. But please, do not hesitate to call upon us at any time. As you can see, we are master craftsmen and builders. It is part of our nature. We will be happy to take on any project or task you deem fit for our meager talents."

"You can hardly call us 'master craftsmen' and then describe our talents as meager in the same sentence, Ostium,"

Melodium, Tug's older brother and Oberon's General, chuckled as he walked over to join them. "But he is correct in one thing, Jessica. You have only ever need call upon us, and we are yours to command. Second to Oberon, of course. No task is too large or small for our notice."

"I appreciate that, Melodium," Jessie returned the giant ogre's smile. "Hey, I do have something to ask you."

"How may we be of service?"

"I don't know how much you know about what's going on, but Greta and I have to confront a vampiric cult tomorrow night. Can another ogre stand guard with Elisian until we get back? Most of the pack will be here, but I don't trust the cabal to not take advantage of our absence and come after Caroline, Christopher, and Jared."

"I am aware of the vampire cult's activities as well as the cabal's interference," Melodium scowled. "It would be our honor to defend your apprentices."

"Can we have two ogres?" John asked quickly.

"Why two?" Jessie turned to him in surprise.

"Because then Elisian can go with us and call on the ogres to help us win the fight. That way I won't have to worry quite as much about you hobbling off to your doom. I'm just respecting my elders."

Jessie stared at him for a moment.

"I will never hear the end of that, will I?"

"Nope," he smirked.

"The two of you are an endless source of amusement. Consider it done. And now, ogres, let us return home so that our Lady Witch may revel in the fruits of our labor," Melodium bellowed, turning back to the crowded room.

The answering roar hit Jessie and her friends like a shock-wave, and then the ogres popped out of sight.

Chapter 19

Jessie stood stunned and slightly deafened.

"Well, that's something you don't see every day," LaSalle remarked.

"Indeed. I must admit, I am quite impressed. We were only away from the bar for perhaps an hour?" Rupert asked. He was too awed to feign indifference.

"Not even that long," Chris said.

Caroline moved to the bar with Jared and Christopher close on her heels. As they started to look over the restored glassware and beer taps, Cassie paled and then darted behind the bar, disappearing from sight to make sure that the ogres had not disturbed her precious equipment.

"They even built a case for the new router," she exclaimed, her voice slightly muffled. She popped up, grinning from ear to ear.

"Well, that's a relief," John said. "I don't know how we would continue without a new router case."

He pulled Jessie into a hug as he spoke, making sure to put her between himself and the now glowering Cassie. Cassie was deadly accurate with any thrown object. She said it came from years of practice while growing up in a large family.

"Oh, no. You brought this on yourself," Jessie laughed and pulled away before she grew serious. "Hey, everyone, I need to let you know what Mara found out. It's not good. Where's Charlie?"

"Right here. I tell you what, that was something to watch," the ghost drifted through the ceiling, glowing a faint violet. "I couldn't keep track of them, they moved so fast. One minute one of them would pick up a piece of furniture, the next minute another one would put the piece down whole again. If I could have farmed like that, boy, I would be sitting pretty, let me tell you! Or would have before I died anyway. What's up, Jess?"

"I would love to find a way to have you show me what you saw because that sounds really impressive," Jessie said. She, like most outsiders, had never had a chance to watch the fae in action at their various trades and crafts, but now was not the time to engage her scholar's brain.

"I just wanted to make sure you're okay," she continued. "And when we get back from Tennessee, I have a business proposition for you."

"For me?" Charlie went pale green with surprise.

His color changes were so faint that they were only perceptible if you knew to look for them, but once Jessie discovered that he could express his emotions through colors, it was as obvious as sunlight through a window. Sometimes she wondered how she had never noticed them at all.

"Yeah. Mara put the idea in my head. But you have to wait until we get back to find out what it is," she teased.

"That's not fair," he objected. But he turned that faint dusky rose that meant he was pleased.

"You're not giving him the bar, are you?" Jared asked with some alarm. "Not that I would mind working for Charlie, but I don't think he can legally have his name on the deed to this place."

"No," Jessie laughed again. "And I don't think he can either. Sorry, Charlie. But it's just as good, I promise."

"Jess, I left a message for the Pisgah pack leader, Kathryn," John said. "She should get back to me when she gets home from work, probably in the next half hour or so."

"What does she do?" Jared, ever curious, asked.

"She's a park ranger if I remember correctly," John said. "Our kids go to the same werewolf summer camp in the mountains."

"A camp for werewolves. How quaint," Rupert murmured as he groomed his already immaculate tail.

"It helps them learn how to adapt when they start the change. They can wolf out and explore their lupine side and learn how to control it in an environment where they don't have to worry about hurting humans," John shrugged.

"Dude. They even replaced the liquor bottles!" Jared was awed. "I wonder how they did that."

"Fae magic, which is not something you can poke around in or use for experimentation," Jessie nipped his obvious line of thinking in the bud.

"I wasn't going to–" he started to protest before Caroline interrupted him.

"You absolutely were, and you know it." She crossed her arms across her chest and fixed him with a stern look.

"Okay, fine. Maybe I was a little curious."

"Good move getting Tug to go with us," LaSalle slapped John on the back.

"Yeah, that will help," Jessie agreed. "Hopefully Draig will be there too."

"Because what every party needs is a dragon," Renard agreed.

Jessie looked out the window at the gathering gloom.

"And the day after tomorrow's the solstice," she whispered.

"Why don't you go tonight and surprise the cult?" Jared asked. "I mean, if we can get everyone together in time."

"Greta and Stefan are too weak. They drained their magical resources when they lost control and rampaged," Jessie replied. "You have to remember that vampires are physically a lot stronger and faster than witches. Our only advantage over them is our magic. We all need to be at the top of our game, so going up tomorrow night is the best we can do. It still puts us ahead of their schedule, and I'd like to have our attack underway or finished by the time the solstice begins. If we time it right, we'll have all of the strength from one of our sacred days when we need it most."

"Plus there could be at least a hundred of these vampires," John added. "We don't want to show up until we can gather as much information and as many assets as possible."

"Yes, in fact we need to make sure we have a fast exit out of there when we win," Renard said. The concept that they might not win was never an option where he was concerned.

"Draig can help us with that," Jessie said with more confidence than she felt.

"What did Mara say?" John asked.

"Humans are bankrolling the cabal in exchange for a promise that they'll get access to our magic."

A stunned silence followed her words before everyone started talking at once.

"What the hell?" LaSalle demanded.

"Is she certain?" John asked sharply.

"*Merde*," Rupert swore.

"This is all my fault," Christopher whispered, and Cassie turned on him, fierce as ever and spitting mad.

"No, it is not! I will kick anyone's ass who says otherwise, no matter who or what they are!"

"Yeah, we all will," Jared slung his arm across his friend's shoulders.

"Everyone, calm down!" Jessie yelled. "Chris, it is not your fault. Zach's family was already involved with the cabal when he found you. That's how he got the idea to try to siphon your magic to begin with."

"Exactly," LaSalle nodded. "And right now, we need to focus on Robert and getting Greta's family back. We'll take care of these humans when we finish wiping the mountains with the cult."

"Well, since the ogres took care of the bar, Caroline, Jared, and Chris, I want you to practice attack and defense strategies until it's time to open," Jessie told them. She pushed thoughts of impending doom out of her mind and moved to stand by the foosball table, which had miraculously survived Greta's rampage unscathed.

"But I want to see how the ogres rebuilt the— okay, strategies, got it," Jared hastily changed his argument when he saw Jessie's eyes narrow and her jaw set.

"You can figure out all of that later. I'm sure they'll even show you in slow motion. Now I want each of you to build a shield out of your element and get familiar with it. You're going to learn how to use your element to your advantage from a defensive standpoint."

"Ooh, can I watch?" Riza said from behind Jessie.

Jessie grinned over her shoulder.

"Of course. You can help throw missiles at them."

Chris blanched, and even Caroline looked nervous.

"Hey, since I'm going to be your babysitter for the next day or two, you might as well get used to battle training. And I'm not nearly as nice as Jessica," Riza said. She pulled a stool next to Jessie and plopped down. Then she paused, looking around the bar.

"Hang on, this place should have been condemned. How did you fix it already?"

"We didn't," Jessie said. "Tug called in the ogres."

"Yeah, they did all of this in less than an hour," Jared added.

"Shit, really?" Riza looked around in admiration. "Will they do any building?"

"It never hurts to ask. I'm sure they charge very reasonable rates," John said. "Hey, Caroline, will you give me a couple of beers?"

"They even fixed the gas pressure in the tap lines!" Caroline exclaimed as she drew two perfect beers. "Can we call them every time something goes wrong?"

"How did you have gas pressure problems when one of your apprentices is an air witch?" Riza asked, taking one of the beers from John.

"I wonder," Jessie shot Jared a dark glare. He had the grace to look embarrassed. It had not been a good day when she walked in to find him dismantling the tap box to see how the lines worked.

"Ah," Riza let it drop. "Hey, before we start blistering your students with fireballs, who else will be here with us while you're gone?"

"Two ogres for the door and the wolf pack plus anyone in the neighborhood who happens to drop by and wants to lend a hand. Tug's going with us so he can call on the ogres if we get in trouble."

"So it's just the seven of you and Tug?" Riza looked at them in disbelief.

"And Matthias, Tam, and Draig."

"Oh, that makes me feel so much better," Riza didn't try to hide her sarcasm. "You realize there are easily a hundred vampires as far as we know, right? And the cabal's going to be nipping at your heels."

"Thank you for reminding her," LaSalle said before he took a long pull from the goblet. "I'm sure she has no worries at all about the entire situation now."

"I'm also waiting to hear from the Pisgah pack leader," John reminded them. "We'll have back up, even if I have to make Jared create a hundred of those little stone statues to march on Butler."

Everyone stopped, picturing the town overrun with six inch stone men, and Cassie started giggling, followed by Caroline until they all roared.

"Okay, ready guys?" Jessie asked, wiping tears of mirth from her eyes.

"No," Chris muttered.

"Too bad," Riza grinned. "And go!"

She lobbed a fireball at the trio, and for the next hour she and Jessie ran the apprentices through defense exercises. Caroline learned how to use water to transmute other elements and send missiles flowing around her body, Jared learned how to use air streams to deflect trajectories and create the illusion that he was in different places of the room, and Chris learned how to burn up missiles in mid flight and surround himself in flames without burning his skin or the newly refinished bar floor.

"Fire is better for attacks, but it can also work for defense," Riza told him as she walked him through dismantling the fire dart she threw at his shield.

"You can attack with water or air too. They're great for biological warfare like suffocation or drowning," Jessie added.

"Yeah, Jared, your mom wrote the book on using water as a weapon. Literally. It's one of the most read books in the Council library," Riza told him, enjoying the look of surprise on Jared's face.

"You can also use air to fling objects at your target, or you can overwhelm them with water," Jessie continued the lesson.

"Like this," Riza tossed a glass of water at Chris. Even though her element was fire, she controlled the water with little effort and drenched him from head to toe.

They had just enough time to clean up the mess from their magic lesson before they opened for business, welcoming the first of the regulars as Charlie's nephews and one of his cousins joined the ghost along with Mary Jo Sutton. A few of Chris' new admirers sidled up to the end of the bar while some of John's pack mates pulled up bar stools next to his human off-duty deputies. Little by little the communities in the town were learning how to live side by side, and it looked like Jessie's bar was a good start.

"Isabel called and wants to know why you're not resting like you promised her you would," John murmured in Jessie's ear as he slid his arms around her waist from behind.

"I had to train my students," she protested.

"You have two choices. You can get some sleep on your own, or I will sit on you until you do."

Jessie paused, craning her neck to look up at him.

"But you're bigger than me," she objected.

"That's the point."

"Fine," she huffed and turned to their friends. "Everyone, I'm calling it a night. You are welcome to stay here as long as you like, but get some rest before tomorrow. Renard, call me as soon as you get anything out of Butler in the morning."

"Will do. I plan to put the girl on a plane back here and then wait in the wings for you and the rest of the cavalry to appear."

"Sounds like a good plan."

"Kathryn called while you were training your already very capable apprentices," John said. "Her pack will be by our side, and two Appalachian cryptids already approached her about what they saw as a menace to their mountains. They will fight with us too."

"Who?" Jessie asked, startled.

"The Tennessee Red Cheetah and the Wampus Cat," he replied.

"I've never heard of them," Cassie said.

"Me either," Jared shook his head.

"The Cheetah is bigger than an ogre and twice as vicious," John said.

"The Wampus Cat contains the spirit of a Cherokee named Running Deer. She killed the evil spirit Ew'ah. It fed on children's dreams and drove her husband, Standing Bear, mad," Jessie told them. "Knowing she'll be there makes me feel a lot better."

"She is excellent to have on your side," John agreed. "Neither she nor the Cheetah communicate verbally, but Running Deer should be able to speak telepathically."

"We'll figure it out," Jessie said, this time with real confidence. "She was a smart woman. I have faith in her."

"Great! So are you going to go home and go to bed willingly? I can make myself really heavy and hairy when I want to."

Jared made gagging noises behind John's back, and Jessie giggled despite herself.

"Fine! If you and Isabel–"

"And Riza," Riza waved her mug in the air with a warning glance.

"— and Riza are all going to gang up on me, then I'll go home and get some sleep."

"Great. I'll drive you," John said. He grabbed her coat from the new, very ornately carved coat rack mounted by the door.

Jessie stared at him.

"How did my coat get here? What exactly did those ogres do?"

"Fae magic," Jared said with a straight face. "Don't poke around in it. You'll be sorry."

"You may be Isabel's student now, but you'll always be my apprentice," Jessie reminded him. "Don't forget that."

"Me?" Jared's angelic face made her laugh again, harder this time.

"Okay, everyone be safe tonight. Caroline, set the wards the way I showed you when you all leave. Riza, Greta's asleep in the Library. Do you want to hang out in there with her?"

"No, I'll go to my own Library," Riza replied.

"Sounds good. Tomorrow you'll have two new ogres to watch the door for you. Tug's going with us."

"I know. You explained this already."

"And I told you about–"

"Jessica! Get your coat on, leave the building, get in the car, and go home!" Riza yelled.

"But–"

That was as far as she got before Isabel stumbled, retching, through a portal into the bar. Everyone stared at her in shock.

"Jessie, Riza, I need you!"

At the same time, Tug turned toward the voice shouting from the parking lot as a witch wearing a Council guard uniform barreled through the door, panic written all over his face.

"Lady Riza! Lady Jessica! Come quickly! You must hurry!" He shouted as he tried to get through Tug to reach the bar.

Riza was on her feet and running before Tug could do anything more than push the witch back through the door.

"Wait, let him through! He's one of mine. What's going on?" she demanded.

"There was a prison break! The cabal members we imprisoned are gone!"

Chapter 20

"**N**o!" Riza cried. "Jessie!"

Uneasy muttering broke out around the bar, and Caroline cleared her throat, her impressive magic lending her the power she needed to get everyone's attention.

"Everyone calm down. Jessie, Isabel, and Riza have got this, and besides, no one would be stupid enough to mess with all of us, am I right?"

She tossed her blonde ponytail over her shoulder and flashed a dazzling smile. To emphasize her point, John sauntered to the foosball table and raised an eyebrow at a kitsune who casually sipped their beer before baring their teeth in a wicked grin and taking up a position at the other end of the table. Jared gave a theatrical groan and started to pull replacement statues out from a box under the bar while Cassie laughed. Slowly the tension started to ease from the rest of the customers, although a few humans still shot uneasy looks at the poor Council guard before Riza gripped his arm and practically dragged him down the hall to Jessie's office.

"Come on," Jessie paused long enough to help Isabel regain her footing and followed Riza. Once they were through the door, she turned on the guard.

"Did it ever occur to you that maybe barging into a mixed species establishment and blurting out that dangerous criminals escaped what was supposed to be a high security prison was a stupid idea?" She hissed, fury written across her face.

"I'm sorry, Lady Jessica," the guard stammered. "It all happened so fast, and my captain ordered me to find you as soon as I could and get you back to the Council."

"Don't blame him, Jess," Isabel interrupted. "He's just doing his job, and while there's a time and place for everything, I don't know that any of us would have done better. We can worry about the right and wrong way to handle something like this later– we need to go now!"

Jessie led the way into the Library, barely sparing a glance for the still sleeping Greta, and then they were through Isabel's portal and into the Council once more. The first thing they noticed when they stepped through the portal was the acrid smell that filled Isabel's office. When Riza wrenched the door open, the smell made them gag.

"Dear Goddess," Jessie gasped, covering her mouth and nose with her sleeve as her eyes watered.

"Burnt wormwood," the guard, who Riza still half-led and half-dragged, coughed.

"Come on," Isabel ordered and took off down the hallway toward the cells.

"What happened here?" Riza asked as they ran.

"We don't know, my lady," the guard stammered. "Somehow they blew out the wormwood and by the time we got to the cells, Zelda and Astrid were gone."

"Who else?" Jessie asked.

"No one," the guard said. "Everyone else is accounted for."

"As far as we know," Riza shot Jessie and Isabel a sharp look. "They could still be making necromancers and golems."

"The remaining cells are still intact," a second guard joined them. "They struck when the guard changed, so they didn't have time to get anyone else."

"How did they get inside?" Riza demanded.

The two guards shared an uneasy glance.

"We're not sure," one of them said. "The captain ordered a head count and identification screening of all the guards until you and Lady Isabel could get back here. So far two are unaccounted for."

"How much do you want to bet they're dead and the cabal put disguised witches in their place?" Jessie asked.

"Not taking that bet," Riza snapped before she stopped running and turned to the guards. "Hold out your hands."

They reached for her without question. She took their hands, whispering under her breath, and sigils glowed on the inside of their forearms just above the wrist.

"Well, at least you two aren't imposters. Let the captain know I'm here," she ordered. "I'll be at the cells."

"Yes, ma'am," the first guard said with a shallow bow before he turned and dashed down the hallway, the second guard hot on his heels.

"After the end of the first cabal war, we put those sigils on the guards," Riza explained to Jessie as they hurried toward the cells once more. "They appear after the guards swear their oath to protect the council, and they can't be replicated, transferred, or tampered with. If a guard breaks their oath, the sigils burn off and leave a scar."

"Smart," Jessie nodded.

They reached the cells at the base of the tower, and the acrid smell grew until all of them fought to see through streaming eyes. Jessie's throat felt like it was closing up.

"Here," Isabel gasped with a wave of her hand, and they breathed sighs of relief as the air around their faces pushed the poisonous wormwood away.

The doors were still closed and locked, but the wormwood that lined the cells was charred almost beyond recognition.

"We should get Robin in here to see if he can detect fae magic," Jessie said.

"I already can," Riza scowled. "The magic signature here is so subtle that you can't easily pick it up, but I was trained for it. This is not a witch's magic. Something else got them out."

"Damn it!" Jessie swore. "Where's Gertrude? Surely she or Olav knows something."

"Yeah, where is she?" Riza swung around like a bloodhound on point.

"Let's check her quarters," Isabel gestured toward the door and surged forward without waiting for them to catch up.

It didn't take long to find her room, but they heard the heartbroken wailing before they saw the door. Astrid's mother clearly had no illusions about the fate her daughter faced.

"I'm going to guess she didn't see this coming," Jessie winced as they pushed open the door.

Gertrude was in a crumpled heap on the floor, Olav, her fae Nisse companion, nearby wringing his hands.

"Please, help her," he looked up at Isabel. "Please!"

"Shh, Gertrude, we'll find her," Isabel knelt and gathered the much larger witch in her arms.

"They'll kill her," Gertrude sobbed. "She gave us information. You know they'll kill her. They'll trigger whatever the thing is that they put in her head, and she will die!"

"We don't know that," Jessie sat down on the floor. "She was too smart to give us anything good we could work with."

Jessie was being generous. Astrid, Gertrude's spoiled, entitled, sulky daughter had been an easy mark for the cabal; her mother's reclusiveness coupled with her overrated self-importance made her the cabal's perfect target both as a dispensable scapegoat and a means to attack her very powerful mother who had walked away from the cabal after they suffered their first defeat at the hands of Jessie and the Witch Council.

"Riza, I still think Robin should come. He might be able to narrow down the type of fae that did this," Isabel said.

"A fae is behind this?" Gertrude turned her tear-stained face to Isabel.

"A fae got them out of the cells," Riza told her.

"Ah. That makes sense. What are you going to do? How do we get my daughter back?"

"I think Isabel's right," Riza looked at Jessie. "We are trained to sense the presence of fae magic, but Robin or Mara might be able to give us more information. Jessie, can you reach out to them?"

"On it," Jessie pushed herself off the floor and pulled her phone out of her pocket.

She dialed Mara's number first. After all, she would probably love a chance to help get revenge on those responsible for killing her beloved Dain.

"Hello, Jessica. Something tells me this is not a social call," Mara greeted Jessie when she picked up.

"I take it you heard about the jailbreak?"

"LaSalle told me. I guess it's safe to assume you wouldn't call me about it unless the fae were involved?"

"The cells are lined with wormwood. A fae burned it out so they could get to Astrid and Zelda."

"And you're certain it was a fae?"

"Riza's trained to pick up the magic signature, but she can't tell what type of fae it was."

Mara sighed into the phone.

"I figured. You understand I had to ask though," it was a statement rather than a question.

"I know. Do you think you or Robin can narrow down the type of fae?"

"I can. I'll meet you at your bar now."

"Okay, port into my office. The less people who know you're involved the better," Jessie said and then hung up. "I'm going to get Mara. Riza, do you want to escort us?"

"That's probably for the best," Riza rose from the floor in one graceful, fluid motion.

It wasn't long before the witches and the Duchess stood in front of the cells. Mara concentrated, brow furrowed before she took a step back, baffled.

"This signature... I don't understand," she said.

"What?" Jessie asked.

"I don't recognize it. It's ancient beyond my understanding, and it's so dark and so cold. I've never come up against anything like this before."

"Would Oberon be able to tell?" Riza asked.

"Perhaps, but it's fading too quickly for him to get here in time. I'll return to my Court at once and reach out to Robin and my uncle. Between the three of us, we can certainly discover who is behind this."

"Thank you, Mara," Isabel said, ignoring the normal taboo against thanking one of the fae.

"Of course, dear friend. Jessica, you have enough to deal with in light of your task tomorrow. You must put this behind you, however much you can, and get rest tonight."

"I'll go sit with Gertrude and see if she knows anything that matches that signature," Isabel added. "Jess, go to bed. Let me know as soon as you leave tomorrow night."

"I will," Jessie promised. "And I think it goes without saying, everyone should keep this to themselves as much as they can."

"Agreed," Riza said grimly. "Happy hunting, old friend."

"You too," Jessie gave an equally grim smile and then was gone.

Chapter 21

Despite Jessie's worries about their impending doom, she slept like a log until early the next afternoon. She suspected that Isabel had spiked her tea with a time-release sleeping spell, but John refused to give her a straight answer when he showed up at her house to return her phone that she had left at the bar in her haste to get to the Council. Her hair was still wet from her quick shower when she met him at the door with her coat in hand.

"You're taking me to get coffee," she informed him as they climbed into his battered red Jeep where she told him what scant information she knew about the prison break while they drove to the cafe. "Poor Gertrude. I can't imagine how she must be feeling right now. Did you talk to Renard?"

"Yeah. The museum didn't have anything about the vampires, but Belladonna found a couple of old timers willing to talk to her. I guess she can be personable when she tries."

"Well, she's a barista. As much as I dislike her, I have to admit that's a hard job. You have to be even nicer than a bartender, so she probably has a lot of experience dealing with people."

"True. Anyway, they swear by the vampire infestation story, and get this— they told her that they noticed activity in the mountains to the north of town. Lots of strange lights and noises, and it 'feels' off to them. Everyone's been avoiding it."

"Hopefully that means the town itself is safe," Jessie said in relief. She did not want to show up to a massacre.

"It sounds like it. Renard put her on a plane in Asheville, and she's headed back here now. Do you want to talk to her when she lands?" John asked as he pulled into a parking spot in front of the Naga's cafe.

"No, I don't want to deal with Hartsfield today. Besides, we need to get a move on," Jessie said, remembering Mara's advice. She climbed out of the Jeep and walked over to stand by him.

"I wish we could get a break," he said, taking her in his arms.

"Me too," her voice was muffled against his shirt. "You're squishing me."

"Shh, there, there," he soothed, squeezing harder until she started to giggle.

"I liked it better when you were solemn and quiet all the time," she complained as she pulled away.

"Really?" He raised his eyebrows. Jessie thought for a moment.

"No, not really," she admitted. "Did you talk to Greta yet?"

"No. The bar was dark when I drove by, so she might still be asleep. I have to get back to work, but I'll meet up with you at the end of my shift," he drew her in for a kiss.

"You'd better," she said with mock sternness.

It was a beautiful day, and the sun glinted off the bare tree branches, warming them with golden light. The bell on the door chimed as she walked into the cheery, neat cafe, and she was soon surrounded by the Kumar family, the children slithering around her knees in excitement as they vied for her attention.

"Children, please! Let Miss Jessie through," their father ordered with a laugh. He wound his way around the wrought iron chairs and tables that took up the cafe's dining room and positioned himself behind the pastry case. A red espresso machine gleamed on the dark wood counter behind him.

"It's fine, Rahul. You know I love them," Jessie smiled. "Three coffees and one cappuccino please."

"Coming up," he replied.

When he handed the tray of coffee to her, he thrust a paper bag into her hand.

"For Greta. And for you! You must keep up your strength for the fight ahead."

"Thank you," Jessie was touched by the gesture, although it was not wholly unexpected. The Naga were half-snake, half-human, and all heart, making them some of the kindest people she knew.

She enjoyed the short walk to the bar until she had to juggle the scalding hot coffees and bag of pastries to dig her keys out of her pocket. Moments later, she opened the portal to the Library where Greta sat with the disoriented look of someone who slept so long and hard that they don't know where they are.

"How do you feel?" Jessie asked.

"Like I slept a hundred years. What day and time is it?"

"December nineteenth and around three in the afternoon. Want some coffee?"

"I would love some coffee," Greta said through a gaping yawn. She tossed the quilts off of her, and the cats scattered. "Did you feed them breakfast and I missed it?"

"Nope," Jessie grinned. "They must have given up trying to get you to wake up."

Sunny immediately let out an ear splitting yowl, and the rest joined in.

"And there they go," Jessie laughed. She handed Greta the cappuccino and started to pull out food bowls. "Go get dressed and I'll feed them. Then I'll let you know what's going on. Wait until you see what the ogres did to the bar!"

"Did they fix it?" Greta asked, hope shining in her eyes.

"Go! I'll show you when you get back," Jessie ordered.

"No, I want to see it now!" Greta jumped over the back of the couch and through Jessie's portal to the office, leaving Jessie to trip over six screeching cats who demanded their food right now, and how could Greta (and, by extension, Jessie) let them starve for so long?

"Holy shit," Jessie heard her best friend yell before Greta ran back into the room.

"They did all of *that*? Why didn't we ask them for help months ago? Now I don't have to worry that your desk is going to collapse on you!"

"Hey!" Jessie protested.

"You know I'm right," Greta was off again.

Jessie shook her head and fed the cats, trying not to break her neck in the process. Sunny, Ace, and Spot just had to be under her feet the whole time.

By the time she was done, Greta had oohed and aahed over the ogres' handiwork and looked more like herself than she had since the nameless man delivered the letter to Matthias' hut.

"Yes, it's lovely, go get dressed! Wear something warm," Jessie interrupted. "And get in touch with Stefan. We need his aerial shots so we know where to put our portals, and we have a lot of catching up to do."

"What kind of catching up? Exactly how long was I asleep?" Greta looked bewildered.

"Just call him!"

"Fine!" Greta flopped on the sofa and dug out her phone before looking up, a chagrined expression on her face. Jessie stifled a sigh of frustration.

"Your phone's dead, isn't it?" she asked.

"Yeah, I forgot to charge it. I'm sorry."

"It's fine. I'll use mine. But seriously, go get dressed unless you want to fight the most serious threat we've dealt with in centuries wearing flannel pajamas."

Greta tipped her head to the side, considering. Jessie paused, eyes narrowed. "Then again, it would really throw them off," she said.

"It would, wouldn't it?" Greta giggled. "But it's probably too cold. I'll go change."

She opened her portal to her little flat in London and disappeared from sight as Jessie pulled up Stefan's number.

"Hey, Jess," he said when he finally answered. He sounded as groggy as Greta had. "What's up?"

"We're leaving in a few hours, so I wanted to see if you got the aerial shots," she said.

"Hang on," he muttered. Jessie heard shuffling in the background and the sound of keys tapping.

"Yep, got them right here. I'll get dressed and meet you at your Library."

"Great. I grabbed coffee. Do you want–"

"Yes. Please. I would desperately love some coffee."

Jessie chuckled as she hung up.

About half an hour later, Stefan joined them in the bar's main room. Greta wore dark green cargo pants, a black, fleece lined peacoat, and hiking boots. Stefan had on black jeans and a gray wool sweater under his navy blue jacket. He also had a utility knife on his belt.

"What's the plan?" he asked.

He gave Jessie a grateful smile as she handed him a cup of coffee. Greta sipped her second cup with a sigh of contentment while Jessie poured the bag of pastries out onto the bar top. They each grabbed one, Greta and Stefan wolfing theirs down as if they hadn't eaten in days. Jessie let them eat while she filled them in on Mara's discovery about Zach's family, the prison break, and, finally, the plan to defeat Robert and get Stephanie back.

"The Pisgah Forest pack leader, Kathryn, enlisted two Appalachian cryptids," she finished. "The Tennessee Red Cheetah and the Wampus Cat."

Greta's eyes widened.

"Okay, that was a lot for one night. I agree that we need to put a pin in everything else and focus on Robert for now," she said, shaking her head. "I'm so glad the Wampus Cat will be there. Running Deer is one of my personal heroes. That's amazing!"

"What about the bar?" Stefan asked, brow creased in worry.

"When we walked in on the ogres finishing their amazing repair work last night, Melodium agreed to loan us two ogres to keep watch while they're gone, which means Tug can come with us. Plus Riza will be here along with some of the pack."

"That makes me feel better about leaving the kids behind," Greta said around a mouthful of chocolate croissant. She licked powdered sugar off her fingers, ignoring her brother's sigh of dismay as he thrust a handful of napkins at her.

"Yeah, me too," Jessie said.

"How's Rupert?" Greta asked.

"Fine, although if being, what was the phrase, 'off-kilter' means that I get all of this extra attention, then perhaps I should mope about more often," the Matagot answered as he strode through the front door and paused for a deep stretch. The sunlight coming through the stained glass windows reflected off of his gleaming coat. Jessie suppressed a shudder as she remembered the arrow sticking out of his wing when he fell into her arms after the cabal shot him down.

Rupert cocked his head and regarded her with his green eyes.

"Never fear, Jessica. I meant it when I told Jared that your concern and care helps. You keep me more centered to myself than you know."

"Good. I'm glad," Jessie smiled. "And while it's just us here—"

"You will be the first to know if I feel that I must remove myself from battle," Rupert finished her thought. "Now, if you'll excuse me, you're interrupting my sunbath."

He jumped on the bar, knocked Greta's empty coffee cup to the floor with an irritated twitch of his tail, and sprawled out in the sun.

"Well, that answers that," Stefan said with a smile.

"Okay, now what?" Greta asked. She bent over to pick up the cup and looked mournfully at it.

"We need a coffee maker for the bar," Jessie shook her head. "Now we just wait for everyone else to get here, and then we move out."

"Do we have everything we need?" Stefan asked.

"Yes," John said as he walked through the door carrying several large packs. "Rations, first aid kits in case you need to save your magic, and bottles of water."

"And don't forget that we can port back here to get anything we need," Jessie reminded him.

"Yes, but isn't this easier than hauling food and water for seven or more people through your portal each time or wearing out your portal rings?"

"Hopefully this will all be over tonight," Greta said. "I don't want to drag it out any longer than we have to. It's better to hit them fast while we're fresh."

"Agreed," Rupert lifted his head long enough to look at them before dropping it back to the bar with a soft thud and closing his eyes.

To pass the time, John and Jessie played foosball while Greta and Stefan watched. Every time John's eyes started to glow yellow, Jessie made his players catch fire, which Greta thought was hilarious.

"That's very unfair," he complained in the glowing light of the sunset through the windows.

"And you going wolf on me isn't?" She raised her eyebrows.

"Looks like we got here just in time," LaSalle belched, passing the goblet to Riza who followed behind him.

"I really need one of these," she took a swig and passed it back.

"Keep our kids safe and I'll see what I can do," he said with a wink.

"Deal," she smiled.

"What did we miss?" Jared asked. He walked in with Chris tagging along behind him. Caroline and Cassie brought up the rear, hand-in-hand.

"Just me leveling the playing field. You might need to rework some of your little statues though," Jessie told him.

"Why are they charred? What did you *do*?" He demanded, outraged.

"Just make them fireproof," John shot his beloved a dirty look.

"But not too fireproof," Jessie batted her lashes back at him.

"Okay, we need to get a move on," Greta jumped up and started to pace. Everyone groaned, which she ignored. "Who are we missing?"

"Mikael, Nicky, and Tug," LaSalle counted off on his fingers.

"Can they meet us there?"

"We'd rather not if that's all right with you," Nicky replied.

He and Mikael walked through the door wearing plain black leather pants and black cotton turtlenecks under black utility coats. They even had black gloves to match their rugged black boots. Greta looked them up and down.

"Are we robbing a bank and no one told me? All you need are a couple of ski masks and you'll be the perfect criminals."

"Glad to see you still have a sense of humor," Nicky rolled his eyes.

"Look who we found," Mikael moved to one side.

Behind him stood a tall, well built man wearing the same outfit as the vampires. His black hair hung in a long braid down his back and glinted with green and gold highlights in the setting sun, and his eyes were a startling emerald green shot through with gold flecks. A dragon's tail peeked out from under the bottom of one sleeve– the tattoo that contained his true form.

"Draig!" Greta cried as she launched herself into his arms with so much force that he rocked backwards.

"Hello, love," he smiled down at her, his deep voice softened by a Welsh accent. "I'm sorry I couldn't get here sooner. But don't worry, we'll get her back. Hello, Jessica and Stefan. It's good to see you both again."

"Good to see you too," Stefan smiled as he came forward and clasped Draig's hand.

"Same," Jessie agreed.

There was a moment of confusion while everyone rushed to meet the last known Celtic dragon, introductions were made, and Caroline had to pull Jared back after he tried to figure out how the tattoo that held Draig's true form worked.

"Has anyone heard from Tug?" Jessie asked.

"I am here," the ogre replied, stepping through a portal. In the distance they could see a marble avenue lined with workshops. Oberon's version of the ogres' home was quite a step up from the primitive world the cabal had dropped them in years ago.

"Great," Stefan said with obvious relief.

"Okay, here's the plan," Jessie said. "The cabal is supposed to stay out from under our feet and maybe even lend us a hand if it looks like the cult is winning. They supposedly want Robert gone as much as we do."

"But don't trust that," LaSalle warned them.

"Exactly. Always watch your back. This could be the perfect opportunity for the cabal to kill two birds with one stone. Renard is already there. He sent me the coordinates for the town and the location where the locals said they saw and felt 'weird stuff'. His words, not mine. Stefan, did you get the satellite images?"

"Right here," he pulled it up on his phone. "We can port in there," he pointed at a clearing about ten miles to the north of the town.

"Great. We get in, get Stephanie, defeat Robert, round up the rest of the cultists and turn them over to the vampires, and hope we make it out in one piece. John loaded us up with supplies in case we need them, but we'll also be able to port back here if there's a problem. Any questions?"

"Is that the only opening into the cave?" Draig asked.

"As far as we know," Stefan said.

"When we reach the mountain, Greta and I will search for another entrance. If I can come up from underneath Robert, then we'll have a flanking advantage."

"That sounds like a great plan to me," LaSalle smiled. "Just for that, you get a turn with the goblet."

"It's very nice. Quite rare," Draig's eyes turned gold and a sibilant hiss underscored his words.

"Watch it, buddy. You can get your own goblet when we get back," LaSalle scowled as he snatched the cup out of the dragon's hand.

"Okay, enough stalling. We need to get going," Greta gestured toward the hallway. "Come on."

She marched down the hall to the Library, their little party following behind.

"Stefan, let me see the pictures and map," Greta turned to her brother and held out her hand.

He passed his phone to her, and she looked at the image, memorizing the details, before she opened a portal. They could see dark woods beyond a small clearing under a cloud covered sky.

"Not ominous at all," Nicky murmured. "Last one through is a rotten egg!"

He jumped through the portal with Mikael, Draig, and Stefan close behind.

"Guess that's you since you have to keep the portal open," Jessie grinned at her best friend as she and John followed. Greta scowled at their retreating backs.

Chapter 22

John's right hand wolf, Seanan, was part of the group left behind to guard the bar, but Jessie recognized the three wolves that jumped through the portal with them as seasoned fighters, although she didn't know them well. LaSalle, Rupert, and Tug were close behind Jessie, until Greta stood alone before she jumped through last, closing the portal as she went.

"I need to call Renard and let him know we're here," Jessie said.

"What about Matthias and Tam?" Greta asked LaSalle.

"They should be close. John, do you have a lead on your pack leader buddy?"

"I texted her the coordinates for this clearing before we left," John said, "She should be here any minute."

"I'm surprised you haven't brought half the forest on our heads with all the noise you made," a woman said as she walked into the clearing behind them. She was short and wiry with copper colored curls that hugged her scalp. Her pretty face was tan with a hawk nose and piercing blue eyes, and her teasing grin belied the criticism in her words.

"Kathryn?" John asked, coming forward with an outstretched hand.

"That's me. You must be John's lady. He has good taste, if I dare say so myself," Kathryn answered with a strong handshake and a nod to Jessie, who stood in the protective half-circle of John's arm.

"You can say that as much as you want," Jessie grinned back before shaking Kathryn's calloused hand and getting down to business. "John told us about the Tennessee Red Cheetah and Wampus Cat. Do you know when they'll get here? We were kind of hoping to get things underway sooner rather than later."

"See for yourself," Kathryn turned back to the woods and waved her hand. "Come on out, guys."

Jessie caught her breath when the branches parted. Out of all of the supernatural creatures, cryptids were the hardest to pin down and the last to wish to make their presence known; too many would be the target of trophy hunters or worse. She was used to werewolves, werepanthers, centaurs, the Lamia, and the Naga, but she could honestly say that nothing prepared her for the two cryptids that walked into the clearing.

The Tennessee Red Cheetah was massive, towering over everyone except Tug. He looked down at her with intelligent, golden eyes as he padded toward them, his deadly claws leaving deep ruts in the loam. The ochre streak down his back, the broad shoulders, the piercing gaze, and the huge jaws all spoke to immense power and strength.

Behind him came a creature that made Jessie's friends gasp. The Wampus Cat was almost as big as the Cheetah. Half cat and half dog, she walked toward them on her hind feet, dropping to all fours when she drew closer to Jessie. Out of the corner of her eye, Jessie saw Draig give a deep bow to the Cats, who inclined their heads in return.

"Who was harmed by those who would poison our world?" a calm voice that hinted at magic older than the stars rang in Jessie's head.

"They were," Jessie pointed at Greta and Stefan before she realized what she was doing.

The cat sat on her haunches and looked at the siblings for a minute. Greta rushed forward and threw her arms around the Wampus Cat's neck before falling back with a choked sob. She wiped her eyes and squared her shoulders, lifting her chin with a determined set to her jaw.

"We will stand by your side," the Cat spoke to Jessie again. "You will not fail as long as I am here. I defeated one demon in these forests, and I will not let more stand. We love these mountains. They will not be spoiled by the likes of this Robert."

"Thank you," Jessie smiled, realizing at the last minute that may not be wise. Thanking the fae implied an obligation. She had no idea what it meant for a powerful Cherokee cryptid spirit.

The Cheetah and Wampus Cat disappeared into the woods, and LaSalle let out an explosive breath.

"That was something," he marveled. "Did you feel her power?"

"Indeed, I am also in awe," Rupert admitted. "It has been too long since I felt the presence of a spirit who calms me as much as she did. Perhaps... well, enough said for now."

"Yes, you can come back," Jessie whispered and was almost knocked off her feet when he head butted her.

"What did she say to you?" Stefan asked Greta.

"That no one would ever use me like they did again," she replied.

He nodded.

"Good. Kathryn, what do you need from us?"

"Just tell me where to go," she shrugged. "My pack is standing by. We don't want these bastards here any more than you do."

"Can anyone get a signal?" Nicky asked, exasperated. "I have no bars, and I can't get in touch with Renard."

"Good thing you're pretty," Kathryn laughed. "We're in the mountains. You always want a satellite phone up here. Cellphones are pretty much useless unless you need a paper-weight."

"Oh, look. John packed one," Jessie grinned. "And he included everyone's numbers."

"Well goody for John," Nicky snapped and stomped off to sulk against a tree while John laughed.

"It's about time," Renard's voice came through the line. "I expected your call an hour ago."

"We just got here," Jessie said. "And we had to meet our allies. Would you like to know where we are so you can join us or are you going to keep snipping at me?"

"I'm not... never mind. Just give me the coordinates."

Jessie hung up after she told Renard where they were and turned back to Kathryn.

"We can head out after he gets here," Jessie told the were-wolf.

"I thought there was going to be a dragon," Kathryn looked around with a frown.

"He's right there," Greta pointed at Draig.

"You're a bit smaller and less... fiery than I pictured," Kathryn shot Draig a skeptical look.

"I get that a lot," he returned with a straight face.

Greta rolled her eyes.

"Dragons are a type of were-creature," she told Kathryn. "He's a lot more impressive in his natural form."

"Hey," he protested and gestured at himself.

"Yes, you're a very nice man," Greta stood on her tiptoes and patted him on the head. He scowled and joined Nicky to sulk together.

The rest of the group huddled around Jessie while they waited, and she let a steady stream of fire energy radiate out from her body to keep them warm in the cold December night.

"We're definitely not in Georgia anymore," LaSalle muttered.

It wasn't long before they heard a soft flapping overhead, and a vampire bat dropped from the sky. Renard landed on his feet with a grandiose bow.

"I have arrived! We can now continue with the next stage of our journey."

Draig beamed at his progeny while Mikael shook his head and pushed into the woods. Stefan and Greta followed close behind. Kathryn bounded ahead, woman one step and large white wolf the second as she guided them along a narrow game trail that led to the heart of the slope.

Around them, Jessie caught white, gray, black, and red shapes as the rest of the mountain pack flowed through the brush as easily as if they were fish in a stream. She couldn't tell how many wolves there were, but she felt a little better about their chances. John and his three streaked by her like ghosts, disappearing into the underbrush to join their brethren.

"Vito sends his wishes for your success," Mikael told Jessie as they climbed. "And he wishes he could be here."

"Does he really wish he was tromping through the mountains in December?" she asked.

"No, but it's the thought that counts," he smiled.

Greta used her earth magic to muffle their footsteps as they moved deeper into the woods. After they had climbed about a hundred feet, Jessie spotted a small light flickering through the trees.

"What's that?" she pointed.

John slipped through the brush, and then they heard startled yells.

"It's okay," he called out. "I think we're expecting these two."

Kathryn led the way to a tiny clearing where John stood facing two witches, a girl and a boy who looked younger than Jessie's apprentices. They huddled against a tree, the remnants of a small campfire at John's feet. The witches looked unkempt and dirty, and they eyed Jessie's pack with undisguised hunger. A meager pile of nuts sat on the ground, and Jessie suspected that it had been a while since they had a real meal.

"Are you supposed to be our backup?" she asked in disbelief. She knew the cabal wouldn't go out of their way to help, but she would rather have no one show up than two half-starved novices.

"No, we're just supposed to keep an eye out for you and then let someone know you're here," one of them sniffled as snot ran down her face. She shivered in her thin robes.

"How long have you been out here?" Kathryn demanded.

"Since yesterday," the other one said. "There's a stream nearby, and they told us how to forage for food. We accidentally set a bush on fire, so we're not allowed to use fire magic. But my dad taught me how to build a fire once, so I think we're okay. Just, you know, it would be nice to eat something other than nuts and berries."

"Who are you supposed to notify?" Draig asked. His eyes glowed gold, and anger underscored his voice. He was just as unhappy about the witches' conditions as Jessie and the rest of the group.

"There are some other witches waiting for you close to the cave," the girl said. "They're the real thing though. Not novices like us."

"Ever think that maybe you joined the wrong team?" Stefan crouched down until he was eye level with the pair.

They exchanged a nervous glance.

"We can't leave now," one said.

"If we do, then they'll hurt us," the other added.

"Hurt you how?" Greta asked.

"They didn't say."

"Did they do anything to you or just make threats?" Jessie asked.

The witches looked at each other again.

"I don't think they did anything to us— yet," the boy said. "They just told us we'd be sorry if we didn't do what they said and that we need to prove our worth before we can be members. But we saw them do something to the older witches' heads. It must have hurt because it made them cry, and one of them threw up."

Jessie, Stefan, and Greta exchanged a quick glance, as if coming to a wordless agreement.

"I know we need to move," Jessie began.

"It can wait a few more minutes," Greta cut her off. "Go get Isabel. Or better yet, find Ivan, His water magic can tell if their heads were messed with better than her air magic can."

"Isabel gave me a way to summon her. It only gets one use, but kids are worth it," Jessie said. She pulled out the feather and concentrated.

The novices looked at each other, baffled.

"You see, some of us believe that young witches like you should be treasured, taught, and protected," Stefan, still crouching in front of them, said as he examined his fingernails.

"That was fast," Isabel stepped through a portal. The barred owl glared at Jessie and then flew off of his perch and snatched his tail feather from her hand before the portal shut.

"Well, something came up," Jessie gestured to the kids.

"Who are they?" Isabel asked with a raised eyebrow.

"The cabal sent them to look out for us," Greta said. "Notice that they're so young that their hair isn't even gray."

"And they have no food," Nicky pointed out. "A pile of nuts doesn't count."

"Or any supplies or warm clothes at all," LaSalle added.

"Can you do something for them?" Jessie asked.

"Hi, I'm Isabel. I'm the head of the Witch Council. Don't be scared, we just want to help you," Isabel said. She knelt next to Stefan in front of the frightened novices who flinched away from her. "Do you want to come back with me to the Witch Council? You'll have to stay in a cell while we get you checked out, but it's warm, the food is pretty good, and no one can touch you while you're in there. If you decide you don't like it with us, then you'll be free to go."

The young witches exchanged an uncertain glance.

"I don't know," the boy stammered. He was so young that his face still had acne. "They– the cabal, I mean– said the Council is pretty bad and tries to brainwash novices. They made us stay out here because they said we have to prove ourselves worthy to join them. How do we know you're any better?"

"I guess I can't convince you right now unless you're willing to give me a chance," Isabel said, her voice sad. She plucked thick cloaks and a burlap sack out of thin air. "At least take these. The cloaks will keep you warm no matter how cold it gets, and the bag will give you whatever food you want. They will only work for the two of you. No one else can use them."

"Really?" the girl sounded like she could hardly believe their luck. The boy lunged forward and snatched the sack out of Isabel's hands, and a stack of burgers and fries fell into his lap. The girl cried out as she started eating so fast that Jessie was afraid she would choke.

Isabel stood up and rejoined Jessie.

"That's all I can do for now," she said with a shake of her head. "Hi, Draig. Glad you could make it."

"Isabel, a pleasure as always," Draig inclined his head.

"I'll look for them on our way back," Jessie assured her friend. "Who knows, maybe they'll come to you on their own."

"One can only hope. I can't recharge your feather until midnight."

"It's okay," Jessie said with more confidence than she felt. "Your owl stole it back anyway. Worst case scenario, I do a series of jumps to get to you if we really need help."

"Can you bring Ivan back here to just check these two out?" Greta asked. "I want to make sure they're okay."

"Of course," Isabel replied. "But not until this immediate threat is handled. I'm sorry, but it would be unwise for him and me to wander around alone in the dark up here, and if we brought a guard detail then our presence might alert Robert and his followers."

Greta frowned.

"I feel as bad about them as you do," Isabel touched Greta's arm. "But I have to be the voice of caution."

"I know. That doesn't mean I have to like it," Greta sighed.

"I look forward to your return," Isabel told them before porting back to her office.

The two young witches looked up at them and huddled around the sack and cloaks, as if their good fortune was about to be snatched away. Jessie heard a deep growl in the underbrush and saw the firelight reflected off of the Wampus Cat's eyes.

"No evil will remain in my lands," her voice spoke in Jessie's head, this time with an undercurrent of anger.

"I think they'll be fine," Jessie said. "Let's keep going."

John nodded before shifting. Jessie ignored the questioning looks from the others and pressed on behind the russet wolf. Stefan paused long enough to leave one of the packs John brought with the kids before hurrying to catch up with the rest of the group.

The cave loomed closer when John emerged from the brush and shifted again.

"There are two more witches up ahead," he whispered. "Pretty sure they're not here to offer moral support. How do you want to handle this?"

"Can we go around them?" Greta asked.

"Not really. Even with you masking everyone's noise, you can't make all of the two footers invisible."

"Then let's say hello," Stefan said with a shallow bow to the wolf.

"Right this way," John grinned. Kathryn sat on her haunches behind him, tongue lolling out in a silent chuckle.

These cabal witches were much older, and they clearly did not expect Jessie and her friends to stroll out of the woods when they did.

"Damn it," one swore, jumping to her feet. "I thought the novices were supposed to warn us."

"If you mean the half starved, shivering kids back there, we went around them," Greta lied.

The other witch scoffed in annoyance.

"They'll be fine," he snapped. "If they can't keep themselves warm and fed, then they don't deserve to be part of our cause."

"You know our pact only makes sure that we stay out of each other's way while we try to stop Robert, right?" Stefan asked in a voice that was so cold that it made Jessie shiver.

"And does not include the rest of us?" Mikael bared his fangs. Draig's eyes turned pure gold and smoke drifted from his nostrils.

"Okay, enough," Jessie cut in. "We have a job to do, and that doesn't include teaching these jackoffs a lesson."

"We're here to cover your rear," the first witch offered. "I'm Mary and he's Peter."

She couldn't keep the nervousness out of her voice as she eyed the vampires and wolves. Kathryn sat on her haunches nearby, a soft growl rolling out of her throat.

"Of course you are. I just love being sent in as a sacrifice," John said as he rolled his eyes.

"Who better to serve that purpose?" Peter sneered, but his false bravado fell flat when he backed into a tree after LaSalle unslung his axe and tested the edge on his thumb with a meaningful glance at the two cabal members.

"Let's just go," Jessie began to lose her patience. "You two stay out here. I'd rather have you be bait for any nasty Appalachian creatures than worry about what you're doing behind me."

Peter stiffened.

"By our honor–" he began.

"Of which you have none, or kids wouldn't be in danger of dying from exposure fifty feet from your campfire," Greta cut him off. "Stay here or I will bury you in a rock slide if you try to follow us. Your choice."

Mary sat down, ignoring Peter's glare.

"I'm fine where I am," she muttered to no one in particular.

Kathryn's tongue lolled out again, and she glanced at the two cabal witches before looking back at Jessie, her ears cocking forward.

"Yeah, let's go," Jessie said. "I'd rather get away from the stench of entitlement and shitty people."

Peter opened his mouth to retaliate until Nicky hissed in his face. The witch shut his mouth with an almost audible snap and dropped to the ground by his companion. Mary looked at her feet and turned red as she hugged her knees to her chest. John shifted, and Jessie, Greta, and Stefan turned to follow Kathryn back into the woods and toward the cave.

"What the…" Peter gasped.

Jessie glanced over her shoulder to see the Tennessee Red Cheetah and Wampus Cat emerge from the dense undergrowth, moving with predatory grace. Peter tried to climb over Mary to get away from the cryptids, but he wasn't fast enough.

The Cheetah looked contemptuously over his shoulder and then, to Jessie's absolute delight, sprayed Peter who shrieked, gagged, and tore his robes off revealing a thin black t-shirt and boxer shorts underneath. He stood shivering in the cold night air while Mary hid her laugh with her hand and caught Jessie's eye. Jessie gave her a nod, and she nodded back. Jessie made a mental note of the witch's face. Robert's followers weren't the only ones that would need deprogramming if they could pull this off.

"Why do they join this cabal?" Kathryn, in human form, asked Jessie as they crept forward.

"Probably because the ones heading it up made a lot of promises of power, riches, and who knows what else," Jessie answered. "What those novices said though, I wonder if they're doing something to guarantee good behavior."

"Like the magical aneurysms they did to the ogres?" LaSalle asked.

"Yeah," Jessie nodded.

"I would very much like to see the cabal come to a nasty end," Rupert growled.

"As would I," Tug rumbled. The ogre was very quiet in the woods, and Jessie remembered that he served as Oberon's tracker.

"Wait!"

Jessie turned, surprised. Mary crashed through the underbrush, swearing as she tripped over branches and got stuck in a patch of briars.

"There's something you need to know," she said when she pulled herself free and reached Jessie. "This cave is one of our– my– the cabal's storehouses. The vampires didn't give us time to empty it out."

"Okay," Jessie wondered where this was leading. "Is it booby trapped or something?"

"No, not any more. But you need to know..." the witch hesitated and looked at Rupert. "There are... things... there. I'm sorry. I'm so, so sorry. I wish I had known everything the cabal really stands for, but it's too late for me. But you can save those kids, and you can save him."

"Him who?" Stefan frowned. "Rupert?"

"I'm sorry," she said again and plunged back into the trees. Her footsteps shattered the quiet night, and then she was gone.

"That doesn't sound good," Greta said. She cast Rupert an uneasy glance. "I wonder what she meant."

"I think I have an idea," Jessie said. An unpleasant thought formed in her mind, and she looked at the Matagot.

"Rupert, I need you to think very, very hard about this. She came back to warn us about something in this cave that relates to you, and I can only think of one thing that could be. I'm sure you can too. Are you certain you want to keep going with us and can maintain your composure? No one will think any less of you if you need to bow out now."

Rupert looked at her for a long moment, and then he was gone, vanished somewhere in the spirit plane so fast that Jessie didn't even see a portal open.

"You think they have his kins' pelts in that cave, don't you?" LaSalle leaned on his axe.

"Can you think of any other reason why a cabal witch would warn him about their storehouse?" Jessie asked.

"No," Tug said in a soft, sad voice. "Will he be all right?"

"We'll find him when we're done here," Jessie kept her voice even. "Let's move."

They didn't have much farther to go before John fell back to nudge Jessie with his nose. She looked up at the cave that lurked in front of them, dark except for a dim flicker somewhere in its depths.

"You good?" Jessie heard Stefan ask his sister.

"Yeah. You?"

"Yep. Let's go get our family."

Chapter 23

The entrance to the cave yawned, forbidding and dark.

"Greta, can you look for another opening?" Draig brought the party to a halt. "I want to come up underneath the cult if possible."

"Yeah, hold on," she concentrated.

She opened her eyes with a small smile and walked to a point about ten feet from the cave entrance where she knelt in the dirt, beckoning Draig to follow her.

"Look," she pointed at a foot wide crevice buried under leaves and moss. "This leads to a large chamber about thirty feet underneath Robert and his followers. From there you should find a tunnel that comes up behind his throne. According to the Earth, it will be big enough for you to get through, although it's going to take some time. It winds around, and it can get pretty narrow."

"His throne?" Nicky choked on the word.

"Yeah, according to the Earth, the asshole has a throne," Greta wrinkled her nose.

Draig made a small sound of disgust before he closed his eyes and shifted into a salamander. In seconds he had worked his way into the crevice and disappeared from sight. Greta brushed off her knees as she rejoined the party and looked at the cave entrance.

"Everyone, stick close to me," Greta said. "The Earth is going to show me the way."

Jessie had a brief flashback to Charlie's rescue when the Earth led Greta down into the depths of the mountain behind Gertrude's small farm. She shuddered. That was not something she had wanted to relive any time soon. Her skin tingled, and she knew Stefan had cast an illusion over the group.

"That itches," LaSalle complained.

"Sorry about that," Stefan said. "It's a spell to hide us. I'm going to try to mute any noise we make, but we still have to move quietly. So be careful."

"And I'm asking the Earth to muffle our footsteps, but don't forget vampires have exceptional hearing," Greta reminded them. "Come on."

She led the way into the cave and the wide tunnel that was carved into the back wall. The party could comfortably walk single file, although Tug and the Cheetah had to duck to avoid banging their heads more than once.

Robert's followers had mounted torches at intervals on the walls, and the guttering light cast shadowy illusions that made everyone jumpier than they already were. The Cheetah slunk ahead of the group and sniffed out the sentries posted in their path. For the most part, Jessie and her friends were able to pass by undetected. There was one harrowing moment when the corridor narrowed dangerously close to a vampiric guard until Tug tossed a loose stone down the passage and lured the sentry away from them.

After what felt like hours of creeping deeper into the mountainside, the Cheetah paused and sniffed the air. He swung his massive head toward a side passage that was concealed behind a boulder. If he hadn't shown them the way, they never would have seen it.

The passage was as black as a moonless night. Either the cult didn't know it existed or Robert didn't care enough to use it. As they moved forward into the inky darkness, the air grew colder and stale.

"Everyone hold hands and stay close to me," Greta whispered. "We can't risk light yet, and I don't want anyone to get lost up here."

Jessie felt John take her right hand and figured the small but tough hand in her left had to be LaSalle's. Eventually, the path leveled out, and they stood in an uncertain huddle.

"Jessie, can you give us some light?" Greta asked.

"Watch your eyes, everyone," Jessie warned the group. She concentrated, bringing in the flame slowly to let their eyes adjust. It was still piercingly bright after the darkness of the tunnel.

"Oh no," Greta said, her voice full of dread.

Jessie looked up from her fireball. They had found the cabal's storeroom.

The room was medium sized and roughly hewn from stone with a ceiling that rose far overhead. Tug gave a snort of disgust as his critical eyes moved over the walls and obvious lack of any attempt at craftsmanship. On one side, piles of magical artifacts and tomes leaned against the wall. It was the other side of the cave that made Jessie's gut clench. Pelts so black that they absorbed the light from her fireball were stacked along one wall. LaSalle let out a low whistle.

"Sure glad Rupert left when he did," the Nain Rouge pushed his cap back on his forehead and shook his head.

"Are those–" Nicky started to ask.

"Matagot coats? Most likely," Jessie said in a sickened voice.

The wolves growled, hackles raised, and pressed against the group, forcing them away from the grisly scene. The Matagot weren't the only casualties on display. Jessie saw silver and purple dragon scales, unicorn horns, and trophies from countless other creatures. Nicky made a wordless sound of dismay and sorrow at the stone remains of a gargoyle just on the edge of Jessie's light.

"We must continue onward. The time for revenge will be upon you soon enough," the Wampus Cat spoke in their minds, her words underscored again by anger.

"We need to let the Council know about this place when we're done," Jessie told Greta.

"Yeah, and we need to reach out to cryptid and fae creatures to see if they want the remains of their loved ones," Greta said.

"Agreed, starting with Draig," Jessie nodded at the scales.

They left the horrible room behind and climbed further into the dark. Jessie and Greta led the way, and the wolves brought up the rear. When light appeared ahead, too bright to be torches, Jessie extinguished her fireball, and Stefan tightened his illusion on the group. They crept forward and found themselves in an alcove overlooking a vast cavern. When Jessie peeked over the side, she swore under her breath.

The cavern was filled with vampires, and Jessie could make out Robert on a cheap, wooden throne that sat on a dais overlooking the throng. Guards flanked an opening in the wall opposite the dais, and Jessie guessed that she and her friends would have come out at that opening if the Cheetah hadn't found the side passage. She saw a smaller tunnel to the left of Robert's throne directly across the cave from the alcove where she and her friends crouched. Crude stone steps led up to the tunnel.

Robert's black, wavy hair, olive skin, and annoyingly handsome face were clearly visible, even from their vantage point, which was about thirty feet above him. He wore gleaming white robes that stood out in stark contrast to his followers' filthy rags, and he lounged in his seat with a quarterstaff by his side while four vampires wearing mismatched, rusted armor, and who looked healthier than the crowd milling about on the floor, flanked his throne.

Rather than seek his true death when he was turned against his will, Robert had set out on a mission to create an army capable of annihilating any beings he considered an affront to the church until he cleansed the world of all blasphemers. Jessie personally doubted that his God considered witches, vampires, or any other cryptids and fae offensive, not that her opinion mattered to Robert.

His army looked not only dirty, but lost. Jessie could make out dark splotches on many of the vampires' bodies where they had been bitten and turned, the blood left to dry on their skin. None of them looked as though they had bathed in weeks, and their unwashed stench wafted up to Jessie and her friends, carried on the updraft from a dozen guttering torches mounted in the walls.

"That's where Draig will come up," Greta whispered, pointing at a gaping black pit behind the dais.

"We may not have to wait for him. Robert's army will be easy to break," Mikael whispered back.

"How? There's well over a hundred of them," Jessie said.

"They're being denied their true nature," Renard explained. "While they might have typical vampiric strength, the war they fight within themselves will weaken their focus in battle. It gives us a huge advantage."

"Especially if we show them their real potential," Nicky added. "I can sense their lack of experience and mental weakness. Mikael and I are direct descendants of our ultimate sire. We will be able to overpower them."

"Are you going to speak to them out loud or telepathically?" Stefan asked.

"We do it verbally," Mikael replied. "We can charge our voices with hypnotic suggestions."

"Then I'll use my air magic to carry your words so that the whole throng hears them," Stefan jerked his chin at the waiting horde below.

"Shh, listen," Greta waved them to silence.

"Where are they? They should be here by now," Robert's nasal whine floated up to them. His face might be pretty, but his voice was not.

"They should be close, my lord," one of his lieutenants, a pretty blonde vampire who stood to his left, told him. She sounded exasperated as if they'd had this conversation more than once today. John nudged Jessie's ribs with his elbow.

"She matches the description of the vamp who gave that guy the letter for Greta," he whispered.

Jessie started to reply, but the vampire was speaking again.

"Do you want me to send someone to scout around outside again?"

"No, go fetch the prisoner. I want her here when her pathetic family arrives," Robert dismissed the lieutenant with a wave of his hand.

"We need to follow her," Greta hissed.

"We can't all go," Jessie objected.

"You, me, Stefan, and Nicky," Greta decided.

She plucked a hair from her head and wrapped it around a pebble, concentrating briefly. It glowed green before dimming back to gray.

"Here, take this," she handed the pebble to Mikael. "When we reach Stephanie, it will flash green. If it flashes red, we're in trouble."

"Got it," he said as he took the stone.

"Before we set our plan in motion, I believe some back up would be appropriate," Tug said.

"Do it," Jessie gave him a decisive nod.

He nodded back and opened a portal to the ogre's marble city where Melodium stood waiting for them along with half a dozen ogres. Once they reached their battle rage, their skin would become diamond hard and impenetrable, making them nearly invincible. Most carried battle axes, although Melodium preferred a great sword that he wore strapped across his back.

Even with their size and weaponry, the ogres were almost completely silent as they stepped into the alcove and lined up behind their general.

"Good to be by your side," Melodium whispered.

"Any word on Matthias and Tam yet?" Greta asked LaSalle.

"They have something planned, and that's all I know," LaSalle shrugged. "Knowing those two, it could be anything."

"They know we're supposed to keep as many vampires alive as possible, right?" Greta couldn't hide her anxious tone. The last thing they needed was a bunch of vengeful fae running rampant through the cave.

"They know," LaSalle reassured her. "They're not going to do anything half-cocked. I hope."

"Who are Matthias and Tam?" Kathryn asked.

"Some of our fae friends. Matthias is a Fir Darrig and Tam is a leprechaun."

"You made friends with one of the rat fae? Our odds are better already!" Kathryn's admiration was genuine.

"For that, you get the goblet," LaSalle said with a bow. She grinned and took a swig.

"There is one last thing you need before your battle begins," the Wampus Cat turned to Jessie and Greta. "'The blood of the covenant is thicker than the water of the womb'. The love the two of you share makes you closer than any sisters. Use this to your advantage, for the ways in which your magic complements each other can be most formidable."

She reared back on her hind legs, and when she came down, Jessie felt a hot ripple pass under her feet. The Cat stepped back, and two swords and two daggers slid out from the rock where she had stood.

"Take one of each," she nodded to the weapons.

Jessie and Greta obeyed, and Jessie gasped almost audibly when the dagger glowed dark green like moss along a river bed and the sword burst into flame. Greta's weapons did the same, but her sword was as green as a pine tree in winter and her dagger glowed orange with fire.

"You can now call the powers of earth and fire to act on your command without depleting your own magic," the Wampus Cat told them. "These weapons cannot be destroyed or given away. They will appear by your side whenever you need them."

"That's something you don't see every day," LaSalle said as he drew closer to admire the witches' new weapons.

"We can make scabbards for you," Melodium offered. Jessie smiled despite herself when she saw the big ogre's fingers twitch as he looked at the weapons, clearly longing to take them apart and figure out how they were made.

"And they will not break or be dismantled," the Wampus Cat added, shooting Melodium a stern look.

"I wasn't going to do anything," he protested.

"No, but you were thinking about it, brother," Tug grinned.

"I can never thank you enough," Greta said to the Wampus Cat.

"Save the children. That will be all the thanks I need."

"Let's go," Greta said, tucking the weapons in her belt.

She led the way as their small group crept along a path barely a foot wide that wound along the wall high above the dais. Jessie suspected that it hadn't always existed. The Earth loved Her children, and Greta was all Hers.

As they passed behind the dais, Jessie looked out over the vampire throng that surged over the cave floor. From her vantage point she could see what Mikael had been talking about. The vampires had strength in numbers, but that was about it. While it was obvious Robert had kept this new batch of recruits fed, it was also obvious they weren't feeding enough. Starvation and the toll fighting their nature took was apparent in their uncertain and exhausted gazes, gaunt faces, and sluggish movements.

They finally reached the small tunnel entrance. Jessie let her fire rise to her fingertips, and Greta drew both of her blades, the hilts sliding easily into her hands with the faintest whisper of a sound. Nicky silently began to turn, and Stefan strengthened the illusion around them as they entered the tunnel.

Jessie could hear the murmur of voices ahead of them, and they came around a curve to see a pair of shabbily dressed vampires leaning against a wall. One held a torch, but they weren't armed.

"*No weapons,*" Greta projected to Stefan and Jessie.

"*They probably didn't think they had anything to fear from a teenage witch who was missing a finger,*" Jessie thought back.

"*A teenage witch, no. Her relatives though? Let's make this quick and quiet,*" Stefan thought to them.

Stefan dropped the illusion just as Nicky ripped out the throat of one vampire with his fangs and simultaneously pulled the other's throat apart with his claws. They fell to the ground, gurgling, and Greta, with a pushing motion, sealed them in the cave walls.

"By the time we get them out they'll have healed," Nicky whispered.

"Nice," Stefan whispered back.

"He was one of the best assassins in Europe for centuries," Greta whispered to Stefan. "That's why I wanted him to come with us."

"Was?" Nicky protested.

"We can discuss this after we get Stephanie out," Jessie rolled her eyes and pushed past Nicky to creep on silent feet down the tunnel.

After coming around another bend, they reached a ledge overlooking a small cave at the bottom of a steep incline. Jessie held her hand up to stop the group and snuck forward, peering down at the darkness. Her heart sank in dismay.

"*Shit*," she projected.

"*What?*" Greta asked.

"*Stephanie isn't alone.*"

"*Yeah, the lieutenant is down there.*"

"*No, I mean she's not the only kidnapping victim.*"

"*What?*" Stefan's startled voice joined in.

"There are five other kids," Jessie whispered for Nicky's benefit. "We need to make this really fast and take out the lieutenant and her guards before they can get to any of the children."

"How many guards are there?" Greta asked.

"Two. Come see the layout, but be careful."

"I get the lieutenant," Greta said before her brother could call dibs. He glared at her for a moment.

"Fine. We need to get between them and the tunnel entrance. On my mark, we drop down and cut them off. Jessie,

I'll suck the air out of them so they can't yell and then I'll use it to fuel your fire."

"And I'll create an earth barrier inside the bars of the cell so the kids are safe," Greta added.

Nicky's eyes glowed red when he saw the huddled group of children in the cell below them. The youngest looked about seven, but they were all so dirty that it was hard to tell. In front of them stood a tall, dark haired teenager who bore a striking resemblance to Greta, her chin lifted in defiance, and her fists by her side. Jessie's heart wrenched at the sight of the filthy, bloodied bandage wrapped around one hand. Stephanie wasn't the only injured prisoner either. At least two other kids cradled hands wrapped in bloodied, dirty strips of cloth.

"Now," Stefan barked out loud, and they dropped from the wall to the cave floor.

Before the vampires could react, Greta made a snapping motion with her wrist, and a wall of earth flew up between the startled children and the bars of their prison. The vampire lieutenant started to yell, but Stefan cut off all of her sound with a wave of his hand. With a snarl Greta made the lieutenant's bones wrench apart, leaving her head dangling at an awkward angle from her neck until Nicky leapt forward and ripped the other vampire's head off of her shoulders as Jessie's fire darts incinerated her body.

The other two vampires fell backwards, looking for escape. Nicky stepped forward and locked them in his gaze. Unable to resist the older and more powerful vampire's stare, the two fell to their knees trembling.

"You will remain here," he told them, mesmerizing compulsion rolling off his voice like a wave. "When I return, I will help you learn how to accept your true nature or help you accept your true death."

"I don't want to die," one of the vampires, a young boy who had probably been no more than fifteen when he was turned, whispered.

"Then wait for me," Nicky turned away and caught Jessie's eye with a nod to the prison. "We can let them out now."

Greta dropped the earth barrier and softened the ground around the bars until Nicky could pull them apart. Stephanie launched herself into her aunt's and uncle's arms, shaking.

"I knew you would come!" she babbled through the tears. "I knew it! I told everyone you would come."

"Of course we were going to come," Stefan said. "It's going to be okay. We're going to get all of you out of here. But we still need to deal with Robert. Can you wait here with the rest of the kids until we get back?"

"No," Stephanie took a step backward, her eyes flashing green.

"No?" Greta was startled.

"No. We're coming with you. We'll stay out of his reach, but we all deserve to see this to the end."

"She's definitely Greta's family," Nicky murmured to Jessie.

Greta and Stefan looked at each other over Stephanie's head for a moment before Greta sighed in resignation.

"Okay, come on," she gestured to the rest of the kids. "But you have to stay quiet!"

The kids let out muffled cheers and started to run toward the tunnel. Jessie had to throw up a wall of flames to stop them before they gave away the witches' position to every vampire in the cave.

"Hold on," she warned the children. "We have to be very quiet or they'll hear us. Our allies are on the other side of Robert's throne room or whatever he's calling it. When we reach the end of the tunnel, Steph, you and the kids wait there with your uncle and Nicky. Greta and I are going to sneak back across. We'll signal when we're about to attack."

"I understand," Stephanie nodded. "We'll be quiet, right, guys?"

The smallest boy nodded solemnly, clutching Stephanie's skirt with a grubby fist.

"Save some for us," Nicky said with a cocky grin and a broad gesture that included most of the young witches.

"Just remember not to–" Greta started.

"— kill anyone, yes, we know. And don't forget you buried two of them in the wall," Nicky reminded her.

"Oh, right. I'll get them when we're done."

Ignoring the children's shocked looks, Jessie and Greta led the little group back down the tunnel until they reached the entrance. Jessie could see the rest of the party on the far side. She held her finger to her lips to caution the children to stay quiet before she and Greta crept back to their friends.

"We found Stephanie along with five other young witches."

"Five?" John was outraged.

"We can make arrangements to get the kids to safety when we're done mopping the floor with that jackass down there," LaSalle snarled. His bushy eyebrows came together in a thunderous scowl. He took a swig out of the goblet and passed it to Renard who took a long drink before passing it to Kathryn and the ogres. "Matthias and Tam are in place, whatever that means."

"Still have no idea what they plan to do?" Jessie asked.

"No, but they said it's going to be good."

Jessie paused, looking at the ogres, an idea forming in her head.

"You can port," she said.

"We can," Melodium agreed.

"And you can take people or, say, vampires to other places."

"Vampires like the lieutenants down there?" Melodium grinned.

"Exactly."

"Anything else before we go kick some vampire ass?" Greta asked, her body as tense as a coiled spring.

"Do we actually have a plan other than getting the ogres to abscond with the lieutenants?" Kathryn asked.

"Other than Matthias and Tam's idea that no one will share with us? Nope. Let's do this," Jessie raised her fire sword in salute, and with a wild cry, the two witches launched themselves over the side of the alcove and right into Robert's lap.

Chapter 24

To say Robert did not expect them to drop down from above was a huge understatement. Before he could do more than shriek at his lieutenants to do something, the cave floor in front of the dais shook and fell away, dropping at least half of the vampire throng into the depths of the mountain. The rest hesitated in shock at the sudden assault.

"No," Greta cried as she ran to the edge of the hole.

"Wait, look," LaSalle yelled to her.

He and the ogres had ported in behind the dais, and before Robert could react, two of the ogres had pulled Roberts lieutenants through their portal and back into Oberon's city. Jessie heard Melodium bellow to keep the vampires under lock and key until he returned.

"Works for me," she muttered and stepped out of the way as the rampaging ogres rushed past her toward the throng.

Robert, finally realizing that his plan to subdue Greta was dangerously close to going up in smoke, tried to lunge after her, but Jessie knocked him back with her flaming sword.

"Uh uh," she said with a nasty smile. "She's not yours, pretty boy."

"Matthias, you are the most amazing fae in the world," Greta called out.

"Yes, I know. Now go kick that asshole vampire's ass for interrupting our dinner," Jessie heard the Fir Darrig call back. She wanted to see what he and Tam did, but Robert took all of her attention.

Robert snarled, his handsome face turning gray and leathery as fangs protruded from his mouth. His fingers elongated into vicious claws, and he swiped at Jessie, who danced back out of his reach. Like all vampires, he was incredibly fast and strong, and it would be unwise to turn her back on him for even a second.

"Defend me! Stop the infidels!" Robert shrieked at what was left of his followers.

As Jessie later found out when John enthusiastically recounted the battle, the cultists hesitated and then rushed forward around the edges of the hole until, with wild screams, the Red Cheetah and Wampus Cat leapt in front of them. The front edges of the horde skidded to a halt, looking wildly around for a way out, but they found themselves plummeting into the hole and whatever magic Matthias and Tam dreamt up when the rest of the vampires, unable to stop themselves, plowed into the frontrunners. The wolves made the jump to the ground below in one smooth leap, aided by Stefan's air magic, and flanked the throng on one side with the ogres on the other, keeping the cultists away from Robert. Mikael, Nicky, and Renard, in their true vampire forms, descended on the horde, and Mikael's hypnotic power rolled through the cave.

"Look upon us and obey, for we are true power," Mikael bellowed.

The thralls began to slow down, Robert's hold weakening against the much older vampire's call. But it was still roughly seventy cultists against three fully powered vampires, and it wasn't hard to see that Mikael, Nicky, and Renard had their work cut out for them. As their power flowed over the horde, the cultists swayed like wheat caught in a storm; sometimes taking a faltering step toward the dais, sometimes falling back to peer up at the older vampires, sometimes shaking their heads and breaking out of their daze and trying to surge forward again. A few attempted to change shape, but with their lack of experience– and a decent meal– they only succeeded in elongating an ear here and there or turning a peculiar shade of gray.

John and Kathryn led the wolves in lightning fast attacks, darting in and out and harassing the cultists to keep them distracted before they could heed their sire's cries for aid while Stefan used his air magic to amplify Mikael's call and hide Robert's voice from his thralls. Jessie's favorite part of the story was when the Cheetah batted cultists over the edge of the hole like a house cat knocking things off of a table. Every time he did, a sizzling sound and screech of pain echoed through the cavern. Moment by grueling moment, the horde was subdued until only a pocket of defiant hold-outs remained, surrounded by wolves, ogres, vampires, and the Cheetah.

Meanwhile, the Wampus Cat cleared the cave in with one jump to land by Jessie's side, and, along with Greta, they closed in on Robert. Jessie felt the adrenaline course through her like fire, erupting from her fingers and blasting fire arrows at the vampire. As fast as Greta could rip pieces of stone and earth from the cave floor, Jessie melted them into white hot molten lava and flung them at Robert. Each time he lunged for the witches, the Wampus Cat lashed out with her huge paw, sending him skidding backward, closer and closer to the edge of the ravine behind the throne.

"What are you going to do when I kill your precious children?" Robert snarled after the Cat buffeted him backward for the third time. He looked around frantically for any means of escape, and Jessie realized that he was unaware that his lieutenant never made it back.

His voice was shrill, and Jessie heard the current of uncertainty beneath. He knew they would never put Greta's niece in jeopardy, so if they were willing to meet him head on in a full out assault, they must know something he didn't. Greta's gaze broke from his for a split second to flick upward, and then she let the cruel, cold smile spread across her face.

He was done. He was theirs.

His final mistake (other than stealing anyone Jessie and Greta cared about) was looking away to follow her gaze. And there was Stephanie by Stefan's side with the pale faces of the other children crowding around them. Stephanie shook with rage as she stared down at Robert with death in her eyes.

"You got this, sis?" Stefan called out to Greta.

"This one's mine," she replied, and then her sword and dagger appeared in her hands. "Ready, Jess?"

"Fuck him. Let's go," Jessie raised her own weapons in a salute and launched herself forward with no warning, Greta beside her. The Wampus Cat jumped over the throne, and the three of them had Robert cornered just as they heard the deep rumble from under the dais. Draig was coming, and Robert had nowhere to run.

Cut off from his followers and with no means of escape, Robert howled in fear and rage. He barely had time to get his quarterstaff up before Greta and Jessie were on him, and he fumbled to parry Greta's thrust and swipe Jessie's sword away from his torso in the same motion. His initial shock over, he concentrated on deflecting the two witches while darting away from the Wampus Cat, his vampiric reflexes and speed giving him an edge.

The edge lasted right up until Jessie, with a snarl of frustration, dropped down to duck beneath his swing and slice up with her fire sword in one hand as she blasted a wave of fire arrows at him with the other hand that set his robes and staff aflame. At the same time, Greta jumped back and drove her earth sword into the dais floor, causing the ground to shift and rise under Robert's feet.

Knocked off balance, he dropped the flaming staff and grabbed Greta's blades, crying out as the fire burned through his hand from one and earth soldered his flesh to the other while his skin blackened and bubbled beneath the burning robes. As he writhed in agony, Jessie nimbly danced to one side and behind him. She screeched in rage as she buried her blades deep, one either side of his spine. Fire and earth energy erupted from her weapons and coursed through his body, making him scream in agony.

Meanwhile, Greta dropped her blades to one side, spun under them, and at the last minute aimed a kick with both feet at his middle that ripped his earthbound hand from his arm and sent him flying almost to the very edge of the pit.

Robert tried to get past the witches and Wampus Cat, but no matter what, he couldn't find a way out. When the dais shook again, he fell to his knees at the edge of the pit. Greta closed in on him. Her eyes were solid black, and his death was the only thing on her mind. But in her single minded rage, she underestimated the crazed vampire. Vampires didn't just have superior strength– they could heal themselves.

As she swung her blades down, he lunged to his feet and grabbed one of her wrists with a hand that was no longer burned. He morphed the blood covered stump at his wrist on the other arm into a jagged bat-like talon and jerked her to him, intent on eviscerating her while dodging her attack with lightning speed. She was able to twist to one side, but it wasn't enough. His talon raked across her hip, slashing down her thigh.

"You will be mine or no one's," Robert screamed, fangs bared.

Greta froze in shock for a split second as the ground shook again. She gasped and clutched at the wound; blood bubbled around her fingers before she recovered enough to glance at the pit. She smiled, a cold, ugly smile that bared her teeth in a pain wracked grimace.

"Okay," she said. And then she threw all of her weight against his chest, and they both went over the side.

"*Greta!*"

As she fell, looking up at the shrinking light, Greta prayed that if she came out of this alive, she would never have to hear Jessie scream like that again.

Jessie was out of her mind. Mikael, Renard, and LaSalle leapt forward and grabbed her while she fought, using everything in her arsenal including fire, to free herself. The Wampus Cat had to throw herself between Jessie and the edge of the pit to stop Jessie from launching herself in the abyss after Greta.

"Jessica, stop," Stefan's voice rang out across the cave, laced with his own fear for his sister. "Do not lose control or you will kill us all! Draig's coming, and she's an Earth witch. Earth will not let her die like this!"

This time when the ground cracked, the sound was deafening and the aftershock knocked the remaining vampires off their feet. The dais began to break apart, and Mikael froze.

"Get back! He's coming," he yelled in panic before bodily picking up both Jessie and LaSalle and throwing them as far away from the platform as he could.

Nicky flew back up to the ledge in time to pull Stephanie to the ground where he tried to cover her from the falling stalactites and rocks, and Stefan used the air to build a shield that could protect the rest of the kids.

All of a sudden, the ravine erupted in a stream of green and gold, and they looked up, stunned, as the gigantic Celtic dragon came up, up, up out of the ravine, to circle the top of the cave.

In one claw he clutched a small, huddled shape. With the other, he threw a still screaming Robert down on the throne and descended on the vampire, a stream of fire that made Jessie's look like a candle flame erupting from his gaping maw. Robert's scream choked off. He was ashes in seconds.

Draig roared, circling again before landing in front of the dais. He cast one huge golden eye over the huddled group, and then he reared his head back. Through her tears, Jessie saw his throat move as he took in a huge gulp of air, and then he blasted his fire again. The fire bathed the last of the horde, but it did not burn them. Instead, the thralls stood dazed, looking around as if coming out of a dream. Kathryn and John lunged forward with strangled yelps, but their wolf packs were unscathed.

"Dragons can control and direct their flame," Mikael called to them. He let go of Jessie and started to run toward Draig who cradled Greta to his chest.

"I'm okay! Mostly!" Greta called out as the dragon carefully lowered her to the ground. She tumbled out of his grasp and staggered, clutching her ribs while blood soaked her pants from the wound on her hip. Her left arm dangled, and even from a distance Jessie could see that it was probably shattered. Jessie took off running and skidded to her knees as Greta collapsed and the two fell into each other's arms, crying.

"She was too far away and falling too fast for me to safely catch her," Draig apologized. "I'm afraid she hurt herself rather severely."

Jessie looked up, trying to see through her tears, at the dragon who had shifted back into his human form, only now wearing designer jeans, silver tipped black cowboy boots, and a royal purple silk shirt with a turquoise and silver bolo tie. The tail of his dragon tattoo peeked out from under one rolled up sleeve.

"We'll get her to a healer," Stefan reassured Draig. "You saved her life, and that's all that matters."

He and Nicky led the children and the two vampire guards Nicky had spared down to the floor of the cave.

"What took you so long?" Jessie demanded through her sniffles and hiccuping sobs.

"The tunnel was more narrow than we thought," Draig replied. "I had to do a fair bit of crawling and shapeshifting. I really had planned to get here sooner."

"Is it safe to come up?" Matthias called to them. Jessie had almost forgotten he was there.

"Yes," she called back.

"Oh, yeah. You didn't see what they did," Greta laughed and then clutched her ribs again, wincing. "Ow."

Jessie's eyes widened as Matthias and Tam's heads appeared, rising slowly out of the hole in the cave floor, and then she started laughing through her tears. They drove what was, for all intents and purposes, a wooden tank that dragged a glowing net full of vampires behind it. The vampires cried out when they came in contact with the glowing strands, and Jessie could see ugly burns on their arms and legs.

"UV net to keep everyone out of your way," Tam beamed.

"We took a page out of Greta's book only, you know, without burying people alive," Matthias added.

"I don't bury people alive," Greta protested.

"That's because Jessie makes you let them go," Nicky pointed out. "Speaking of, you still have to get the last two vampire guards out of the tunnel."

"Oh, right," Greta furrowed her brow and concentrated, and a moment later, two dazed vampires staggered to the tunnel's entrance and almost fell to the cave floor.

"Thanks for coming along and saving me," Greta sniffled, looking up at Draig.

"Always. I have never had many friends, and I need to keep the ones I have left safe," he smiled, crouching down by her side.

"What did you do to the vampires?" Jessie asked with another hiccup. Neither she nor Greta could ever be called "pretty criers". She waved at the horde which huddled together, talking softly. Some cried, some laughed, and most looked ashamed.

"I took away Robert's hold on their minds. And now, he's gone forever," Draig replied.

"Damn it, I wanted to hit him," Stephanie scowled.

"She's your niece all right," LaSalle chuckled to Greta, who smiled.

"I know. We're all very proud of her."

"Can you save the vampires Matthias captured?" Jessie asked.

"Of course," Draig replied.

Jessie looked at him, waiting.

"Oh, you mean now?"

"Yes. Please. That would be great."

"Oh, right. Um, if everyone could step back please," he rose to his feet and looked around, uncomfortable with all of the attention on him.

He flowed up and out, his beautiful dragon form filling the dais. Kathryn yipped and jumped back when his barbed tail nearly came down on her head. With a white hot blast, he burned out the last of Robert's poisonous influence, leaving the vampires stunned and silent.

"What will you do with them?" he asked as he turned back to a man.

"We're taking them to the Vampiric Council where they will get the option of either adapting to their vampire nature or taking the true death," Mikael said, coming to stand next to the dragon.

"Good," Draig nodded with a glance at Mikael. "Call on me if I can be of assistance with that."

"Of course, Sire," Mikael bowed his head.

"Don't call me that," Draig grimaced.

"As you wish," Mikael's tone was mild, but Jessie suspected he hid a smile.

Draig sat down cross legged next to Jessie and Greta.

"What about you two?" he asked.

"We need to get her to a healer," Jessie nodded to Greta. "And we need to let Isabel and Vito know what happened. I'm sure Isabel is frantic with worry by now."

"Can you do anything about the vampires who are part of the cabal?" Greta asked.

"I'm afraid not," Draig said with a sad smile. "I was able to burn off Robert's influence because he had tried to corrupt and subvert all that it means to be a vampire. Unlike Robert, the vampires who joined the cabal are acting according to their nature. Vampires, like dragons, are drawn to wealth and power. I can't change their personalities or make them meet your definition of 'good'."

"What now?" LaSalle asked. He, Renard, and Kathryn passed the goblet back and forth, and Draig eyed it again, a golden glint flashing across his eyes.

"Oh, no, dragon. Go steal your own goblet," LaSalle scowled.

"He probably has a dozen of them stashed somewhere," Renard grinned.

"True," Draig admitted. "But I could always use more."

"Hey, there's something else I need to show you," Jessie touched the dragon on the arm. "Stefan, can you float us back up to our hiding place?"

"I can fly us up, you know," Draig looked amused.

"I wasn't going to make you turn into a dragon again," she protested.

"I don't have to," he laughed.

He stood and then bent down to swoop her up in a bridal carry. Jessie squeaked and held on for dear life as he bent at the knees and then launched himself up toward the alcove.

"Does he know he looks like Superman when he does that?" she heard Kathryn ask Greta.

"Probably. Don't make me laugh. Pretty sure I broke all of my ribs," Greta replied.

Chapter 25

"What did you want to show me?" Draig asked as he set Jessie down. She glared at him.

"Warn me next time!"

"I'm sorry," he looked down. "I don't always think things through."

"I know, but you have to if you're going to be more in this world, and I don't think you get to go back into hiding now that all of the vampires here have seen you," she said. Her gentle tone took the sting out of her words.

He frowned.

"I wasn't hiding. I just got busy."

"Draig, I'm not criticizing you, but you didn't even know how many vampires exist now until Vito had to ask you to help us find Robert."

"It's different for me, Jessica," he objected. "I've always been aware of the vampires. They hover on the edge of my consciousness. They just don't need me to be present all the time. Vito does a great job with the Vampiric Council, and he can always find me if there's an emergency. But I have to be careful. There are still humans out there who would love to boast that they bagged a dragon, and there aren't that many of us left."

Jessie felt uneasiness curl in the pit of her stomach as she thought about what lay in the storeroom ahead.

"What do you know about the cabal and their activities?" she asked.

"Enough to know that they're dangerous and put the balance of the world at risk. Vito told me about Nicodemus' gargoyle lover. I suspect his role as a guardian played more of a part in his death than most suspect," Draig answered.

"Speaking of, what exactly are the guardians? Or who?" Jessie asked.

"You got me to bring you up here to ply me with questions about my existence?" Draig raised an eyebrow.

"No, but I'm curious."

"As are many."

"Fair enough," Jessie shrugged and started to lead him down the tunnel. "Draig, I have to tell you something. Do you remember when the cabal witch in the woods warned Rupert that there might be Matagot pelts here?"

"You found them?" He winced.

"Yeah," Jessie stopped him right before they reached the entrance to the storeroom. "But that wasn't all we found."

"No," his voice was flat and dark, and his eyes suddenly glowed a fiery orange, pupils narrowing to slits. Jessie felt heat radiate off of his body.

"No?" She was startled.

"I feel her. My youngest sister and most beloved of my heart and nest."

"Then you know what's in there," Jessie pointed at the dark entrance.

He pushed past her, and her heart clenched when she heard his heartbroken wail that deepened into a coughing roar. She flattened herself against the wall just in time before the chamber walls exploded out, blasting a hole through the mountain, and she saw his huge dragon form silhouetted against the night sky as he flew away. She clambered over the rubble into what was left of the room. The dragon scales were gone.

"Jessie! What's going on! Are you okay?" Stefan shouted as he and Nicky shot up to meet her on his air puff.

"What the hell..." Nicky stared at the hole in shock.

"The dragon scales belonged to his sister," Jessie told them.

Stefan shook his head.

"Poor guy," he murmured.

"Yes," Isabel's voice said behind him.

"When did you get here?" Jessie asked, startled.

"Stefan called me to help with Greta. Are there really fae and cryptid remains in here?" Isabel looked sick.

"See for yourself," Jessie stepped aside.

"This is horrible," Isabel looked at the stacks of trophies, tears in her eyes. "We will do everything we can to reach out to the fae and cryptid communities so that these poor victims can be laid to rest."

"Starting with Rupert," Jessie said. "He's not going to handle this well."

"Let's go back down and regroup. There's still a lot to do," Isabel said. "I brought Vito with me to help with the vampires."

"What happened?" Greta twisted around with anxiety written all over her face when Isabel and Jessie floated back to the dais. "Where's Draig?"

"He took the scales and left. We'll find him when we get out of here," Jessie said as she knelt by Greta's side. "How are you doing?"

"She would be better if she would stay still," one of the healers Isabel brought with her snapped. She continued working on Greta's arm while muttering about certain earth witches who were determined to get themselves killed.

Greta's hip had stopped bleeding, and Jessie could see ugly scabs forming through the torn pants. The healer glanced up at Jessie.

"Whatever made the slashes on her leg was highly poisonous. It will take longer for the scabs to heal, and they'll leave scars. She needs to take it easy for at least a week or she might reopen the wounds."

"It was a vampire," Jessie told her. "She had ripped off his hand, but he managed to grow his arm into some kind of talon."

"Vampire blood is toxic to witches, so that would explain it."

"I'll keep her in our Library and my house," Jessie promised. "At least until the scabs are gone."

"Hey, Jess." Ivan slung an arm around her shoulder. "Don't worry, we'll get her fixed up in no time. Again."

Jessie stood up and looked around the cave. Melodium and Tug held a portal open into the Vampiric Council chambers where the vampire throng filed through, and she spotted Vito off to one side talking to Mikael. She made her way over to them, skirting the rest of the ogres who oohed and ahhed over Tam and Matthias' wooden tank. The leprechaun and fir darrig beamed as they showed off their handiwork.

"We saved all of them except one lieutenant and Robert," Jessie told Vito when she reached his side. "The other three lieutenants are Oberon's prisoners, courtesy of the ogres."

"A most admirable accomplishment, my dear," Vito nodded in approval. "We'll recover the lieutenants later. Much later, I think."

He linked his arm in Jessie's and led her back to Greta's side where Stefan joined them.

"Where are the Cheetah and Wampus Cat?" Greta asked. Her voice sounded groggy, and Jessie raised an eyebrow at Ivan.

"To help with her pain," he explained. "On top of the vampire cut, she has at least three broken ribs, a fractured femur, a sprained ankle, and her arm is in a million pieces. What did she hit?"

"She fell down that hole and landed on a dragon," Jessie pointed at the pit behind what was left of the dais.

"Of course she did," the other healer shook her head. "Is that where she got these burns?"

"No, I had to do that when she lost control after the cult sent her Stephanie's finger. Stephanie's her niece, by the way. She's over there with the rest of the kids we rescued and could use some help too. They all could."

The healer paused and looked over at the rag tag group who followed Stefan around like puppies. Stefan looked very uncomfortable.

"Oh, Goddess. The poor things! Where are their mothers– no, don't answer that. I heard about the graves. Ivan, we have to take care of them next."

"You can go now. I'm a-okay," Greta giggled.

"No, you're not, but you will be," Ivan laughed.

"You still didn't tell me what happened to the Cheetah and Wampus Cat," Greta complained to no one in particular. She tried to pout and then started giggling again.

"Yeah, where are they?" Jessie looked around.

"They left. They said that it was an honor to fight beside you and their claws and teeth are yours should you ever need them again," Kathryn said as she walked up. "I have to say, this was not what I expected and quite an eye-opener. My pack is also yours if you ever need it, and I will spread the word about the cabal up the Appalachians into Canada."

"Do you think there are werewolf pelts in the cave?" Jessie pointed up.

"We turn human when we're killed. That's not to say some of our kind aren't dead somewhere because the cabal tried to get their hands on our skins," Kathryn scowled. "But no, I didn't sense any wolf kind up there."

"Coooooool," Greta said. "That's a cool word. Coooooool."

And then she was out like a light.

"Thank you," Jessie said with some relief.

"Oh, believe me, it was my pleasure," the healer laughed.

"That's the last of them," Mikael called.

"Excellent. I should return myself," Vito said. "Jessica, I'll let you and Greta know what happens with their deprogramming."

"Thank you," she hugged him. "I appreciate that."

"I know, my dear. Mikael, Nichodemus, Renard, take care of our favorite witches," Vito said as he turned to leave.

"Oh, you had better check on Draig too," Jessie stopped him. "The cabal had his sister's scales, and he kind of blew out the side of the mountain when he found out."

"I see. I will reach out," Vito sobered. "This is not good for him. He has such little family left."

"Tell him he can join our pack," Jessie said.

"I shall," Vito smiled. He kissed Jessie on the forehead and stepped through the portal which closed behind him.

"We still need to get those novices off the mountain," Stefan reminded them.

"And see if we can help Mary," Jessie added.

"Who's Mary?" Isabel asked, brow furrowed.

"One of the cabal witches who had a change of heart."

"We'll try to help her, but if she's a full fledged witch then they've already wired her brain," the healer working on Greta looked up with sad eyes. "She may already be dead."

"What does that mean?" LaSalle asked. "What do they do to the brain?"

"They rig a spell into the mind that acts like a small bomb for lack of a better term. They can detonate it or use it to inflict pain. It's how they stop anyone who gets cold feet or second thoughts from leaving the organization."

"That's horrible," Tam was aghast.

"I'm working on a way to neutralize it," Ivan said. "If Mary is still alive, then I'll help her as much as I can."

"Jessie, I hate to ask this, but let's go back to that chamber," Isabel said. "I want to get a catalog of everything that's in there and get it someplace safe."

"Okay, but I want to check in at home first," Jessie said. More importantly, she wanted to make sure Rupert was safe. She had a bad feeling about what would happen when he found out about the pelts.

"Do that, and I'll start going over everything with Isabel," Stefan ordered, moving away from his little group of new-found fans with some relief.

The healer finished setting Greta's arm and cast the final healing spells to start the shards of bone knitting back together before she turned to Stephanie.

"Now, then, let's take a look at you, my dear. Oh, your poor hand!"

"Vito gave me the finger in case you can reattach it," Mikael held out the small box with some distaste.

"Oh, excellent. Such a wonderful vampire," the healer beamed.

"You or Vito?" Nicky asked in a stage whisper.

"Me, of course," Mikael tossed his head.

"If you have everything wrapped up here, my pack and I are going to head out," Kathryn said.

"Thank you for everything, Kathryn. It was an honor to fight by your side too. And, if you're feeling a little parched, I am heading to my bar to check in. I owe you at least ten rounds." Jessie shook the werewolf's hand.

"You don't owe me a thing," Kathryn shook her head. "That vampire would have come after us and the people around here sooner or later, and then we would be on the cusp of an even bigger war once humans start to think that maybe cryptids aren't such a great idea after all. How about I take you up on that drink another time?"

"Sounds good," Jessie clasped the werewolf's hand.

Kathryn shifted back to a white wolf and lifted her muzzle in a howl as her pack swarmed around her and loped out of the cave.

Jessie twisted her portal ring and opened the portal to the Library.

"Can she be moved?" she asked Ivan, nodding at a comatose Greta.

"Oh, yes. She would probably be more comfortable there," he nodded to the entrance.

"Lucy, get back," Jessie scolded the little cat who peeked out into the cave. "Mikael, can you..." she gestured at her best friend.

"Of course," he knelt and gently lifted Greta, who whimpered in her sleep.

"Easy," Jessie said as they passed into the Library and he laid Greta on the sofa. Jessie covered Greta with blankets and scooped Lucy up, dropping the calico on top of her favorite witch before Mikael stepped back in the cave and Jessie opened the portal to her office.

She almost fell over Riza, who had decided to take up residence in her desk chair while Jared paced across the length of the room. The relief on their faces when they looked up at her brought tears to her eyes.

"Well?" Jared asked, unable to keep the anxiety out of his voice.

"We got them."

Chapter 26

"Oh, thank every higher being," Riza's shoulders sagged, and she lunged out of the chair to grab Jessie in a tight hug. Jared wrapped her arms around the two of them from Jessie's other side, sandwiching her between them.

"I can't breathe," Jessie choked.

"Wait, why are you alone," Riza pulled back with a frown.

"Greta's healing, and everyone else is helping Isabel. Have you seen Rupert?"

"Why does Greta need healing? Rupert's in the bar. Does this have anything to do with why Seanan thinks his scent is off?"

"She fell onto a dragon and broke a bunch of stuff. What do you mean his scent is off?" Jessie frowned.

Riza stared at Jessie.

"I love how you make statements like that seem normal. Yeah, Rupert's been weird ever since he came back. He won't tell us what's going on. He just showed up out of nowhere and started pacing back and forth and growling. He was making the customers uncomfortable, so I made him go outside until he could calm down. Seanan pulled me aside and told me that he smells sour and musty. His real scent is under there, but it's changing."

"That's not good," Jessie said. She felt dread like a cold fist around her heart as she pulled out her phone and thumbed through the contacts until she reached Madame Blanche.

"Hey, how fast can you be here?" Jessie asked when the White Lady answered.

"I can move through the spirit plane and be there in moments. What's going on?"

"I'm afraid we're going to lose Rupert. Get here as fast as you can," Jessie hung up and turned to Jared. "This is going to be really bad. Who's in the bar?"

"Caroline, Cassie, the Suttons, and the ogres Tug left here along with John's pack," Jared replied. "There are some vampies, too, and a couple of kitsune. Why?"

"Are the vampies the only humans here?"

Jared thought for a moment.

"No, I think a few of Charlie's old friends came by to see him."

"Get them out of the bar," Jessie ordered. "I don't care what excuse you have to make, but hurry.

""Because that doesn't sound at all ominous and like something I need to prepare for. Jessie, what's going on?" Riza demanded.

"I would like to know as well," Madame Blanche added as she appeared by Jessie's side.

"We ran into a witch who warned us that the cabal kept a storeroom with fae and cryptid trophies in the cave," Jessie told them. "Rupert chose to come back here and wait for us, and now I have to tell him that his kin's pelts were in a stack on a floor somewhere in the mountains."

"This is very bad news," Madame Blanche said. "Where is he now?"

"At the bar," Riza said. "One of the wolves John left behind told us that his scent is changing."

"*Merde!* We must hurry," Madame Blanche cried.

"Wait," Jessie grabbed the White Lady's arm. "There are too many humans here. I love Rupert, you know that, but we need to keep everyone safe. Give Jared a minute to get them out."

"Bar's clear," Jared came back into the office a few moments later. "But we owe Charlie's friends a round tomorrow night."

"Deal. Let's just get this over with," Jessie set her shoulders and started out the door.

Madame Blanche pushed past Jessie as they moved into the hall. She ran surprisingly gracefully in stilettos. Jessie had a moment to be impressed before running after her.

But the minute they reached the bar and Rupert looked up at them, Jessie knew he was lost. His pupils were so wide that his eyes were almost black, and he took one look at her and gave a screeching yowl, ears flat to his head, fangs bared, and claws extended.

"You were there!" he howled. His pain distorted his voice. "My kin! My family! You reek of their death!"

"Rupert, I'm sorry," Jessie started to step forward.

He attacked so quickly that she almost missed it. She barely had time to stumble back and raise an arm to protect her face and chest before his claws came down, and she felt the immediate burning pain as they raked across her skin and ripped her arm open to the bone.

"Rupert! *Arrête ça tout de suite!*" Madame Blanche cried.

She shoved Jessie to one side and darted forward, seizing Rupert's paw when it started to come down again. For a moment the entire bar froze in stunned silence, watching the grappling match between two immortal cryptids, and then Rupert vanished, taking Madame Blanche with him.

No one moved. The only sound was the drip of Jessie's blood on the polished floor. Then, shaking her head as if waking up from a bad dream, Seanan leapt into action and launched herself over the bar to grab a handful of towels before running to Jessie's side. She pushed the towels as hard as she could against the wound.

"Someone find John," she yelled to Jared and Caroline, who were still frozen. "*Now!*"

"He's still in the cave where we rescued Stephanie," Jessie gasped.

"How do we get there?" Seanan demanded.

"We have to go through the portal in the Library," Jessie said. She swayed on her feet as blackness crowded around the edges of her vision.

"Fine," Riza snapped as Seanan scooped Jessie up. "Keep those towels on your arm and bear down. Lift it above your heart."

They made it to the office in record time, and Jessie pushed the knothole that opened the Library with bloodied, trembling fingers.

"What the hell happened?" John yelled when they burst back into the cave. He ran forward and met them at the portal entrance, pulling Jessie from Seanan's arms.

"Rupert," Riza told him in the no-nonsense tone she used when she was really mad.

"Are you fucking serious?"

"Can we talk about that later?" Jessie asked, teeth clenched against the pain. The towels were soaked through, and she shivered uncontrollably as she started to go into shock.

"She needs a healer fast. She's losing a lot of blood," Seanan snapped.

"Isabel! Ivan!" John yelled, turning and running for the cluster of witches huddled around the children.

"What the–" Isabel started to say when she looked up at John carrying a blood drenched Jessie in his arms.

"Here, give her to me," Ivan ran to them.

"Isabel, Rupert might come here for the pelts. He's changed. It's bad. He attacked me just because he could smell them on me, and I didn't even touch them," Jessie tried to talk around the healers.

"Get everything out of that cave and hurry," Isabel snapped at her guards. "Riza, go with them. Put everything in one of the safe rooms that only you and I can access. We'll get it all back to the rightful owners later."

"By the Goddess, what is it with you and Greta? Ivan, stop the bleeding so I can get the cuts to close," one of the other healers ordered. For a moment the healers worked together in silence until the blood flow finally died down to a trickle and Ivan breathed a sigh of relief.

"Thank you for saving us," Stephanie came over to Jessie and sat down. "I knew Greta would come, but I'm glad you did too."

"Of course," Jessie mustered a smile around the pain. "How are all of the kids?"

"They'll be okay," Stefan said as he joined them. "We'll make sure they all have somewhere to go where they're safe."

"I don't know how you're going to pull that off, but I trust you," Jessie sighed in relief as the deep claw marks closed and the pain started to abate in her arm. Then she grimaced as the wounds started to itch. "I hate the itching. Why does there have to be itching?"

"Because that's how we know you're all better," Ivan told her. "Maybe if you and Greta would stop throwing yourself into danger all the time, you would itch less."

Jessie chose to ignore that.

"We need to find Mary and those cabal kids," she said with a worried look on her face.

"My wolves went back for them. The kids are over there," John pointed at the half-starved, filthy teenagers huddled against a wall while some of Isabel's healers looked over them with kind faces and words. "Mary, though..."

Jessie bowed her head to hide her tears of anger and sorrow. Another pointless loss in a pointless war. When would it end?

"How is it you went to check on the bar and came back bleeding?" Nicky sank down by her side next to Stephanie with a mixture of admiration and horror on his beautiful face. LaSalle was right behind him.

"It was Rupert," she told them what happened in the bar. "He looked deranged. I don't think he knew who I was. Madame Blanche fought him off, and they disappeared together."

"The thing about being 'chaotic neutral', as you always put it, is something like this can happen with no warning,"

LaSalle looked at the ground and shook his head. Like the Matagot, the Nain Rouge could also shift their natures on a whim depending on how they were treated. "He's going to need all of our love to come back from wherever the dark places of his mind took him."

"I know," Jessie said. John scowled, and she shot him a stern look. "I know you're upset because he hurt me, but you have to forgive him, John. I mean it. He's our family. Our pack. We will not abandon him."

"I know, but I get to be upset with him right now," John met her eyes with an angry glare.

"Yes, you do. So do I. But we will not shun or embarrass him."

"What now?" Nicky asked.

"We need to get the kids to safety and check in with Vito," Jessie said. She gingerly sat up with John's help. "And we need to find Draig and Rupert. Draig is hurting just as much, and he needs us too, especially after he saved Greta and helped clean up Robert's mess."

"First you and Greta need a good night's sleep," Ivan interrupted. "And you need to drink a lot of rosehip tea and orange juice to start regenerating all of that blood you lost."

"Like that will happen," one of the healers muttered.

"I can get a good night's sleep," Jessie protested. The healer just gave her a long look and went back to the task of closing one of the kid's wounds.

"I'm honestly amazed that you can even stand up right now. I have this under control," Isabel said as she walked over to them. "We have almost everything out of the cave, and I have sentries posted at the entrance and throughout so we can keep excavating over the course of the next week or two. I'll let you know if we find any other caves or rooms."

"Okay, then I think I would like to go home now," Jessie said. She felt a wave of exhaustion crash over her and threaten to pull her under.

"You do that," Isabel smiled. "Stefan and I will finish up here, and we'll all sit down and talk tomorrow."

Chapter 27

"More tea?" Jessie asked Greta who was ensconced in multiple quilts and blankets on the sofa.

"Jessie, if you give me any more tea then I'm going to float out of here," Greta pushed the offered cup away. "I'm fine. Honest. Everything is almost healed."

"Give some to Stephanie," Stefan said with a little smirk.

"I don't want any more tea!" Stephanie protested, sitting up straight from her seat by her aunt. "Don't you have any soda or something?"

"No, that stuff's bad for you," Jessie wrinkled her nose.

"Whatever," Stephanie rolled her eyes before snuggling back into Greta's side.

"We'll take you to the Naga's cafe after we catch up on what's going on and get some hot chocolate," Greta told her niece. "Isabel, what did you find out?"

"The novices we rescued have been asleep since yesterday. When they wake up, eat something healthy, and feel better then we'll give them a chance to join us or leave. As you know, Mary didn't make it. The cabal left her body outside the cave for us to find."

"I hate them," Stephanie said to no one in particular.

"Join the club, kiddo," Greta agreed.

"What about all of the stuff you recovered?" Jessie asked.

"We contacted the Alliance last night after we got everything out," Isabel said. "They're sending fae and cryptid scholars to help identify the remains so we can get them back to the right people. Hopefully that will be done next week. We still have sentries posted while we make sure there aren't any other storerooms or surprises. We hoped some of the missing artifacts would turn up, but if they were in the cave then the cabal probably got those to safety before Robert took over."

"Well, damn," Jessie said as she put her own cup of tea on the coffee table. As much as she loved it, even she had to admit she was growing tired of the stuff after almost twenty-four hours of drinking infused brews to reclaim some of the blood she had lost and accelerate her healing.

They always figured that the cabal had spies throughout the Witch Council, but that hypothesis proved true when dangerous artifacts went missing from its high security vault. One of those artifacts showed up in Jared's parents' garage: the portal his uncle Theodore used to exile the ogre race to a new world. Luckily for Jared's family, Isabel had secretly tasked Greta with making and hiding a full inventory of everything the Council seized at the end of the Witch rebellion, thus proving that they were innocent.

"Keep us posted on that," Jessie said with a nod to Greta. "We have centuries of research documented in our Library and can probably help."

"I will if I need to, but you have enough on your plate," Isabel fixed Jessie with a grim stare. "You can't deny that you're especially targeted by the cabal. They have their sights set on you, and you know it. We have to put a stop to this before someone else gets hurt or worse."

"I know. You're right," Jessie tried to hide the twinge of guilt when she thought about the filthy children huddled behind Stephanie or Rupert's rage-maddened eyes.

"I wouldn't mind a beer," Stefan announced. "Jess, can you open the portal?"

"Yeah, I think we'll all feel better around our friends," she agreed and opened the door to her office where they all trooped behind Stefan down the hall and to the bar.

"Wait, is that–" Greta stopped and stared at the door in surprise.

"Draig took us at our word when we said he has a home here," John grinned as he met them at the entrance to the hall. "Happy Solstice!"

Jessie felt tears fill her eyes as she took in the scene. Draig, LaSalle, and Tug stood at the door in animated conversation, the dragon waving his arms around as he described something to his new friends. Tam and Matthias raised a toast with Riza, and the three of them sang some long-forgotten Yule drinking song in such off-key tones that Caroline winced and Cassie covered her ears. Jared scolded a shamefaced Renard who tried, once again, to hide the shattered remains of a stone foosball player with his foot, and John's beer sat on the window sill across from the Fox.

Fatima, the Naga matriarch, slithered toward the witches and pressed a bag in Stephanie's hand.

"Chocolates for our littlest witch," she said with a wink. She gave Jessie and Greta kisses on the cheek and rejoined her consort. Rahul smiled and raised his glass in their direction.

"Ooh!" Stephanie's eyes grew wide as she opened the bag.

"Lucky," Greta laughed before she went to join Draig, LaSalle, and Tug.

Isabel looked around and lightly touched Jessie's arm.

"I'll be right back. I know someone who needs to be here even more than we do tonight."

"Who?" Jessie asked, startled.

"You'll see," Isabel smiled before opening her portal and darting through.

Stefan strolled over to Jared and looked down at the figurine that valiantly tried to climb the table and get back on the field, despite the fact it only had a torso and one arm.

"You know what you do," he interrupted Jared's rant. "Start charging them."

Jared stopped in mid-yell to look at Stefan in amazement.

"Why didn't I think of that?" he exclaimed. "Yeah, they have to rent the players from me and pay a deposit!"

"Hold on, now," John started to protest in alarm.

"No! I will not! This is the fourth set I will have to make because you can't control yourselves. Do you think I have time to just sit and carve these figurines? From now on if you want to play, then you're gonna pay!"

"I thought you were my friend," Renard gave Stefan a look of utter betrayal.

Stefan shrugged.

"Don't look at me. You're the ones who keep breaking things," he said with a grin before handing Jared a business card. "Hey, Jared, give me a call sometime. I have a business proposition for you."

"Oh yeah?" Jared took the card and looked at it.

"Yeah. You saw first hand what happens when a witch rages. What if we had a safe place to go so we can lose our shit and blow some stuff up? Let's talk."

Jessie made her way to Greta's side and hugged Draig.

"Good to see you," she greeted him with a smile.

"Thanks, you too," he smiled back. "I'm sorry for blowing out the mountainside. I hope I didn't hurt you."

"You didn't. I'm sorry that you had to find her scales like that."

"Yes," he sobered. "I will lay her spirit to rest at the next new moon. And my claws and teeth are yours for this fight."

"Speaking of claws and teeth..." Jessie's voice trailed off.

"We can't find him," LaSalle told her. He couldn't hide the unease and sadness in his voice. "Not even Madame Blanche knows where he's gone. She's been chasing after his trail all night and day. If she can't get to him then no one can."

"We have to help him," Jessie insisted.

"Aye, I know that, but what can we do to a beast spirit who doesn't want to be found?" LaSalle asked.

"We'll think of something," Greta reassured him. "We always do."

They chatted for a moment more before Jessie moved away and started to join Riza at the bar.

"Hey, Jess, what did you want to talk to me about?" Charlie appeared at her elbow, curiosity coloring him navy blue.

"How would you like to be my bar manager?" she asked.

"Wait, really?" He was so surprised that he turned pale green.

"Yeah, it was Mara's idea, but I like it. You know how everything runs, you already help keep the place going, and I can pay you. Well, it would go to your family, but you know what I mean."

"Wow, Jess, I would be honored!" A huge grin split his face as he reached to shake her hand. She winced when his hands passed through hers. It felt like being submerged in murky, cold soup.

"Oops, sorry. So when do I start?"

"How about tomorrow? We can go over things you can do and how to make this work," Jessie smiled at his enthusiasm.

"Great! Man, I can't wait to tell Mary Jo. Oh, there she is. Hey! Mary Jo! Wait until you hear this!"

He waved the succubus down as he floated across the bar with more purpose than usual, and Jessie laughed.

She felt the ripple in the bar's wards when Isabel reopened her portal, and turned with a smile to greet her friend, only to come up short in surprise. The last thing she expected to see was Isabel dragging Gertrude's tall form through the portal. As far as Jessie knew, Gertrude had not left the Witch Council since Greta found her nearly dead outside of Brigitte's home a few months ago. It felt like it had been decades.

"She needs to get out of her room and out of her head. She won't stop beating herself up about Astrid and the cabal," Isabel announced as she dragged Gertrude through the crowd by her wrist. It was quite a sight since Isabel barely came up to Gertrude's shoulder. Jessie hid a smile as Isabel pointed at a bar stool and snapped, "Sit."

"I fail to see how this could help," Gertrude protested as the *völva* obeyed the tiny witch.

"It's easier not to argue with her," Greta said as she joined them and accepted a non-alcoholic beer from Caroline while Isabel placed drink orders for her and Gertrude.

"Clearly," Gertrude sniffed.

"Jess, how are the listening spells in here nowadays?" Isabel asked.

"Better in my office. Do we need to go in there?" Jessie asked.

"No, hang on," Isabel's brow furrowed in concentration and the air around them shimmered as the sounds from the bar became muted. Caroline looked startled when she tried to pass Isabel and Gertrude their drinks and came up against a solid barrier.

"Oops, sorry," Isabel shot Caroline an apologetic smile and reached through to grab a martini for herself and a cosmopolitan for Gertrude.

Gertrude eyed her drink with distrust.

"Is it supposed to be pink?" she asked.

"Yes," Isabel grinned. "You'll love it."

"If you say so," Gertrude muttered as she took a cautious sip. Her expression showed her surprise and then a little smile played at the corners of her mouth.

"We need a way to get more information," Greta said. "Robert was dangerous, and involving him in this showed that the cabal has no idea what they're playing with. Whoever is heading it up this time is doing a half-assed job. Isabel, did you get anything out of that talisman we recovered?"

"Its magic matched that of a missing witch who we suspect was used to make a necromancer," Isabel scowled. "He's probably dead by now."

"I don't get it," Jessie shook her head. "Why are they so sloppy this time? They keep leaving loose ends all over the place. It's like they're not even trying to hide what they're up to."

"I agree," Gertrude frowned. "When I joined during the last conflict, it was tightly reined in. We did not know anything the leaders did not wish for us to know. I was firmly entrenched from the beginning and even I was unaware of the fae's or vampires' involvement. And we never made such sloppy mistakes or poor errors in judgment. We certainly would never have entrusted a green witch barely old enough to be an apprentice to take out seasoned witches like yourselves."

"What if the witches aren't the only ones in control this time? The fae have little concept of how the modern world works. Reviving the cabal could have been their idea, and, as Draig pointed out, it's in the vampires' natures to be power hungry and attracted to wealth. They could easily bankroll the cabal along with the humans." Jessie pointed out "Gertrude, do you know anyone who might have gotten out like you did but who might have more information?"

"I wish I could help you, but I had very little interaction with other witches in the cabal after I left it. As far as I'm aware, Morgan Le Fey is the only other one to walk away and not die. But I doubt she would be useful. She was invested for her family's sake. She did not care about the cabal's promises of prosperity and power."

"I just hate feeling like we keep chasing them. It would be nice to have the upper hand for once," Isabel sighed.

"We keep holding our own," Greta pointed out. "That says something. And we have some pretty strong allies."

"And we have the twins," Jessie said.

They fell silent and watched Caroline and Chris behind the bar. The two moved as if they were halves of one unit, each complementing the other's actions and always aware. The vampies watched Chris too. His goth good looks caught the eye of quite a few of the vampire groupies who were considering switching their allegiance to the shy, quiet witch who carried an air of mystery that even he was unaware of. The attention made him acutely uncomfortable, and more often than not, Caroline came to his rescue when one of his fawning admirers got too close.

"Have there ever been triplets?" Greta asked.

"The Norns and the Fates," Gertrude replied, sipping her drink. It was almost empty, and she gave Caroline's inquiring eyebrow a nod.

"So there really are three of each?" Greta asked, surprised. Even for a witch, the legends were maddeningly obscure.

"Yes," Gertrude told them. "Each is more powerful than any witch alive and together they hold the power of foresight and prophecy. They can control a man's fate with the snick of a pair of scissors and not think twice. Gods begged their favor, and they ruled the stars."

"Wow," Jessie gave a low whistle. "What happened to them?"

"No one knows where the Fates are," Gertrude told them. "But the Norns scattered. The younger sister was struck down, and the oldest… let's just say she is one who should remain lost. It was she who drew me into the cabal in the first place, and I do not doubt that her powers of foresight allowed them to locate Greta's whereabouts the night that man arrived to give her Robert's letter."

"And the middle?" Isabel asked.

Gertrude put down her empty glass and looked at the bar for a long moment. When she looked back up, her eyes were white from end to end.

"Well," Gertrude said with a sad smile. "You're looking at her."

"Wait, what?" Greta broke the stunned silence.

"How did I never see this?" Jessie marveled. "It's so obvious. You're one of the oldest and most powerful witches in the world who originated in Scandinavia."

Gertrude chuckled as the white bled out of her eyes, leaving the pale gray-blue irises.

"There are still quite a few old, powerful Scandinavian witches, Jessica," she said as she shot Jessie an amused glance.

"But don't you have the power of foresight too?" Riza frowned. "How did you miss Astrid's betrayal? Not to bring up a sore subject or anything," she added with a wince.

Gertrude's smile faded.

"I have foresight, but my eldest sister cursed me to always be blind to my family's fate after our youngest sister was lost to us. That was one of the reasons why I isolated Astrid and myself during her childhood."

"What happened to your younger sister?" Greta asked, leaning forward on her stool with her knees drawn up like a young girl getting ready to hear a story.

"She fell in love with a hero," Gertrude said with a half-shrug as she turned back to her drink. "It was I who saw the tragedy that would befall her should she leave our side for his, but she refused to heed my warning. She asked me what kind of happiness would she find in a broken heart instead, and I could not answer her. When the time came for him to face the frost giants, she stood by him, and when her string unraveled from ours, my eldest sister cursed my sight."

"So she's dead?" Greta whispered.

"Not quite. You see, like many of the 'bad guys' in legend, frost giants are not inherently evil. They just wanted to be left alone, but heroes will do what they must to build a reputation for themselves. The giants did not realize my sister's identity until it was too late. When she fell, they froze her body and encased it in ice to try to preserve it as much as possible in case she could ever be restored, for she is still a Norn. It takes a lot more than a physical blow to destroy us. One day, perhaps, she might return. We can only wait and see."

"What about your oldest sister?" Jessie asked. "Why did she join the cabal?"

"Ah, yes. She was bitter and angry and still mourned our sister. She blamed humans for our loss, you see. She raged against humanity's determination to ignore our warnings and seek out their own destiny in the name of heroism and greed, and she desired above all else to wipe out the human race. We have not talked since I left the cabal to go into isolation. No doubt she foresaw my daughter's betrayal and believed it to be a fitting punishment for me."

"But how was it your fault?" Greta objected. "What were you supposed to do, tie your sister up and keep her with you? Or brainwash her? She was a grown witch."

"Grief does different things to different people," Gertrude gave another shrug. "Why didn't my eldest sister try harder as well? Perhaps she feels guilty because she was also incapable of forcing the youngest to see reason and wishes to lash out at me rather than face her own shortcomings."

She turned back to the bar and downed her cocktail in one gulp.

"I would like to talk about something else now," she said in a voice so low that it was almost a whisper. She spun the martini glass around by the stem, staring sightlessly at a scene far in the past.

"Of course," Isabel replied and gently laid a hand on Gertrude's arm. The *völva* flashed Isabel a grateful smile and then twisted her stool around so she could see the room.

"So this is what your bar looks like, Jessica. It suits you. There is a good blend of comfort and peace."

"And the occasional argument," Jessie added as a scowling Renard handed Jared a stack of bills and the remains of yet another foosball figurine.

"Nice doing business with you," Jared grinned and handed Renard a new miniature statue.

"Do humans ever come here?" Gertrude asked.

"Sometimes," Jessie replied. "Once Charlie's friends and family figured out he was haunting the place, they started coming around to spend time with him. Most of them are cool with Mary Jo too. And little by little more people from town started to stop by for happy hour and such. Most people in town are okay with us. There are a few who think witches and cryptids should go back where they belong, but so far no one has tried to do anything about it."

"I suppose that will always be the way of the world," Gertrude sighed. "After all, the original cabal formed because witches wanted to get rid of humans."

"True," Jessie stirred her sweet tea with her straw as they fell into a comfortable silence until it was broken by a chime from Jessie's phone.

"Who is it?" Isabel tensed.

"Mara," Jessie frowned. "She sent a text. Why is she reaching out? It's the Solstice and Yule."

"Maybe she just wants to say hello," Riza sipped her beer, her alert gaze belying her casual words.

Happy Yule, my dear friend. I have a potential lead (Annie assures me that is the correct terminology). Meet me at the Hill tomorrow evening. Bring Greta, Isabel, and Riza.

Jessie looked up from her phone and held it out to the others.

"Looks like we're taking a field trip."

Chapter 28

T he setting sun gilded the bare trees and forlorn cathedral when they stepped through Jessie's portal to the Hill's parking lot where Annie waited. Her normal cheerful smile was missing, and her skin was a decided shade of green. Jessie peered at the little brownie.

"Are you okay?"

"Fine," Annie snapped and then winced. "Sorry, girls. My Ian got his hands on a very potent batch of orcish liquor, and let's just say that its effects the day after imbibing it leave something to be desired."

"Wow, I didn't know the fae could get hungover," Riza marveled.

"Is that what this is called? Because I can think of many other better terms. Like walking death. Why must the world keep spinning?"

"I'm sorry, Annie," Jessie gasped, trying her hardest to keep her laughter at bay. "I hope it goes away soon."

"Drink lots of water," Greta advised. "And don't listen if anyone suggests the hair of the dog."

"Why on earth would I want a dog's hair?" Annie stared at them, baffled.

"No, it means to drink more," Riza started to explain and then stopped when Annie blanched. The brownie gestured toward the familiar path that wound into the gardens before hurrying into the hall with a hand clamped over her mouth.

Despite the lack of snow in the outside world, white flakes dusted the gardens except where rose bushes bloomed with out-of-season crimson glory. The fae were creatures of pure magic and answered only to the universe; if Mara wanted roses in the middle of winter, she was going to get roses in the middle of winter.

The witches followed the path to Dain's bier where Mara waited for them. She rose gracefully from her cushioned seat on the stone bench to greet them before gesturing for them to sit and settling herself back down. LaSalle's face when he mentioned Mara sitting vigil by Dain's side in the cold rose unbidden to Jessie's face, and she closed her eyes, concentrating. Mara made a startled sound as heat crept up the stone and into her cushion.

"I can leave it," Jessie offered. "I can turn the cushion into a talisman."

"You are kinder than I deserve," Mara gave the fire witch a grateful smile. "My strength lies in illusions, and it would cost me a great deal of energy to keep a fire going throughout the winter."

"You deserve much more kindness than this small token," Jessie shook her head.

"I'll make sure to mention this to LaSalle," Mara said with a wink before her smile faded. "I have news about the prison break at the Witch Council. Oberon thinks he knows the magical signature I discovered."

"Who is it?" Isabel asked.

"Oberon believes the Erlking is our culprit. Of the other three fae rulers capable of performing magic like this, the Morrigan's magic is as wild as fire and hot as battle, Titania's magic is spring flowers and bird song, and you have all met my uncle and know his magical signature to be similar to a forest in summer."

"And you're sure that there are no other fae rulers this strong anywhere in the world?" Greta asked. After all, the fae's prejudices against each other had worked in the cabal's favor so far.

"There are other fae rulers this strong, but none who are as skilled in illusions, deception, and manipulation like the Erlking, the Morrigan, Titania, and Oberon, " Mara replied. "And certainly no others with the same magical signature. When it comes to the ruling fae, we at least know that much about our species."

"What do we know about the Erlking?" Riza asked Mara.

"He has the most to gain and the least to lose," Mara told her. "Older even than Oberon, he has never liked humanity's encroachment on the world, and if he could upend the Alliance, then all the better. He was a god of tricksters and king of winter, and he would happily bury humans if it meant he could have his natural order restored. He compares humans to cockroaches and parasites and believes mankind is determined to destroy nature and the world. I think it goes without saying that you have all of our resources at your disposal in this fight. We don't wish to see this world ended any more than you do."

"For starters, we have to figure out where they took Astrid and hope we can get her back in one piece," Jessie fidgeted on the bench and crossed her legs. It had been a long week. "Gertrude dropped a bombshell on us last night, and we have to presume the Erlking is going to want the middle sister of the Norns in the palm of his hand, even if he has to use her daughter to make it happen."

"I'm sorry, what?" Mara stared at Jessie.

"Oh, yeah. Gertrude is a Norn," Jessie shook her head and then filled Mara in on Gertrude's sad story.

"I wondered what happened to them," Mara said thoughtfully. "And she does not know where her younger sister's body lies?"

"I don't think any of us asked her," Isabel admitted. "My guess would be with the frost giants though."

"I wonder..." Mara's voice trailed off and she stared off into the distance, a line creasing her perfect forehead between her eyebrows. After a moment, she shook herself, coming back to the present and looking around at the witches who watched her expectantly.

"Never mind about that for now," she said. "What are our next steps?"

"We have to figure out how deeply this rot spread throughout the fae realm and what other cryptids are involved," Isabel said. "And we can't rule out the ogre's world either. I wouldn't put it past the cabal to try to use it to stockpile resources or even prisoners."

"True," Mara agreed. "My uncle still has an active portal to that world."

"Yes, he has helped coordinate a number of fae and witch security patrols to weed out the cabal's supply and weapons caches," Isabel told her. "But not even all of our best efforts can put our people in every hiding place on that world at once."

"And don't forget the newest members of the cabal," Riza reminded them. "Humans. Think about it– the cabal keeps turning and killing necromancers and witches. It makes sense that they wouldn't want all of that magic to go to waste, so they promise some rich humans that they can siphon magic, get them to figure out a way to do it, and then bam, the cabal has the magic at their fingertips."

"That's a damn good reason to get humans involved," Greta agreed.

"Mara, did Oberon's spy find out if whatever Zach's family built to capture our power will only be used on witches? Or do they think it can work on cryptids and the fae too?" Jessie asked.

"I'll find out," Mara replied. "And let's schedule a meeting with Oberon soon. He will want to hear all of your news and discoveries from your own lips."

"I want to see this human's house for myself," Riza said. "Can we make that happen?"

"I suppose I could," Mara replied. "We must be careful that we are not detected, but it should be easy to do. Perhaps in a week once Jessie and Greta are fully healed we can pay a visit to my satyr sentry."

"We'll set it up," Isabel promised.

"Oh, and I believe LaSalle promised this to you in exchange for keeping the apprentices safe while everyone else dealt with Robert," Mara grinned as she plucked a goblet out the air and handed it to Riza.

Riza took it as her face lit up with a delighted smile.

"I had forgotten about that! This will be put to good use."

The witches bid Mara farewell as they walked back to the parking lot with a promise to return as soon as Jessie and Greta had recovered. A week later, they found themselves at Dain's bier once more, although now it was midnight, and they were all dressed in black.

"I know being placed under a fae spell is less than ideal, but in this case, it will be necessary for both Isabel and me to cast invisibility and glamour spells to keep us all from being detected," Mara told them. She wore a black cat suit, for lack of better term, and the costume was incongruous to her normal flowing gowns.

"If we have to do it, then let's do it," Jessie nodded. Her skin crawled as she felt the layers of both spells settle over the small group, and Riza sneezed.

Mara led them into a copse of hawthorn trees next to the gardens and pressed a knot on one of the trees, opening a portal to the same expensively manicured lawn Jessie remembered from a few months before. A vintage Jaguar was parked in the sweeping driveway that curved in front of the house, and the streets were quiet. Atlanta's skyline loomed in the background.

The satyr waited for them on the other side.

"Milady," he gave Mara a flourishing bow and cheeky grin.

"Any activity tonight?" she asked with one perfectly arched eyebrow.

"See for yourself."

He gestured across the immaculate landscaping toward the mansion, the front of which was partially concealed from the road by an English laurel hedge. The building was a

"Yes, and I recognize the elves from Oberon's court," Mara agreed. "The one who looked toward us is one of the spies my uncle sent to infiltrate the cabal."

"Will he be safe?" Jessie's brow crinkled in worry.

"Don't worry, he can take care of himself," Mara reassured her friend. "He's a landless noble with quite a bit of time on his hands, and he spent most of the last two hundred years or so studying magical defenses."

"Gertrude's sister certainly had no problem joining the twenty-first century," Isabel remarked.

"No, she looks like she's done very well for herself," Greta agreed. "Mara, do you think Oberon's spy can find out what she's been doing with her life since she and Gertrude parted ways?"

"I'll ask," Mara promised.

"Did any of you get a look into the other room?" Riza asked.

"The one the Norn came from? I saw a copper box on a table. I think it had a tube or wire coming out of it," Jessie replied.

"I wonder if that's what the humans built to reclaim magic from talismans," Isabel mused.

"See if our spy has any knowledge about whatever that thing was and let us know as soon as you can," Jessie gave Mara a quick hug and opened her own portal to her Library, stepping back so the rest of the witches could file through.

Greta paused on the threshold.

"Did anyone else notice that Zach's dad wasn't too happy about the way the Norn talked to him? I wonder if we can use that to our advantage."

"That's not a bad idea," Mara's eyes narrowed in thought. "I'll talk to Oberon. Maybe we can get our spy to create a little dissension. I'll send word as soon as I can."

Mara gave them a wave good-bye before the portal closed, leaving the witches in Jessie and Greta's Library.

"Now what?" Isabel couldn't hide her exasperation as she pulled her chiming phone out of her back pocket and pushed the talk button. "Hello?"

"No, you talk into this part," Jesse, who was standing next to Isabel, heard Olav snap.

"Olav, what's going on?" Isabel asked.

"Isabel? Are you there? Am I doing this right?" Gertrude yelled so loudly that Isabel winced and held the phone away from her ear.

"You don't have to yell! Just talk normally," Isabel tried to explain. "Hang on, I'm going to put you on speaker phone."

"What is a speaker phone? Am I not already speaking into the phone?" Gertrude was baffled.

Greta had to hide her face in a pillow to muffle her laughter, and Jessie smacked her friend on the arm. Riza could barely contain her own mirth and had to wipe her eyes.

"Yes, it's– oh, never mind. Where are you?" Isabel glared at her friends while she rubbed at the spot between her eyes.

"Your office. Did I do this wrong? It was very important that I reach out to you, and the guard assured me that this device would be satisfactory."

"No, you're fine," Isabel reassured the older witch. "I'm coming back now. Just hang tight."

She hung up and turned to face her grinning friends.

"You are all terrible," she informed them. "Are you coming?"

"Sorry," Greta giggled. "Yes, we're coming."

Jessie pressed the panel that opened a portal into Isabel's office where Gertrude stood, staring at the phone in her hand. Confusion was written across her face.

"I'll teach you how to use it later," Isabel gently but firmly took the phone from the other witch's grasp. "What's going on?"

"Astrid reached out to me," Gertrude exclaimed.

"What? Are you sure?" Jessie demanded.

"We have a secret code we have used since she was a child," Gertrude explained. "Sadly, that was how she lured me to what was supposed to be my doom."

"Is it possible she could have taught this code to someone else or had it plucked from her memory?" Greta asked gently.

"Perhaps," Gertrude admitted. "But in light of this message, I do not believe that to be the case."

"What's the message?" Riza asked.

"She is safe for now. She is back in the hands of the cabal, and she will learn everything she can to redeem herself in my eyes and make right the terrible wrong she has done to me."

Jessie and Isabel exchanged a long look.

"Do you believe her?" Riza asked. No one questioned her bluntness. The other three looked at Gertrude, waiting for her answer.

"I have to believe she is at least safe for now. As for the rest... well, time will tell."

"Let's see what she can send to us," Jessie decided. "Gertrude, do you have a way to reply to her?"

"No," the *völva* shook her head.

"How did the message reach you?" Riza frowned.

"It appeared in front of the Council door and a guardsman brought it to us," Olav explained.

"That's dangerous," Greta said in alarm. "What if any cabal members on the Council find out?"

"Here, maybe this will make you feel better," Gertrude handed the note to Jessie.

The first thing Jessie noticed was that the parchment was addressed to Olav and signed by someone named Freya. It simply said that he was missed during the harvest, Gertrude's farm was running smoothly, and the reindeer had gotten out of the field again. Jessie looked at Gertrude, baffled.

"This is in code?" she asked.

"Yes," Gertrude beamed. "I am Olav, and Astrid is Freya. You see, no one reading this would think that it was anything other than a message for my seneschal from a friend or family member."

"That's pretty clever," Riza said admiringly. "I suppose the code is embedded in the note somehow?"

"Yes," Gertrude nodded. "We use a combination of characters and words. So you see, she could send a hundred messages to me, and the cabal will be none the wiser."

"Okay, well I guess we finally have some good news," Riza said. "As long as we can keep her out of your sister's clutches, that is."

"Yeah, speaking of, your sister is definitely working with suspected cabal members," Greta added.

Gertrude's lips thinned.

"I had hoped she would give up on this dream of vengeance, but it seems I was wrong."

"I just wish we had a way to warn Astrid," Jessie sighed.

"Me too," Greta agreed. "Will your sister be able to read Astrid's mind and know what she's doing?"

"We can't read minds, but she might be able to deduce that Astrid is up to something depending on her augers and readings," Gertrude admitted.

"That's a risk we'll have to take since we can't warn your daughter," Isabel shook her head. "I just wish her life wasn't on the line for all of this."

"Me too. We're going to go check in at the bar and get some rest," Jessie said. "I'll let you know if Mara finds out anything from Oberon's spy."

"Thanks, Jessie," Isabel hugged her friend.

"Gertrude, stay strong," Greta told the older witch. "We'll do everything we can to get her back."

She didn't make the vow a promise. Everyone knew that Astrid's chances were slim.

"Thank you," Gertrude gave a formal bow.

Jessie and Greta looked at each other once they were back in the Library.

"I'm going to go check with some of my archive contacts," Greta said. "I want to see what we have on the Erlking."

"Good idea," Jessie agreed. "I'm going to see if there's any word on Rupert and kick John's ass at foosball some more."

Greta laughed and was gone, leaving Jessie to smile as she crossed the room and let herself back into the warmth of the bar and the friends who waited for her there.

Epilogue

Jessie glanced across the bar and sighed. It had been a month since they rescued Stephanie, and there was still no word from the cabal– or Rupert. Greta rubbed red rimmed eyes and unsuccessfully tried to hide a gaping yawn. She had worked non-stop since they came back from spying on the humans, tapping into all of her resources around the world trying to find both the escaped witches and the Matagot, but she had turned up very little. The Erlking proved to be equally elusive; she could only find bits and pieces of folklore about the once legendary fae monarch.

Krampus and Santa Claus sat at a table nearby drinking margaritas and comparing notes from their Christmas spoils while some of the local townspeople stared in awe, whispering dares to each other to approach the pair. LaSalle and Matthias kept Tug company at the door, and Madame Blanche made a rare appearance to sip a martini with the Sutton clan.

At the end of the bar Stephanie and Jared were in a heated debate over the best table top games for new gamers while Chris looked on with an amused smile. Stefan stepped through the front door, pausing to shake hands with Tug, LaSalle, and Matthias, before approaching his sister.

"How long has that been going on?" he jutted his chin at Stephanie and Jared, who were now beseeching Christopher to back them both up.

"Oh, about an hour," Greta leaned her head on her hand and looked at the pair. "I have no idea where she gets it."

Jessie and Stefan stared at Greta until the corner of her mouth twitched and she started to laugh. Stefan shook his head and turned back to Jessie.

"Any updates?"

"Nothing."

"Same. I don't like it."

"Neither do we," she sighed and got up to move behind the bar. She had given Caroline and Jared the night off, allowing Christopher to have a little more responsibility and freedom behind the bar with her help. "Do you want anything?"

"I'll take a beer," he took over her newly vacated seat. "Something brown if you have it."

She poured a porter into a mug and passed it to him before taking over the vampies' orders so Chris could get away from the overwhelming attention.

"Charlie, you guys need anything?" she asked the ghost who was joined by his former next door neighbor.

"We're good, Jess," Charlie beamed at her. His transition into her bar manager had worked well. The staff felt supported, he made good business decisions, and it was amazing how quickly he could break up an argument just by walking through the combatants.

The rest of the night was uneventful. Various friends dropped in and out to say hello; no one wanted to be alone right now. When it was over, Jessie smiled good night to Chris, who climbed into Jared's car to go home. Greta had left already, taking her niece with her, and soon she and John were alone in the bar.

"What are your plans now?" he asked, drawing her in for a kiss.

"I need to feed the cats and then I was thinking about home."

"Whose home?" he smiled.

"I'm not picky," she smiled back and started to lean in for another kiss when she felt the air shift. John's eyes flashed gold, and she felt his coat start to form under her fingers.

"He's here," John growled. "Stay behind me."

She didn't have to ask who he meant. Rupert's green eyes glowed like faerie fire in the dark corner behind them where the shadows built until they became a pool of the darkest black. She watched silent and tense as the shadows coalesced into the form of a giant black cat and Rupert slunk forward, ears back, and tail down, almost creeping fearfully along the floor.

"Rupert," she said softly, putting a hand on John's arm as she slowly stepped forward, John moving by her side. If Rupert attacked again, the werewolf was her only defense.

"Jessica..." the Matagot whispered. "I need you. I cannot find myself."

Jessie knelt on the floor and then settled cross legged, facing the big cat.

"You know you are so, so deeply loved, right? I understand why you did what you did. We all do. No, that doesn't make it okay, but haven't we all done something we're ashamed of in all of this?"

"I am so afraid I will hurt you again." Rupert hid under a table, tail between his legs in an oddly canine gesture.

"What about the Wampus Cat?" John asked. "You said you felt peace with her. She would help you. I know she would. We can take you to her."

"That's right," Jessie remembered. "Will you let me take you to her?"

Rupert looked up and for the first time, Jessie saw a gleam of his old self flash across his eyes.

"Yes. Please. And then I will do everything in my power to make up for hurting you."

"Letting me help you is all that I want," Jessie replied.

She held out her hand, and the big cat slunk forward again until his nose touched her outstretched fingers. Then, to her surprise, he pushed his head under her hand until she felt her fingers instinctively curl in the dense, soft fur.

"Come on," she whispered. "Let's go see a Wampus Cat."

About the Author

Eli Rainwater moved from Atlanta to Durham where she lives with her three cats. She moonlights as a bartender at a pizza joint, drinks way too much coffee and tea, and is really bad about things
like sleep or eating real meals. She loves to garden but gave up on making her yard look reasonably manicured ages ago.